VONNIE DAVIS

For years I've been a romance junkie, devouring each one like warm, chocolate chip cookies. Perhaps that's why I adore writing about love and passion. Passion—such a powerful word, don't you think? I'd classify myself as a late bloomer. I started college in my late forties, met the love of my life in my mid-fifties and published my first book in my early sixties. My husband and I live in Southern Virginia. We enjoy spoiling the grandchildren and traveling. My deepest desire is to write saucy, often humorous romances you'll cherish long after you've turned off the e-reader.

You can follow me on Twitter @VonnieWrites.

How to Seduce a Fireman

Book One in the *Wild Heat* Series

VONNIE DAVIS

Harper*Impulse* an imprint of
HarperCollins*Publishers* Ltd
77–85 Fulham Palace Road
Hammersmith, London W6 8JB

www.harpercollins.co.uk

A Paperback Original 2014

First published in Great Britain in ebook format by Harper*Impulse* 2014

Copyright © Vonnie Davis 2014

Cover images © Shutterstock.com

Vonnie Davis asserts the moral right
to be identified as the author of this work

A catalogue record for this book is
available from the British Library

ISBN: 9780008113506

This novel is entirely a work of fiction.
The names, characters and incidents portrayed in it are
the work of the author's imagination. Any resemblance to
actual persons, living or dead, events or localities is
entirely coincidental.

All rights reserved. No part of this publication may be
reproduced, stored in a retrieval system, or transmitted,
in any form or by any means, electronic, mechanical,
photocopying, recording or otherwise, without the prior
permission of the publishers.

To all the fire personnel who keep our homes and our lives safe and to their loved ones who worry about their safety on a daily basis. Thank you.

CHAPTER ONE

Quinn Gallagher was *dead* meat.

Cassie Wolford marched to the side door of Fire and Marine Rescue Unit Thirty-two in Clearwater, Florida. She swiped the entry pass she'd purloined a year or so ago from her oldest brother and yanked the handle when the light in the security lock turned green. Propping her hip against the door, she maneuvered the large box containing the remainder of her birthday cake through the doorway. *Quinn better have a damn good excuse for being a no-show at my party last night.*

She'd asked him twice if he was coming and, both times, he'd used that wicked smile on her before claiming he wouldn't miss her twenty-first birthday for the world. So unless he was inside hobbling on crutches with two broken legs or wore a body cast from face to feet, he was about to get his jaw jacked. *I don't care if he does have a body built for sin and I want to be his number one sinner.*

With both of her brothers serving as firemen in this top-notch unit, Cassie knew her way around the building. She crossed the threshold into the firemen's living quarters, slapped the cake on the large dining room table and pivoted toward conversation floating in from the TV area amid the battle sounds of a warrior game on Wii.

Masculine laughter, deep and sensual, slithered straight to her core before spreading out to spark all her nerve endings. Quinn Gallagher did that to her, no matter if it was his laughter, his voice, or his eyes that fluctuated between blue and grey. *Why Quinn? Why not a guy who is as crazy for me as I am for him? But no, I have to fall hard for Mr. I-Could-Give-a-Shit.*

One quick glance in his direction, and she sucked air. Quinn, in his typically jovial manner, was recanting a story to her youngest brother, Jace, and a new fireman she'd yet to meet. All Quinn wore was a white towel slung low around his narrow hips.

Water drops lazily forged a trail down his tanned and toned body. Moisture dripped from his freshly shampooed dark hair, trailed over his perpetual five-o'clock shadow and plopped onto his collarbone, splatted onto his hardened pecs and washboard stomach, before skiing the hills and valleys over every ridge of his abs. *Oh, to be a droplet of water.*

Even though they'd jogged together often under the hot Florida sun, seeing his tribal tattoo over his broad shoulder, left pec and upper arm still made her fingers itch to touch and fondle, especially that strange indentation between swirls of ink that decorated his shoulder blade.

He was such a perfect specimen of male hotness with those magnetic eyes and firm lips that smiled easily and often, creasing his cheeks with deep dimples. Cassie wanted him so badly, she ached. Yet he treated her more like a little sister or a family friend. She scowled. *Hell, why not spray-paint some black spots on me? Let him scratch behind my ears like he does the firehouse Dalmatian.*

The new guy spied her first. "Hey, how'd you get in here?"

Jace's head whipped in her direction. "Looks like my sister over-rode the security system—again. Somehow she's been doing it for years." Jace strode toward Cassie and wrapped his arm around her shoulder before kissing her hair. "Boyd, meet my baby sister, Cassie. Sis, this is the newest pair of boots in our unit, Boyd Calloway."

She extended her hand. "Nice to meet you, Boyd. Since I turned twenty-one yesterday, I now decree I'm to be classified as Jace's *youngest* sister." Her brother smirked when she elbowed him. "I'm serious, Jace, I won't put up with being called the baby anymore." She patted the cake box. "There was so much cake left from last night's party, I brought it by for the guys. Not everyone who promised to come showed up." She aimed a glare at Quinn.

"Hell, peanut, was that last night?" He shook his head, flinging droplets in every direction.

Did she mean so damn little? She'd had such high hopes for last night. She'd dreamed of a birthday kiss from him, and not one of those baby ones on the nose or forehead, either. A lip to lip, tongue to tongue, make-her-insides-quiver adult kiss. Tears threatened and she fought to blink them away. She would not cry in front of him. "You know damn well it was."

"Hey, when a sexy woman shows up on a man's doorstep with a bottle of tequila and a proposition, he's prone to forget what day it is." Quinn flashed her a cocky grin that flayed the edges of her heart.

The rest of the guys in the unit cheered in affirmation.

Jace's arm tightened around her shoulder, his lips next to her ear. "Don't let him get to you, sis. You know how he is."

Yeah, she knew. Quinn was a player. She wasn't; she'd crushed exclusively on him for three years, waiting for the jerk to notice her. What a fool she'd been to think once she turned twenty-one, he'd accept her as an equal, as a woman old enough to date. The man moved from woman to woman like she moved from one shade of fingernail polish to another. Just how was she to get him out of her system? Maybe she needed to play a little herself. Wasn't that what tonight was about?

She breathed a kiss on Jace's cheek. "Gotta go. Sara and Misty are waiting in the car. We're going to Iguana Ike's. Have some beers. Party a little." She wiggled her hips. "Dance a lot. Girls' night out."

Quinn dared to take a couple steps toward her, his eyes narrowed. Gone was his previous fun-loving insolence. In its place was macho authority. "You're going out, dressed like that?"

Geesh! Talk about mood shuffling.

Jace grabbed the cake box and headed toward the kitchen. "Boyd, let's get some coffee to go with the cake. We'll get the hell out of the way, and let kerosene and a match deal with their inevitable explosion in private."

Boyd glanced from her to Quinn before following Jace. "What makes you think there's going to be an explosion?"

"I know my ba...ah...youngest sister. Two things we don't do with Cassie. One is tell her how to wear her hair. She's a beautician and a damn good one. Second, we don't tell her what to wear. Grab some plates, will ya?"

Cassie fisted her hands on her hips. "What's wrong with the way I'm dressed? This is the outfit Wolf and Becca gave me for my birthday."

Quinn reached to yank the off-the-shoulder sleeve to cover her shoulder. "I'm betting Becca picked this out for you. Cause I know damn well that protective older brother of yours would never allow you out in a black sweater that reveals more than it covers." He propped his hands over the V of his sculptured abdomen and leaned in. "You go into a meat market like Iguana Ike's with all that cleavage hanging out and you'll have sharks circling for the kill."

She pointedly glanced at her siren red fingernail polish with black swirls. "Not that it's any of your business, but perhaps that's exactly what I want. Sharks." Maybe the player needed a dose of his own medicine.

His eyes narrowed for a beat and a muscle ticked in his square jaw. "Don't play with me, Cassie. It's been a helluva day, and I'm not in the mood. We just got back from a marine rescue off Sand Key Park and it didn't go well. Wolf and Barclay weren't able to save a teen. Booze and scuba-diving never mix."

"Oh no! How's Wolf taking it? He gets so upset when he can't save someone. Taking care of everyone else is his thing. It's what keeps him going." He'd certainly taken care of her over the years and had gotten her to face some painful issues.

Quinn pointed toward the hallway. "The Wolf's in a mood, that's for sure. Been banging equipment around. He's in the showers now. I'd love to see what his opinion is of your outfit. Hell, that red leather skirt barely covers the essentials."

"Aw, hell. Here we go. Cassie in a snit is not a pretty sight." Jace's remark drifted in from the kitchen.

"I don't dress to please my brother. Nor will I ever dress to please the likes of a man who can't live up to his promises." She slid the black sweater off her shoulder and down her arm the way she'd worn it earlier. Then she presented Quinn with a defiant glare. "Now that we have that clear, you, Mr. Romeo, can go to hell. I hope the woman who was more important to you than my birthday party gave you a good dose of the clap."

Several fireman hooted and hollered at her snide remark. As usual, the place was wall-to-wall with male ears.

She snatched her purse from the table and took two steps before Quinn's hand vised around her wrist and jerked her against his chest. She was nearly lipstick to pierced brown nipple with his very fine pecs. *God, I'd like to bite one out of sheer spite.*

"Watch your mouth, peanut—"

"Stop calling me 'peanut'. I'm an adult now." She heaved a sigh. *Which would negate my biting his nipple, wouldn't it?*

Quinn's gaze swept over her face for a second, his jaw clenched in annoyance. "All right, since you're an adult, you ought to be able to handle this. I'm tired of you panting after me. I'm not interested. I mean, I love you like a sister and I'd do anything for you. Hell, we jog together often. Scuba-dive. Catch a movie now and then. But we do it all as friends. Nothing more." He exhaled a long sigh and shook his head once. "Dating is out of the question. I want you to stop drooling over me as if I'm husband material."

Oh, dear God. Are my desires that apparent?

He couldn't have said such a hurtful thing. Not her Quinn. Her chest constricted, forcing her stomach to do a free fall to her stilettos. The block walls of the building warped inward for a few seconds and the tile floor tilted. A buzzing filled her ears and her breathing all but ceased in lungs clutched by pain.

Dear God, no.

Since the news of her parents' death no one's words had wounded her so deeply. Evidently she hadn't hid her fascination with him as well as she'd hoped. Not only was Quinn well aware of her yearnings, but he resented them. So much so he felt the need to announce in front of everyone that he held zero desire for her.

He feels no attraction for me.

Happiness limped from her soul on a ragged sigh. Through her veil of tears, Wolf stood, hands on hips, like a storm cloud ready to erupt. Beside him were Jace and several firemen. She'd embarrassed her brothers, too. Had her behavior been so obvious, so humorous to everyone? *What an idiot I am.*

"I...I'm sorry." She fought to keep her voice steady. *God, please don't let me cry in front of these men.*

"Cassie, baby." Wolf advanced, concern evident in his features. He'd resigned his commission in the SEALs to come home to care for her and her older sisters after their parents died. He'd pulled her through many rough days and nights. No one could pull her through this, though. It was time for her to face the cold hard bitchin' truth: Quinn wanted her to leave him alone.

She stepped back and extended a hand in a stop gesture. "I'm sorry I've been such a pain in everyone's ass." Reaching into the outer pocket of her purse, she grasped Wolf's key card. "Here." She extended it to him. "I won't need this anymore."

Wolf shook his head. "Keep it. I've known you had it all along. The Captain knows too. I want you to go to Becca's tonight."

Yes, her oldest brother would send her to the safety of his fiancée's care. Everyone wanted to tell her where to go, who to be with, who to love...or not love. Would they ever accept the fact she was able to take care of herself? Perhaps she needed to prove she could. Hell, she was no weakling. All she needed was some time to adjust to a life without dreaming about Quinn and then move on. *Eight or nine years ought to do it.*

She tossed the entry card onto the table and strode out of the fire station for the last time. *I'm a grown woman. I can do this. The hell with Quinn Gallagher.*

CHAPTER TWO

Quinn's eyes adjusted to the contrasting interior of Iguana Ike's. Lights embedded in the edge of the teak bar, along with those strung around the shelves stocked with liquor bottles, twinkled in an annoying rhythm, while dimness hugged the tables and booths. Strobe lights, programmed to flash in time with the music, caused his headache to pound along with the song's bass beat thumping in his chest. His gaze drifted beyond the wall of glass to the large deck with soft lighting and palms shifting in the evening breeze. Why couldn't Cassie and her friends have chosen a table out there where it was quieter?

Getting last minute personal time off from the station had proven difficult but, hell, not as tough as prying Wolf's hands from around his throat. Quinn rotated his neck and swallowed, the discomfort a reminder of performing the unpardonable sin—hurting Wolf's baby sister.

Truth be told, Quinn wasn't so fucking proud of his behavior either. Seeing the pain in Cassie's almond-shaped eyes and watching the light go out of those green orbs had nearly done him in. But what choice did he have? She cared for him, that much was obvious and had been since shortly after she'd turned eighteen. He couldn't allow her starry-eyed dreams to continue, not where he was concerned. Not when he had cast iron running through his veins. Loving was not in his emotional repertoire. Not anymore. Not since Renata.

If he were a different man, Cassie, the pretty brunette with the heart-shaped face and bright green cat eyes, would be his singular focus. But he wasn't a different man. He was tainted goods with a damaged heart, a thorny background and a cold outlook on life and love.

Even so, here he sat, trying to work up the courage to approach Cassie and apologize. No doubt she'd refuse his request. Not that he could blame the entertaining blend of kitten and tiger. He'd been damn harsh. He twisted the lime over his bottle of Corona, popped the wedge of fruit into his mouth and chewed.

A blonde, with more cleavage showing than she had covered, shifted onto the empty bar stool next to him. Her overdose of perfume nearly closed his sinuses. "Hi, Quinn. I haven't seen you in ages."

He looked at her face, so artificially tanned it was almost leathery in appearance. Damn, he hadn't been drunk enough to get close to that, had he? "Sorry, but I don't recall the name. Have we met?"

Some of the brightness went out of her smile. "Brittany Cook. We dated a couple times last fall."

"Right. Brittany. I'm sorry. Part of my memory's gone. I don't recall women's names like I used to." He pointed to his head. "Had a timber fall on me during a fire. Hell, I can't even recall how to make love to a woman anymore. I've had to go on the 'no sex' wagon for a while. You know, until I get my game back."

She gave him a scathing once-over, huffed an irritated you're-an-asshole breath and sauntered off. No loss there.

Quinn spun the stool around and propped his elbows and back against the bar, his Corona in hand. One sip and his stomach returned a *hell-no* message. Last night he'd consumed an entire bottle of tequila—alone. There'd been no woman, just his worry about giving Cassie the obligatory birthday kiss and the concern that one touch of those plump pink lips wouldn't be enough.

Not that he led a celibate life, far from it. Lately, though, few women captured his attention the way vivacious Cassie did. He groaned and slapped the bottle onto the bar, his gaze zeroing in on the pretty brunette, with that go-to-hell streak of dyed red hair bisecting her dark tresses. By far, she outshone any other female on the dance floor.

When had Cassie matured into such a beautiful woman with curves in all the right places? The first time Quinn had set eyes on her was at her eighteenth birthday party. Wolf had conned him into manning the grill so he could visit with his guests, but Quinn's gaze kept drifting toward little Cassie. She'd been like a bubbly cheerleader on steroids. Animated. A Pollyanna full of joy. Young with so much promise. Even then, he'd known he was a distant barren planet orbiting the sunny warmth of her personality. God, she was perfection, had always been so in his eyes and heart—pure magnetic perfection.

Now she was twenty-one, just as vibrant and as much fun to be around. Her friends, Sara and Misty, were laughing, trying to keep up. Cassie danced with her arms over her head, gyrating with the fast beat of the music, her red leather skirt hugging that fine ass of hers like he had in his last wet dream.

He brought the Corona to his lips to cool his parched throat. *God, she's gorgeous.* To his annoyance, his cock twitched in agreement. The fact his cock paid more attention to Cassie of late was the driving force behind his earlier behavior. He could not use her for a brief fling, not his sweet angel. She deserved more, and he had less than more to give.

If he were honest with himself, which was a bad habit in his opinion, he'd admit how deeply his emotions ran for Cassie. They spent a lot of time together. Whenever anyone questioned or teased him if he was "tapping that", he gave his typical response that he and the kid simply enjoyed doing the same things. His old "we're just close friends" reply wasn't going to work much longer, especially after watching her move that lithe body of hers and wanting to run his hands over every delectable inch.

He'd expected to find his jogging companion in tears, near desolation, not out on the dance floor having a helluva good time. His male ego was taking a bit of a beating. Was he so easily forgotten? Still, on closer observation, her cheeks were flushed. Even from across the dance floor, with that damn strobe light blinking on and off, her eyes held wildness. When the waitress taking care of Cassie's table came to the bar with her next order, Quinn motioned her over. "What are the girls drinking tonight?" He jerked his chin toward Cassie and her friends.

"Two of them are drinking strawberry daiquiris. The other one, the one who's been crying, is doing tequila shots."

"Shots? Cassie doesn't drink shots. A beer now and then." He glanced toward the dance floor again. Cassie stumbled and Misty caught her. "Cut her off. Now." Hell, with her dressed like that, tossing back shots and pissed at him, this could turn into a clusterfuck in a hurry. Her sweetness was rarely marred by her temper, but when it was, she was a pistol to handle.

The waitress leaned back and studied him. "You the asshole who broke her heart?"

"Me?" He feigned innocence. If there was one thing he could do well, beyond fighting fires and saving lives, it was acting. In fact, his whole life had become a three-act play—both tragedy and comedy. "What makes you think that?"

"She's been talking about some blue-eyed heartbreaker, and you fit the bill. Whoever tore her soul to hell and back ought to be hung up by the short hairs. She seems like a nice kid." The chatty waitress filled her tray with the order the bartender set in front of her. "She's thinking of leaving town." Having dropped that effing bomb, she took off.

Christ. Cassie leave Clearwater because of him? This was where her family lived. Where she grew up. Where her clientele resided. Loneliness crept in and wrapped its cold, gnarly hands around his gut and squeezed. She'd been part of his world for three years.

The sunshine of his existence. What would his life be like without her in it?

A group of guys moved in, surrounding Cassie and her friends on the dance floor, their playful intent obvious.

Quinn took a long swig of beer. The horny bastards merited watching.

The blond guy with hair past his shoulders stepped behind Cassie and grabbed her hips, rubbing his groin against her ass. She flashed the sumbitch a smile over her shoulder, and Quinn's gut clenched.

His fingers coiled tighter around the bottle. Hadn't he so much as told her to move on? Still, he hadn't expected her to get drunk and allow the first asshole that came down the pike to put his damn hands all over her.

The music stopped and Cassie sauntered toward a table with her friends. A slow tune started and blond guy grabbed her arm, pulling her into an embrace. His grimy hands slid down her back to cup her ass.

Someone turned off the strobe lights during the bump and grind music, which gave Quinn a clearer view of the dance floor and blond guy's touchy-feeling dance style. Evidently, holding a conversation while dancing was out. Asshole was practically chewing on Cassie's neck.

Possessiveness rolled and burned in Quinn's gut. No one had the right to touch his angel like that, dammit. Not that she was exclusively his. She was the angel in her family and at the fire station, too, if his co-workers' anger at him after he'd blown her off was any indication.

God, his feelings for her jumbled his emotions and created havoc with his mind more and more every damn day. Breaking things off with her before they started had been wise. It was his method that sucked raw eggs. That's why he was here, to explain…what? Why? Hell, he could never explain why.

He expelled a curse and jammed his hand into the front pocket of his jeans. Spinning on the barstool toward the bartender, Quinn slapped a bill on the bar. "Shot of Jim Beam and a beer chaser."

Goddammit, some motherfucker had his hands on Cassie's ass! Wildness burned so hot in him it nearly seared all rational thought—except for murder. Hell, murder was rational, wasn't it?

Shot glass in hand, his gaze ricocheted back to Cassie. She reached behind her to ply the man's hands off her bottom and place them higher on her back. *Good girl.* Words were exchanged. Blond guy acquiesced. Evidently he wasn't as dumb as he looked. Quinn tossed back the shot, hissed a breath through his teeth and ignored his stomach's protest.

If he didn't soon make his move, blond guy would have her out the door and on the way to who knows where. He downed a few swallows of beer and stood. As Grandpa Hudson was prone to say, "Eating crow never comes easy."

By the time Quinn shouldered his way through the crowd on the dance floor, blond guy had his hands on Cassie's ass again. Quinn slowly circled the couple. Her dance partner was too busy getting his rocks off by rubbing up against her to take notice. Cassie, on the other hand, caught sight of him and her eyes widened. Her mouth silently formed his name. She knew his work schedule at the fire and rescue station. Seeing him here must have really shocked her.

So, what was it to be? Option A? Act like a gentleman and tap blond guy on his shoulder, asking to cut in? Or option B? Belt the bastard in the jaw?

Possessiveness could be a volatile bastard, uncontrollable as hell and prone to rear its head at the worst times. The thought of tossing Cassie over his shoulder and carrying her to his Wrangler appealed, which totally went against what he'd told her back at the station.

The band announced they were taking a break and the ensuing silence birthed another option. One Quinn liked even better. Option C for crazy. "There you are, Dominatrix Cassie." He took her hand, bowed over it and kissed her knuckles with feigned reverence.

She jerked her hand to her chest and narrowed her cat eyes. "What are you doing here? Why are you speaking to me now?"

"Is this the submissive you've chosen for our *ménage à trois* tonight?"

Blond guy's eyes lit up. "A ménage? Hell, yeah!" His head bobbed, teeth gleaming in the semi-darkness.

Oh, this was going to be fun. Quinn extended his hand to the man. "Hi, name's Georgio, but most guys just call me Donkey, cause of the size of my dong." He grabbed his crotch. "Not to worry, though. I'll lube you up good first. Your name is?"

The kid's smile dimmed and he shuffled his feet. "Ah...Dustin." His gaze flicked from Quinn to Cassie. "Look, I'm not sure what all's going on here. Maybe you better fill me in."

"Georgio?" Cassie's eyebrows rose, folding her forehead, and her hands went to her hips. "*Georgio?* What the hell are you talking about?"

"I'm talking about those release papers. Did you have Dustin sign them? We don't want another lawsuit." Quinn looked at the blond guy who shook his head and shrugged. "I'll handle this, Dustin." Once again, Quinn captured both of her hands in his and bowed over them. "Dominatrix, at the risk of angering you, need I remind you what you did to Pepe, the last guy you chose for our threesome?"

Her jaw was agape. "The *last* guy?"

Quinn shook his head once and tsked a couple times. He clasped a hand on Dustin's shoulder and leaned in to whisper conspiratorially. God this kid smelled like the make-up counter at Macy's. "You see, Dominatrix Cassie is enamored of hot wax play. After Pepe got naked and stretched out on his stomach, she shoved the unlit end of a candle in big Pepe's ass and lit the wick. While waiting for the wax to melt, she cranked the torture rack—"

Dustin's eyeballs bulged. "Torture rack?"

He nodded. "After she clamps restraints on the man's ankles

and wrists, she cranks his legs and arms out until he screams. If they aren't loud enough, she cranks a little more. Truthfully, she likes it when their shackled hands and feet meet."

"Fuck." Dustin wrapped his arms around his chest, pushed his knees together and scowled at Cassie.

"Liar! I would never hurt anyone like that." She kicked Quinn's shin. "Don't piss me off, bucko. I'm running out of places to hide the bodies."

He fought the urge to laugh. She could be damn comical when she was pissed. "Thank you, Mistress Cassie. I do love it when you discipline me." He winked. "You know how it turns me on." He faced Dustin again. "Back to my story about Pepe. She'd crawled beneath the torture rack so she could force the man's cock and balls into a cage."

"Cage?" Dustin squeaked, his head whipped toward her and he stepped back.

Quinn nodded. "A little one, wired for electrical shocks." His open hands mimicked the size of a coffee mug. "Poor Pepe was screaming, first in English and then in Spanish. Or was it Portuguese? Mistress Cassie thought they were shrieks of ecstasy." He shrugged and lifted his hands in a helpless gesture. "How was she to know Pepe had farted and shot the candle from his ass onto his back, setting his hair on fire." He shook his head again. "Pepe was a hairy bastard. The poor sumbitch went up like a roman candle."

Dustin gasped. "Holy hell."

Cassie jerked the bill of Quinn's ball cap. "Listen you lying idiot. I'm so mad at you right now, I could ram *your* balls into a cage. Although I'd need a bigger one than you claim I used on Pepe." She pointed to his crotch. "See his jeans, Dustin? They look like his crotch has the mumps."

Dustin forked his fingers in his hair. "You're a crazy woman." He pivoted toward Quinn. "Tell me, what happened to the dude, Pepe? Did he…did he live?"

"Oh, he's fine, even with second-degree burns. I was there to put out the fire." He aimed a grin at Cassie. "I've got a fair amount of experience at that."

Dustin pointed at Cassie. "You are one sick bitch." He scurried back to his friends.

Cassie whirled on Quinn. "What the hell was that about?"

He grabbed her elbow and marched her toward her table. "That was me clearing out the shark tank. Get your purse. You're coming with me." Now that his comedy routine was over, his anger returned with a vengeance. Little Miss Cassie was in for one hellacious lecture before he apologized for what he'd said at the fire station and took her home.

"Like hell!" Her plump lower lip stuck out, and she reached for her drink.

He snatched the glass from her hand and slammed it back on the table. "You don't want to push me right now. Not with all the anger I've got rolling around in my gut. What were you thinking to let a strange guy put his hands on your ass?" He glanced at her two friends sitting at the table, both of whom were wide-eyed, having just sucked air over his words. "Which one of you three is the designated driver tonight? And don't you dare tell me it was supposed to be her." He jerked his head toward Cassie.

Sara meekly raised her hand. "I am." She slid her cocktail in front of Misty. The three young women had shared an apartment for over a year. Quinn would sooner Cassie still lived with Wolf, but he understood her need to exert some independence. He'd just wished her roommates exerted a more mature attitude. Hell, if he had his way, her roomies would be a passel of nuns, especially after Cassie's behavior tonight.

"I'll see that she gets home safely, ladies." Anger, scalding hot, seared part of his brain even as he snatched Cassie's wrap and purse from Sara's outstretched hands. He couldn't get beyond the vision of another man touching Cassie. He shook her arm and marched her toward the door. "You'll be lucky if I don't paddle that fine ass of yours once I get you out to my Jeep."

She aimed a finely waxed dark eyebrow at him, her heart-shaped face pulling at the possessiveness in his soul. "You don't have the balls."

CHAPTER THREE

Quinn shoved open the door and Cassie's feet tangled as he jerked her through it, the fresh air a welcome relief on her skin after the stuffiness inside the bar.

"I want you to take a few deep breaths to help clear that booze buzz you've got goin' on." His familiar woodsy cologne overtook her senses when he hauled her against his hard chest and leaned to whisper in her ear. " Cause you just made the foolish mistake of telling me I don't have the balls to do something. Little girl, you have no idea what I've done in the past, or what I'm capable of doing in the future."

In the moonlight, augmented by the parking lot security lights, his eyes glittered an odd mixture of blue-grey beneath the bill of his black ball cap. His proclamation triggered an unlikely concoction of fright and craving that poured through her system like hot chocolate on peanut butter ice cream. The desire to lean into him and curl her fingers into his faded Harvard t-shirt was so keen she had to fight to resist.

"Why are you so angry with me?" In the three years she'd known him, he'd never revealed this aspect of his personality. "And don't call me little girl."

His hands settled at her waist. "Turning twenty-one doesn't automatically make you an adult."

"Yeah, well, bragging about your conquests doesn't exactly make you a good lover either." She was tired of hearing about the females in his life, knowing he'd never give her ten minutes of his time, much less a corner of his heart. Which, of course, was the problem. She wanted his whole womanizing heart, not just a jagged edge. She didn't care how many women he'd had before her; she just wanted to be his last. *Yeah, fat chance, Cassie. Wise up.*

He wound his fingers around her upper arm and steered her toward his Wrangler. "You allowed a man to put his hands on you."

If she didn't know better, she would have sworn he'd spoken through clenched teeth as if he were pissed. But why? "We were slow dancing. People touch when they slow dance, or haven't you noticed?" Earlier, on the dance floor, Quinn had deliberately circled her and Dustin twice, glaring as if he could kill, as if he were… Joy blossomed and warmed her soul. "Wait, are you *jealous* that someone had their hands on me?"

A harsh bark of laughter escaped. "Jealous? Me? Peanut, don't go reading more into this than a good friend merely covering your back. You're grasping at straws."

Maybe. Maybe not. Maybe some overconfident man needed his buttons pushed. "I'm glad, because I do need to move on. Just because you don't find me attractive doesn't mean another man won't feel differently if I give him half a chance."

He stopped for an instant before his hold on her tightened and he marched her forward.

"Dustin gave me his cell number earlier. I'll call him tomorrow and explain your wild story was just that, a *wild* story. Maybe I'll have him over for some homemade lasagna." If Quinn showed no qualms about her making his favorite dish for another man, then she'd have to face reality: the man she'd crushed on for years had no feelings for her.

"Lasagna?" Quinn backed her against his vehicle. "You'd make lasagna for him?"

"Well, yes. You've tasted my pot roast. It's not always the best, but my lasagna—"

He grabbed her upper arms and shook her, his body practically vibrating with anger. "You make lasagna for no one, but me. Do you hear? Me." As if the emotional force behind his words registered, a pained expression narrowed his eyes and pinched his lips. "Dammit, Cassie, you're killing me here." His head slowly inclined. "Killing me," he groaned. "Surely," he kissed one corner of her mouth. "Fucking," he kissed the other side. "Killing me." His lips made contact with hers and all the moisture in the upper half of her body dropped to the apex of her thighs.

Fingers that had dug into her arms seconds earlier now forked into her hair, holding her head while his lips molded and seduced hers, sipping, tasting, taunting.

Cassie backed farther into the metal of the Jeep as if she could absorb some of its steely strength because her legs were quickly turning to jelly. All these years, she'd jokingly called him hot lips, but she'd had no clue. *Dear God in heaven. This is better than I ever dreamed.*

His tongue brushed across the seam of her lips twice. "Open for me, angel." His deep voice sent sensations up her spine like the stroke of a lover's hand.

She did and his tongue swept in to lay claim, as if she hadn't always been his. He tasted of beer and lime and sexual potency. Her arms wrapped around his neck and he stepped closer until their thighs touched, the heat from him nearly frying her brain cells.

His lips left hers and moved across her cheek to her jaw, where he kissed, bit and soothed with his tongue. Warm lips trailed down her neck, sucking, pulling moans from her throat. "When I saw you with that other guy, I nearly went insane. I wanted to get twenty kinds of possessive, no matter what I told you earlier. You've got me so freakin' tied up in knots I can't think straight. All I know is, at this moment, I want to mark you like some wild beast so no male will ever approach you again."

"Yes, Quinn!"

As if her exclamation had carried a bucket of ice water, he broke contact and his hands lifted in a stop gesture. He stepped back and shook his head. "I did not say that."

Her heart beat so fast, she could barely breathe. "Yes...yes, you did." No way was she going to allow him to recant those words. She'd been waiting for three long years to hear them.

"This," he motioned with two fingers from him to her and back again, "is not happening. I'm not...we're not..." He spun and inhaled loudly as if to purge something from his body. "*Fuck.*"

She grabbed his arm and spun him around. Having two brothers, she knew how to get in a guy's face. "Why not? Give me one good reason, because this running hot and cold thing you're doing is driving me nuts." She jabbed her index finger into his pecs. "One minute you tell me you're not interested." Her second finger-jab was harder and his dark eyebrows rose. "Then you show up here and kiss me senseless." A firmer finger-jab made Quinn grunt. "The next minute you're pushing me away again." She curled her fingers into a fist and bumped his pecs—and God knew how she loved them. "You know what, Quinn Gallagher? I think, when it comes to me, you're chicken shit."

He grabbed her fist and wrenched her hand behind her. "Damn you, Cassie." His other hand fisted in her hair, jerking her head back. "Stop pushing me." His handsome face morphed into a mask of dark scowls. "Can't you get it through that pretty head I don't want more than friendship from you?" He leaned his forehead against hers. "God sakes, don't do this to me. To yourself. I adore you," he exhaled a ragged breath, "but as a friend, a jogging buddy, someone to hang out with." He stepped back. "Nothing more."

She took in his tortured expression. Which one of them was in denial here? What the hell was his problem? Her arms wrapped around her waist as if to shield herself from any more emotional blows. She knew what her problem was. It was loving six-foot-three of finely corded muscle with zero capacity for deep emotion. "You can put away your spear now. You've wounded me twice in one evening with the truth according to Quinn Gallagher. I can't take anymore. I'd ask what you're doing here, why you aren't at the station, but what the hell does it matter?"

He slid fingertips into the front pockets of his faded jeans, the muscles of his shoulders and arms shifting under the cotton material of his shirt. "I took some personal time. I need to apologize for the things I said to you. I hurt you and I'm sorry. It was all uncalled for."

"Wolf made you come, didn't he?" This had her brother's imprint all over it. He'd been doting on her since the fire that took their parents' lives. Tears burned the back of her throat and pricked her eyes. "So you took off work to ease tensions with your jogging partner. My feelings as a woman meant nothing." She could play the guilt card with him. Hadn't Misty told her to make him feel like an ass for hurting her? A car pulled into the parking lot, drawing her attention for a beat before she looked at his tense face again. No, playing emotional games was never her thing. "Look, it's obvious I can't hide the way I feel about you. Maybe it's best if we stay away from each other."

"Cassie." There was a deep strain in his voice.

Twin tears spilled over and tumbled down her cheeks. "You can't have it both ways. You can't keep me around for a buddy and then reject my feelings." She tugged her cell from her purse and scrolled through her contacts. "I'm calling a taxi to take me home. Go on back to the station." A hot bath, comfy sleep clothes, a quart of chocolate brownie ice cream and a few hours of crying and maybe...*maybe* she could make it through the night.

Quinn unlocked the door. "Get in. We're not done talking. When we are, I'll take you home."

She couldn't endure one more minute with him, not when she knew how he really felt about her.

"No. We're done. Have a good life, Quinn." She'd made two steps before his arm banded around her waist and lifted her.

"I said we're not through talking, dammit. Now, get your sweet ass in my Jeep." He plopped her on the seat and buckled her in. "If you want me out of your life, my friend, fine. But before I walk away, I have some things to teach you."

She folded her arms over her chest. "You don't have a damn thing to teach me. Although I am a little intrigued how you knew about hot wax play. Isn't that some BDSM shit? Beyond that, we have nothing to discuss."

He shrugged. "We watch the occasional movie at the station."

She glared at Quinn, sauntering in front of his vehicle. So he enjoyed watching dirty movies. What guy didn't? Was that what made him disinterested? Her innocence? She glared out the passenger window and swiped at a tear. Hell, the closest thing she knew to sex games was Spin the Bottle—and if that wasn't damn pathetic, what was?

He settled behind the steering wheel and clicked his seatbelt. "How about a walk on the beach?"

"How about you telling me why I don't do it for you?"

"Peanut." His voice was almost a moan of remorse.

"Don't you peanut me. Am I so ugly, so immature, so annoying?" She lifted her open hands in a helpless gesture. "What? I'm good enough to hang out with, to jog with, to go see a movie with, but not date. Why? You've already humiliated me today, so fess up. Tell me why the thought of our being a romantic couple makes you want to throw up."

He started the engine and shoved the Jeep into reverse. "I never said that. You're overreacting."

She punched him. Once, twice, three times in the arm. "Overreacting? After all you've put me through today? You arrogant asshole." She slapped his arm again and shifted in her seat so her back was toward him. Good god, what a day.

"Would you settle down?" He pulled onto route 60 and sped toward Clearwater Beach. Since he had the top off his Wrangler, the cool evening air blew over them. Cassie wrapped her black knit shawl tighter around her shoulders. Both were silent, the tension between them hanging thicker than early morning fog off the gulf. He hung a left onto South Gulfview Boulevard and zipped into the parking lot at Mossie's Island Grill.

"You're favorite place. Have you eaten, pea...Cassie?" He undid his seatbelt and shifted in his seat.

"Not hungry."

"Well, I am. Come on. Let's get something. You know you love Mossie's food."

I'll never be able to come here again. How often have we come here together?

After placing an order to go, the two of them removed their shoes, locking them in the wheel hub along with her purse. Spending time with him alone on a darkened, deserted beach would have been a dream come true a day or so ago. Now, it was merely another nail hammered into the coffin of her dreams. How many ways could he tell her goodbye?

He removed a blanket from the back of the Jeep and passed it to her before he shrugged into a jean jacket he discovered jammed under some tools. She followed him toward the beach while he carried the bag of food and a six-pack. Gone was their usual jovial rapport. An uncomfortable silence settled over them, and she wished she were home where she could fall apart in solitude.

"How's your soft crab sandwich?" Quinn shoved a curly fry into his mouth.

Is that what she was eating? Her taste buds were suffering from a broken heart, too, if such a pitiful thing were possible. "It's okay." She drained her second beer and reached for a third.

His warm hand covered hers. "Go easy on that stuff."

She popped the top and guzzled, not because she was thirsty, but because she was through taking orders from anyone.

Quinn crumpled the empty French fry bag and shoved it into their take-out tote. His arms angled over his raised knees. "Look, I know you're pissed, but you need someone to teach you a few things."

The can of Coors stilled near her lips. "Oh, really? I suppose you are the fountain of feminine knowledge." She finished off the beer. Between the greasy fries and three beers, her stomach had expanded to the size of Eagle Lake.

"I know enough not to take a drink of anything I've walked away from to use the restroom or dance. Someone could easily slip in a date rape drug. Remember that."

She nodded and belched. "Got it. Quinn is afraid of being raped."

He grabbed her shoulders and pressed her down on the blanket. "You think this is funny?" His breath skimmed her face. "If you're not more aware of your surroundings, one day you're going to wake up in a strange place, naked, sore and bleeding from the rectum. You won't know who or how many men have had you… or in what ways."

How dare he? "I'm not that kind of person." Her stomach rolled in time with the waves.

He tossed his hat aside and his eyes widened in the moonlight. "Are you that naïve? The drug will render you powerless. Read up on it. You dress in scanty I'm-yours-for-the-taking clothes and sashay into a bar? No wonder guys come flocking over. Hell, you're a damn attractive woman, Cassie."

"Just not attractive enough for you."

"Don't you get it? Our problem isn't with you. It's with me."

She pushed him aside and sat. The shoreline seemed to tilt for a few seconds. She glanced at Quinn over her shoulder. "Are you gay?"

"Hell no, I'm not gay."

"Oh yeah? Show me."

He laughed and shook his head. "Oh no, little one. I'm not falling for that challenge."

"And I'm not begging anymore. I'm through." Her pride could only take so much trampling. She stood and bent to gather their trash. It took three tries to grab an empty beer can. Damn thing kept moving. "Take me home, Quinn. My ego can't survive another beating."

He stood and reached for her. "Peanut."

"I'm finished. I love you, but I have to love myself more." She hurried to one of the nearby beach trash receptacles and tossed everything away, including her hopes and dreams. Quinn wasn't far behind as she trudged through the sand toward his Wrangler. She'd lost everything.

First her parents. Then, not long ago, her beauty shop had burned to the ground a mere ten days after the grand opening. Until renovations were complete in the little strip mall where her business once stood, she was working part-time at a national chain of salons in a larger, more modern shopping mall. Now, Quinn had made it all too clear they could never have a romantic relationship. She'd made such a fool of herself, mooning over him at the station, she couldn't step foot in there again.

The world spun for a few seconds, and she wrapped her arms around the trunk of a palm tree to keep from sliding off the planet. Cold sweat beaded on her forehead and neck. She swallowed convulsively.

"Cassie?" Quinn's hands were at her waist. "What's wrong?"

She leaned over and vomited until everything she'd eaten and drank in the last day, or maybe the past week, was purged from her stomach. Quinn scooped her into his arms and ran with her to his Wrangler.

CHAPTER FOUR

Quinn thumbed Wolf's number on his cell. "Did I wake you?"

"No. Watching a flick with the guys. Did you find my sister?"

"I've got her in the Jeep with me. She got sick and passed out. You want to call Becca and tell her I'm on my way with Cassie?"

"What did you do? Get her drunk?"

Quinn snorted. "Hell, she did that her damn self." He ended the call before Wolf could fire off more questions.

The lights were on at Becca's townhouse and the front door hung open. Einstein, her German shepherd, barked from the yard where she walked him. Quinn crouched, bracing himself. "Hey, buddy!" Einstein barreled toward him, his large paws making contact with Quinn's shoulders and pushing him against the front tire of his vehicle. A wet tongue slurped across his face. "Yeah, I like you, too." He stood and the dog sat at his feet, panting.

"Is she still asleep?" Becca leaned to capture Einstein's leash.

"I think it's more a matter of being passed out than asleep. She was doing shots. Then we ate some greasy food at Mossie's and she guzzled a few beers."

Becca's lips pursed and she forked her fingers in her red hair. "Wolf's going to give her such a lecture. You know how protective he is where his family's concerned."

Boy, did he ever. His neck still throbbed at times. "I'll run interference on that as best I can." He glanced over his shoulder at the sleeping form slumped in the passenger seat. The street light in front of his vehicle created a yellow glare over Cassie's pretty face. "I said a lot of things to hurt her."

Wolf's fiancée stepped toward him. "Why? Why do you hold her at arm's length when it's obvious you care for her?"

He shook his head. "No. I don't." Maybe if he told this damn lie enough he'd start to believe it himself. "Hell, Becca, she's just a friend. We hang out. Nothing more."

Einstein whined and Becca bent to scratch his neck. "Who was she?" The redhead straightened and stared him straight in the eyes. "Who was the woman in your past who hurt you so badly you're afraid to care again, to love again?" Her head tilted to the side as if waiting for a name, an explanation. "Because I'm not buying the load of bull you're trying to shovel on everyone."

Quinn forced a chuckle. "You interviewing me for that blog of yours or your newspaper column?" Becca wrote a popular and sometimes snarky blog entitled "The Things Men Do." She'd used it as a stepping stone to getting her own column in the local newspaper.

She glanced down the street, the corners of her mouth slightly upturned. Her open hand gave a dismissive wave. "You forget. I was once in your place. Scarred and scared and determined to outrun Wolf." She shot him a quick glance. "It won't happen, you know. Once one of those Wolfords set his or her sights on someone, that person doesn't stand a chance. I think it's a family trait."

"Didn't take him long to capture you." Less than two months after moving into the townhouse next door, Wolf had a diamond on Becca's finger. He'd storm-crashed through the walls she'd erected around her heart after her ex-husband left her a year earlier.

No one, including the woman in front of him, could understand why Quinn lived behind an emotional fortress. After the cluster-fuck of his mission in Chile, he'd encased his warped heart in cold, hard lead. Renata's betrayal, the ensuing loss of four members of his team and the damage to his reputation with the agency had pretty much corroded the hell out of his soul. Putting a bullet between Renata's scheming eyes had further twisted him so severely inside, he wasn't fit for anyone, much less someone as sweet as Cassie. She was sunshine to his darkness, emotional openness to his secrets, purity to his evil. Yet, damn if he wouldn't give his right nut for things to be different. *Yeah, crap into your ball cap and wish, Gallagher, and all you're gonna have is a hatful of shit.*

He exhaled a long sigh, pushing his dark thoughts to the dank recesses of his mind. "Where do you want me to put Cassie? I need to get back to the station." He had a long night of thinking and planning ahead of him. Before he'd let Cassie leave her family, he'd resign from the fire and rescue station and head for parts unknown—or home. His stomach cramped at that thought. Wouldn't his old man just shit a brick if he returned to the Truman Building, near the White House, or back to the Pentagon, across from Arlington?

"In the guest bedroom upstairs." Becca pivoted and pointed toward her front door. "Ah...there's ibuprofen in the upper cabinet to the left of the kitchen sink, if you can get her to take them. Otherwise she's going to have a terrible headache in the morning. Bottled water's in the refrigerator. If you think you can handle Cassie by yourself, I'll take Einstein for his walk before bedtime."

"Sure. No problem." If Becca and the dog left, she'd take her inquiring mind along with her. Damn if she didn't read him too well.

"Put Cassie in the blue bedroom at the top of the stairs and close the door behind you." She patted her pocket. "I've got my key."

"Okay, will do." He circled the front of the Wrangler and unlocked the door to lift Cassie out. Before he did, he unlocked the glove box and retrieved her birthday gift, shoving it into the interior pocket of his jean jacket. After snatching her purse, he slung his unconscious passenger over his shoulder in a fireman's carry. Gentle snoring drifted from her lips and her appealing fragrance of peaches and cream filled his nostrils, as did the stench of vomit and Dustin's strong aftershave. *Jesus, what an unholy combination.*

Once inside, he strolled through Becca's townhouse to her kitchen to retrieve the water and headache medicine. His gaze drifted to a framed cross-stitch picture of Einstein hanging on Becca's dining room wall. No doubt the crafty person who'd made it was the same individual who'd sewn and framed the fireman's insignia hanging in his living room. Cassie believed in giving gifts she'd made herself. His arms tightened around her legs, molding her to him. He'd never met anyone as selfless as she.

The birthday gift he'd tucked into his jacket pocket rubbed against his chest as he ascended the steps. It was a present he should never have bought her. Yet it was the only thing he'd found during his long hours of searching that even came close to suiting her personality. After all that passed between them tonight, giving it to her probably wasn't a wise choice. He should take it back to the jewelers for a refund. Hell, the thing was solid gold and the diamonds top quality.

He gnashed his teeth in resolve. He'd be damned if another woman would ever wear *her* necklace.

Cassie groaned and shifted on the bed once he laid her down and flicked on the bedside lamp. Her dark hair with a splash of red dye in the front feathered across the pillow. He set the water and bottle of ibuprofen on the table before slipping off her red stilettos. Pretty red toenails greeted him, and he rubbed them, brushing off a few grains of sand.

He rolled her to her side, unzipped the back of her red leather skirt and snaked it down over her hips. Holy hell. He pinched his eyes shut. A red lace thong. One quick yank and he had the skirt pooled on the bottom of the bed. He forked his fingers through his hair in frustration, his need growing greater by the second. *You cannot freaking touch her, man.*

Next would be her sweater. If she hadn't thrown up, he'd let her sleep in it. But waking up reeking of vomit would only acerbate the headache she was sure to have. Lifting one arm at a time, he worked them out of the pullover.

The jostling pulled her from a deep slumber.

"Don't. Want Quinn."

"I'm here, peanut." He tugged the sweater over her head and tossed it on the floor. High, firm breasts nearly spilled from her red lace bra. He allowed his gaze to take a long, slow journey over her body. His cock rose to take a peek too. No little girl ever looked like this. She really had grown up. His fingers flexed. He'd seen her in a bikini many times, but her swimming attire was nothing compared to red peekaboo lace—what there was of it.

"I'll be right back." He slipped off his jean jacket and tossed it on the foot of the bed.

"Don't go." Her lips formed a pout.

If he didn't put some distance between them, he'd have his hands all over her. Hell, he'd be all over her. The last thing he ever wanted to do was take advantage of this sexy bundle of innocence and sweetness.

He stormed into the bathroom and turned on the shower, sticking his head under the cold spray for a good thirty seconds. He gasped and sputtered, hoping, willing the coldness to subdue his cock. Grabbing a towel, he blotted his face and hair dry. He snatched a washcloth and held it under hot water to clean Cassie's face, neck and hands. If he could, he'd wash her all over to cleanse her of Dustin's touch. She should smell of Quinn's scent, not another man's. Never another man's. *Keep your head on straight, man. Pack that possessive shit up and lock it away.*

He sat on the side of the bed and wiped off her face, neck and shoulders while she mumbled and complained in her sleep. "Cassie, open your eyes." He shook a couple pills into his hand and held them out to her.

"Mmm?" Her eyelids fluttered.

He slid an arm under her shoulder and lifted her into a sitting position. "Open your mouth and take these pills."

She stuck out her tongue to accept the medicine.

He exhaled an unsteady breath. His cock grew again with a pink-tongued destination in mind. Cassie was day-by-day, hour-by-hour becoming his obsession. Fighting her off hurt like hell, but giving her false hope of a happy ever after would be damn cruel. That's why he had to leave Clearwater. She was already talking to her friends about moving to get away from him. Her family was here; she needed them. If anyone had to go, it should be him. Really, besides his job, a small circle of friends, and her, what did he have to hold him in this Gulfside community?

He tumbled the pills onto her tongue and held the bottled water to her mouth. "Swallow."

She obeyed, with a tiny stream of water dribbling off her pointy chin.

"Open." He wanted to make sure she'd swallowed them.

She mindlessly complied, her eyes still closed.

Yeah baby, his cock commented, pointing its selfish head in her direction, straining Quinn's jeans to the point of bursting.

"Lie down." He needed to get the hell out of here. Just how much temptation was a guy supposed to take? He slid the covers over her shoulders. "Sleep well."

"Quinn?" The enticing sultry sleepiness of her voice drew him closer like a magnet.

"Yeah, baby?" God, he had to leave.

"I love you."

Even in her sleep, she could rip his heart in two. He closed his eyes and pressed a long kiss to her forehead. After tonight, he'd never see her again. "I love you, too, angel. Be happy. Live well, baby." When he opened his eyes, his gaze fell on a tall, slender form in the open doorway, shadowed in the darkness by the light in the hallway. Einstein pranced into the room and rested his chin on the sheets next to Cassie's arm.

Quinn stood, his gaze slowly sweeping over Cassie for one final glimpse, devouring and memorizing every beautiful detail. He snatched his jacket and removed her birthday present to set it on the nightstand, whispered her name on a pained exhale and did what he did so well—denied and buried the pain.

Becca reached to stop him when he exited the room. "Why won't you tell her how you feel? I can see what this is doing to you and I know how crazy she is about you."

Silent, he shouldered past her and stormed down the steps, abandoning the better part of his world.

CHAPTER FIVE

Quinn slouched in the orange plastic chair, his legs spread, eyes half closed. Despite his nonchalant state, he cataloged his surroundings—like the organized interior of Captain Noah Steele's office and the captain's end of a phone conversation regarding a firefighter's treatment at the emergency room. Muffled sounds of running showers and typical station banter filtered through his superior's office walls. Smoke stench still hugged the lining of Quinn's nose, fainter now after a shower and flushing out his nasal passages. He tilted his head to the right and absorbed Wolf's tense demeanor. The man hadn't stopped glaring at him since he'd set foot in the fire captain's inner sanctum. Evidently Wolf was still pissed over the way he'd spoken to Cassie yesterday.

Requesting a meeting with his two bosses so soon after a three-alarm fire at a high-rise probably wasn't the best timing. The call had come in about twenty minutes after he'd returned from leaving Cassie at Becca's, and the blaze had taken nearly six-hours to contain. Everyone was drained, physically and emotionally. Still, he needed to put his plan into effect before his candy ass chickened out. God, walking out of Cassie's life was going to rip him apart inside, yet he'd been sliced-and-diced before and endured...in a half-assed manner of speaking. No doubt he'd survive another ration of pain.

Noah settled the receiver back on the desk phone. "Boyd's got smoke inhalation, diminished lung function and signs of angina." He stretched his arms over his head, fisted his hands and yawned. "Typical stuff. They're keeping him overnight and running more tests in the morning. He'll be off a week and then light duty for a few more." He leaned back in his chair and locked his hands behind his head. "I want his equipment checked. Should never have happened."

"Maybe Boyd didn't connect everything correctly. His first fire with us. New gear and all." Wolf lifted a shoulder. "Could happen. I'll inspect his apparatus once numbnuts here spills his guts." He jerked his head toward Quinn before slumping farther into his chair and gulping from his water bottle.

Quinn inhaled and searched deep for the right words for his fire captain and the commander of his Marine Rescue Unit. *Hell, just spit it out.* "I'm giving my notice. One more forty-eight hour shift and then I'm gone." He owed them more notice than this, but he had to get away from Cassie before he lost the battle to keep his hands off of her.

Wolf jerked upright in his chair and fired the empty water bottle into the trash can, the plastic clanking against the metal container. "The hell you say." His dark eyes narrowed on Quinn and his broad hands slowly swept up and down his jeans as if he was trying to keep from wringing Quinn's neck.

"First the Drug Enforcement Agency and now us." Noah pinned Quinn with a hard stare. "You're starting a dangerous pattern of not sticking, man. Careful, it'll quickly become a loser's habit." His chair squeaked when he straightened and planted his forearms on the desk. "You better have a helluva good reason for walking out on us like this."

"Wait!" Wolf's gaze hinged from Noah to Quinn, his mouth agape. "You were DEA? Fuckin' DEA?" He leaned forward, his piercing eyes stared at Quinn as if seeing him for the first time and taking his measure.

Unable to hold it back, Quinn laughed at Wolf. "Can't stand being left out in the cold, can you?" Wolf obviously had a nut in a twist discovering he knew so little about his co-worker and friend. He shifted his attention to Noah. "To answer your question, Captain, my reasons for leaving are personal."

"Are you having personnel issues with a member of the squad? Cause if you are, I'll haul his ass in here, and we'll have it out."

Shit, if he did, he'd handle it his damn self. "No. Things here are cool. These firefighters are a great bunch of guys. I'm honored to be counted among them." He shrugged. "Just feel a need to move on."

"*You* were DEA?" Wolf seemed caught on that one nugget. "Why the hell am I just now learning this? Man, we've been tight. I've included you in my family circle. Allowed you to spend time with my baby sister."

"True that." *And I've fallen in love with your baby sister. If I don't get away from her, I'm going to ruin her life, and damn if she doesn't deserve better.*

"Are the pressures of the job getting to you? Part of being a firefighter is seeing everyone's pain after they've lost everything. Their belongings, a pet...family members." Noah exhaled and shot a pained expression at Wolf.

The ex-SEAL crossed a booted foot over his knee and picked at the worn sole, his mouth a firm, straight line. Several years before Quinn came to Clearwater, an arsonist had set Wolf's parents' house on fire, killing them and leaving his four younger sisters orphaned. Cassie had barely been a teenager at the time. From what Wolf and his brother Jace had shared with Quinn over the last three years, it had been a particularly rough time for the family.

Wolf resigned his commission with the SEALs to finish raising his sisters and to keep Jace in college. Cassie went through some major behavior issues, which she nor Wolf rarely mentioned. Quinn always imagined Wolf easing her through whatever teenage angst she dealt with at the time, his steely fingers encased in kid gloves. He still handled his little sister with strict yet gentle commands. The bond the two siblings shared was substantial.

Noah repeated his question, irritation tingeing his voice. The fire captain was ex-military and didn't suffer fools lightly.

"No, I can handle the job stress. I'm thinking of moving up north with my parents." Or not. His dad had never forgiven him for losing his men in Chile and resigning from the State Department. As soon as he was through with this meeting, he planned to email some of his old co-workers to test the waters—at least the ones who'd still give him the time of day.

He'd already emailed his remaining team member, asking if he needed a new fellow on his mercenary squad. T-Bone had turned paranoid after Chile and did strange things to hide his identity. Imagine, an ex-military explosives expert using "SparklePrincess" as his email address. Quinn had to chuckle at the thought. If no openings were to be had with T-Bone's ragamuffin gang of brothers and a couple old Army buddies, or one of the government agencies, Quinn would start an online search at various fire stations in other states.

"You'd move back to DC? Leave the sun and sand? They just got eight…nine inches of snow up there a couple days ago. You feel the perverse need to shovel that shit?" Wolf slung an arm across the back corner of the chair and arched a dark eyebrow. "Or the need to walk away from Cassie?" He exhaled a harsh bark of laughter. "That's what this is about, isn't it, you son of a bitch? *Damn* your soul to hell for the pain you're going to cause her. You think Becca didn't start texting me the minute your sorry ass cleared her doorway? You think I don't know what the fuck she saw and overheard?"

"Wolf, stay on track. This is station business."

"Hell to the no. This is *family* business. My sister is crazy about this lying motherfucker. Hell, we haven't had a family meal or party that he hasn't been a part of. Now I find out he's been hiding a past. Does she know about this shit?" His eyes widened in question. "No, or she'd have mentioned it. And neither did I, dammit. You're one closed-mouthed son of a bitch."

"Calm down, Daddy Wolf. I was working for the government not hanging around some schoolyard, selling red tops to kids." Wolf was obsessively protective of his family. When he and Becca got married and started having kids, Quinn didn't even want to be around. Wolf would be a totally insane parent, micro-managing the child's every movement. Sadness pulled and twisted at Quinn's soul. He wouldn't be around, though, would he? No. He'd be long gone from this city he enjoyed, the angry man across from him, whom he respected like a brother even though he drove him crazy at times, and Cassie—every emotion always brought him back to his heart-faced love. *Man, I've got to pack this shit away.*

Noah scowled and leaned across his desk, his hands clasped and his gaze locked on Quinn. "Does this have anything to do with what went down in Chile?"

Aw hell. Quinn's stomach sank. How did Noah gain access to confidential information? "That's not open for discussion."

His captain's index finger rose like a flag on a pole. "Wolf knows what's said in this office stays between us. When you came here over three years ago with eyes as vacant as my brother-in-law's mind, I got curious. Damned curious. Magna cum laude in college—Harvard, no less—hellacious high scores on the civil service exam and a pristine background check. Exemplary service with the State Department. Yet you wanted to charge into burning buildings?" Noah grunted. "Made the back side of my balls tickle—and not in a good way. I made a few calls to some old Army buddies who work in the State Department."

"What the hell are you two talking about? This man's been my boat pilot for over two damn years, and I'm just *now* hearing he used to work for the Drug Enforcement Agency? Why wasn't I clued in?" Wolf's narrowed scrutiny swept over Quinn like a Mack truck over a pothole. "When were you with the State Department? And what the hell happened in Chile?"

Wolf would expect a full report. Quinn stared at the tiled

ceiling for a few beats, coming to a decision about how much info to share, how much he could, according to the department's confidentiality agreements he'd signed. Hell, he wasn't sharing a damned thing beyond general information.

"I worked for the State Department for two years or more before being assigned to temporary duty with the DEA. Any information beyond that is on a 'need to know' basis. You know how that works. I don't recall you regaling the family with tales of your old SEAL missions."

Wolf scowled for a few beats and then nodded. Quinn could have sworn a new level of respect glistened from his commander's eyes. "I feel what you're saying."

Noah leaned on his chair's two back legs and grinned in that smart-ass way he had. "So, Quinn, if this has nothing to do with your former work experiences—and I don't believe that song and dance for a minute—then what are we going to do with little Cassie after you run and hide?" He smirked at Wolf and winked. "Boyd's newly separated from his old lady. Bet he could use some of your sister's sweetness to help him over this smoke inhalation thing."

Like hell.

Wolf chuckled, *the bastard*. "Yeah, he might at that. I'll have to introduce them, if they haven't met already."

Quinn straightened in his chair, every muscle tensed. *Boyd and my angel? No fucking way.*

Wolf's eyebrows raised in question. "How are you going to feel once the rest of the single guys here find out you've cut Cassie loose? Man, you've got to know they've held back from asking her out because of you. Once they hear you're leaving, especially after the way you cut her down yesterday, they'll be sniffing around her like the horny sonsabitches they are."

A green haze poured over Quinn's vision field like monster goo from Cassie's favorite animated flick and, in a nanosecond, the green morphed to dark red boiling rage. He'd be damned if anyone sniffed around her. Not after he'd gotten a taste of her last night. His chair clattered to the floor as he lunged for Wolf.

CHAPTER SIX

A swath of sunlight burned Cassie's eyelids while some evil fiend inside her head, armed with a blowtorch, scorched her brain cells. She rolled away from part of the source of her discomfort and met Mr. Hangover, the booze beast, the harbinger of queasy stomachs and banger headaches. A long groan escaped as she covered her ears to keep them from tumbling off her head. She pried her eyelids a crack and noted blue and white striped sheets. Where was she?

Toenails clattered on the steps. Einstein, who must have heard her groan, charged around the corner into the bedroom, jumped on the bed and licked her face, whining a wail of concern.

"I'm okay, buddy. Just don't jar the bed, please." Her hand slipped from the covers to pet Becca's German shepherd. How did she end up here? Where were her clothes? Memories of last night slowly crept into her muddled mind.

Quinn.

She'd thrown up and he'd rushed her to his Jeep as if she was about to disintegrate into a bazillion bits of barf residue. He'd kissed her forehead and murmured words of comfort. Then he'd put her shoes on her feet after wiping off the sand. Her hand covered her eyes, gently, because they were about to pop out of her head and roll down her cheeks. *I certainly know how to make a good impression, don't I?*

Footsteps trunked up the steps. "Cassie? You up?"

She gasped and snatched the covers over her head. "Stop yelling, Wolf. And don't come in, I'm not decent."

"You've got ten minutes to shower and get dressed. Becca's at work, but she put some clean clothes on the vanity in the bathroom for you. I'm making breakfast and then we're talking. Don't dawdle."

"God, I feel like I'm fourteen again." How many times had he told her not to poke around, and how often had she done it just to hear him growl. After her parents died, he'd become her rock, her security.

Footsteps sounded on the steps as Wolf descended. "Hell, if you were fourteen, you'd be grounded and on some serious-assed restrictions. Ten minutes and counting."

She rustled under the covers and scratched behind Einstein's ears again. "Big man doesn't scare us, does he?"

Einstein whined and licked her face.

A pink wrapped gift on the nightstand caught her eye. Was it for her? Or was it something Wolf had left for Becca? But why would he put it here and not in Becca's bedroom? She reached for the oblong package and fingered the silver ribbon. A small gift tag read *"To Cassie, from Quinn. Happy Birthday, Peanut."*

Her heart rate kicked into the happy-to-be-me category. He'd bought her a gift. Even if it was something cheap and goofy, he'd thought enough of her to buy it and have it wrapped. So why didn't he bring it to her birthday party? Her eyes narrowed. Oh yeah, his mystery female visitor.

Pushing that thought aside, she slid the metallic ribbon off the box. No way could he have wrapped it so carefully. She slid her fingernail along the taped edge and folded back the iridescent pink paper. The embossed logo on the white jeweler's box impressed her. Had Quinn really gone to *Zales* to buy her a gift? She snapped the lid open and gasped. From a delicate gold chain dangled a filigree heart pendant. An angel nestled within the open scrollwork edging the heart. Small brilliant diamonds covered the angel's outstretched wings.

She blinked back tears. "Oh, Quinn, you *do* care. No matter what you say, you do care." When he'd kissed her last night, he'd called her his angel. Is this how he thought of her? As an angel who'd wormed her way into his heart? She slid two fingers beneath the pendant, the warmth of the gold soaking into her skin like the sun's rays on a bright June day. So beautiful. So fragile-looking and yet solid, just like her feelings for him.

She pressed the white box to her heart and sighed. Her first jewelry gift from a man, and the man was Quinn.

Einstein sniffed what she held and then laid his chin on her shoulder, his black eyes studying her. She ran a finger between his eyes and down his muzzle. "I have an admirer. He's just too scared to admit it yet. Poor schmuck." She giggled with glee and the dog licked her face. "Poor chicken shit schmuck." The canine's tail beat a happy rhythm on the bed.

"Cassie? Six minutes and thirty seconds!"

Her brother's booming voice snagged the dog's attention and he growled deep in his throat.

She placed a hand on Einstein's head. "Doesn't that man know I have a hangover? Why does he have to yell?"

The German shepherd woofed once. He bounded off the bed, charged to the top of the steps and barked as if he were saying, "Shut the hell up! Woman with a hangover up here!"

"Six damn minutes! Einstein? Want some kibble?" Toenails jangled down the stairway. Evidently the canine's stomach over-rode being chivalrous.

Cassie placed the gift from Quinn back on the nightstand and slowly sat, willing her aching body to cooperate. Just to prove Wolf didn't scare her with his macho bossiness, she took ten minutes to shower, dress and put on her angel necklace. Although if she were honest, she had to move slower than normal to lessen the effects of the Westminster chimes gonging in her head—in triplicate. If she lived through this hangover, she'd never drink booze again.

Wolf sat at Becca's dining room table, his rigid body posture familiar. He was about to give her holy hell. His narrow-eyed gaze swept to her before he pointed to the chair next to him. "Tomato juice. Drink. Coffee. Drink. Fried eggs. Eat."

She pointed to him. "Mouth. Close."

"Don't fu...play with me, Cassie. I'm not in the mood. You had no business doing shots and getting shitfaced."

A long-suffering sigh escaped. "I'm twenty-one. I can drink if I want."

He crossed his arms and assumed his faux-father bearing. "Being twenty-one also carries a passel of responsibilities, young lady."

Oh God, he was dragging out the "young lady" speech. She gulped the tomato juice and choked. "Holy hell, what's in this?"

"Two raw eggs, minced garlic, Tabasco sauce and a shot of whiskey." He had the audacity to wink. "Hair-o-the-dawg. It'll cure what ails ya." He made a wiggling motion with his fingertips. "Drink up."

"Will I feel better or worse?" She forced down a little more and her stomach churned and clenched. Then she noticed his winking expression continued. She tilted her head and studied him. "What's wrong with your eye?" His broad hand rose to cover it and she coiled her fingers around his wrist to yank it back. For a few seconds they played tug-of-war in the air until he relented and relaxed his muscles.

She stood and leaned over him, peering closely at his face. "Wolf, your eye is swollen. It's turning black and blue." Her fingers lightly traced the curve of his face. "Your cheek is bruised and your bottom lip is split. Are these work-related injuries?" His silence was telling; so was the fact he wouldn't make eye contact. "Were you in a fight?" This was so unlike her brother. "What on earth happened?"

"Quinn's fist and I had an intimate conversation."

"Quinn did this?" She collapsed in her chair and sipped more of the doctored tomato juice. "Why?" Quinn and her brother were close. Sure they teased, but never got out of hand with it. If either one needed help, the other one was there in a heartbeat.

Wolf gulped his coffee and slung an arm over the back of the chair. "I was pushing him. Trying to find out his true feelings about you."

Her hand covered the golden angel pendant. "And?"

He pointed to her eggs. "Eat those before they get any colder than they already have."

What had Wolf said to Quinn to set him off? Knowing her brother, if she didn't eat, he'd never tell her. She shoveled in a couple of bites and washed them down with coffee. Just to be sure he'd answer her questions, she drank most of the god-awful tomato juice, gagging a time or two. She blotted her lips with the napkin and tossed it at him.

Wolf snatched it mid-air, his normal smirk somewhat crooked since his cracked lower lip grew puffier by the minute.

"Okay, I've done like you asked. Now, it's your turn to tell me what happened between the two of you." She hoped their friendship wasn't ruined because of her. In some ways, Wolf and Quinn were as close as brothers.

Wolf leaned back in his chair, the front legs rising from the floor. "I've always suspected how Quinn felt about you, but after the way he spoke to you yesterday, I wasn't sure. Becca overheard him whispering some things to you after he'd put you to bed last night."

"What kind of things?" So Quinn had put her to bed. Had he taken off her clothes? No biggie, really. They'd gone swimming together before, so seeing her in a bra and thong wasn't the end of the world. Perhaps with another man, yes, but not with Quinn. Still, what had Becca overheard him saying to her?

"You'll have to ask Becca."

She crossed her arms and narrowed her eyes at her brother.

Damn, he could be so annoying. "If you know, why can't you just tell me?"

Wolf stood to retrieve the coffee carafe. He filled his mug and then topped off hers, before setting the empty pot on the table. "Because." He slumped in the chair and brought his mug partway to his lips. "Conversations between a couple are private. You'll learn that one day." He slurped his coffee and shook his head. "Okay, sis, here's the thing…" He ran a hand across the back of his neck and exhaled a long sigh. "Quinn turned in his notice this morning. He's leaving the station, and Florida."

Cold fingers of panic clutched her lungs and wrung every centimeter of air from their spongy honeycomb confines. Leaving Florida? No, he couldn't. Not her Quinn! "He what?"

"He's leaving. He's freaking scared and he's running. The man's in love with you." Wolf pointed to his face. "The fact he attacked me when I teased him about the guys at the station coming on to you after he leaves proves that. I wasn't sure before, but I am now. The thought of another man touching you drove him freaking crazy."

Her index finger caressed her angel necklace. "Why move away? I don't understand." Maybe Wolf didn't either. If she wanted answers, she needed to go to the source. "I'm going to his place. We need to talk." A thousand things, like grains of sand, sifted through her mind. "I've waited on that man for three years."

"Three?"

She stood, gathering her dirty dishes and silverware. "That's right. I fell in love with him when I was eighteen, but I sensed the situation was hopeless. For one, he treated me as if I were too young. And number two, would you have allowed me to date him?"

"When you'd just turned eighteen? Hell to the no. He's seven years older than you, which might not be so bad now, but not then." The sharp tone of his voice caused Einstein to whine.

"Exactly. So, like a good baby sister, I waited until I turned twenty-one." Meanwhile, she'd done the responsible thing. She'd earned her associates degree in business and then her cosmetology license. "If he thinks he's getting away from me now, he doesn't know how damn determined a Wolford can be." She charged into the kitchen, began loading the dishwasher and spun to shake a fork at Wolf. "I will hunt that man down."

Her brother followed and placed his hands on her shoulders. "Listen to me, now. Something happened to Quinn in his past. I don't know what it was, but I get the gut feeling it was bad." He turned her to face him. "*Real* bad, Cassie. I'm guessing it was job-related, yet I get the feeling some parts of it were personal and have warped how or why he can't handle his feelings for you." His brown eyes bore into hers. "If anyone can tear down the walls he's built, I'm thinking it's you. If anyone can show him how to feel again after some catastrophe, sis, it's you."

Tears pooled. "You're talking about my cutting." She extended her arms, studying for the millionth time the faint scars scoring her flesh from her wrists to the bend of her elbows. Because she hadn't been home the night the arsonist started the fire that killed their parents, she'd blamed herself. The worst part was she had lied. Told her mom and dad she was at a friend's pajama party when, instead, she and Renee, both barely thirteen, had gone to a party with some older kids. Her sense of culpability numbed her and she began cutting herself to feel pain.

His hand trailed over her hair. "Don't go back to your dark place, Cassie." Her brother knew her too well, could read her body language. "A lot of kids lie about where they're going. Doesn't make it right, but it happens. Hell, I did it a time or two, myself. The fire was not your fault. You know that."

She nodded. After a couple of years of counseling and an intervention by her siblings, she'd finally released the guilt. "So you think Quinn's in the same emotional place I was? He's always joking and acting a fool."

"Yes, but sometimes a man wears a mask, especially when he can't face the man in the mirror. I bet you dollars to donuts, he's using the laughing disguise to hide his pain. He's a good man, sis. Beneath all the smart-ass attitude, he's a decent sort. Loyal. I'd want him guarding my six any day."

She studied him for a few beats. "What's changed your mind?"

He snatched two sugar cookies from the cookie jar, shoved one in his mouth and tossed one up for Einstein to catch mid-air. "Some things men just don't discuss, you know?"

She poked a finger into his stomach. "You are so full of that macho shit."

Her brother grinned before he enveloped her in his arms for a hug. "Yeah, but my woman digs it."

"Well, not your sister." She punched him lightly in the shoulder and he laughed. Still, what Wolf said made sense. If Quinn was hiding behind a false face of humor, he'd never heal. Hadn't she'd learned that during her intense, often agonizing, counseling sessions? The man she loved would always hurt. Her heart ached for him. If anyone knew the hopelessness of that kind of emotional torment, it was her.

She had to convince Quinn to stay, to face his demons. If he moved away, he'd take a large piece of her soul with him. Her stomach swirled and twisted like a cyclone, the resulting pain making her gulp for air. She couldn't deal with the loss of him or the dream of a shared future.

By damn, she wouldn't allow it.

"I have to go. If that man thinks charging into a burning building takes guts, just wait until he comes up against Cassie Jacqueline Wolford when she's in a full rant. I'm telling you he doesn't stand a chance."

Wolf laughed behind her. "You go, baby girl. Show numbnuts who's gonna be boss of this outfit."

CHAPTER SEVEN

Quinn dragged his tired, sorry ass down the steps of his apartment building, two filled boxes in his arms. He wanted his belongings packed and ready to go as soon as his final shift at the fire station was over. Acid rolled in his gut. Contrary to what Wolf and Noah insinuated, he was *not* running from Cassie or his feelings for her. Not in the way they suspected. Hell, it wasn't commitment he feared.

Thanks to a recent text, it was Cassie's safety.

He hadn't stopped trembling since a text had dropped into his cell's message box not more than an hour ago. *Ur joggin buddy dies if U return 2 the agency.*

No sooner had he read the text twice than rage and panic joined forces. He rammed his fist through the closet door in his bedroom where he'd been about ready to start packing his clothes. Unless he replaced the door with three fist-sized holes in it, he'd probably forfeit his security deposit. *As if I give a good rat's ass.*

The message meant two things. One, he'd been watched for a long time, maybe his entire spell in Clearwater. And, two, one of the men he'd contacted about job openings in the State Department and the DEA was the mole who'd informed the cartel of his team's activities years ago. Renata hadn't been the only person to apprise the drug lords of their progress. And his team had been damn good at ferreting out intel. Working together the way they did, they'd become a very real threat to the drug trafficking in that country.

One might say he owed it to his fallen team members to find out who in the agency had ratted them out.

But he could not...would not risk Cassie's safety to do it. She had to come first.

Returning to the grind of government work was now out of the realm of his possibilities. He'd stick to the adrenalin-pumping, rewarding fire and rescue business. He'd survived for three years without knowing the identity of the mole, but he wouldn't survive for a minute knowing his angel had been harmed.

There'd been three responses to the dozen or so emails he'd sent before his shift at the fire station ended. A few of his previous co-workers at the State Department and in the DEA still cared enough to pass along some contact information. Two referenced security firms that did clandestine work for the government—mercenaries. Another, Lance Blakewell, shared information about an opening within the department, low-level, but it was a foot in the door. He'd considered it until he got the threatening text.

What the hell? Fuck it all, right?

After he grabbed a few hours of sleep, he'd make a list of everyone he'd contacted and contact them again. Put the word out he'd found a firefighting job somewhere.

No, that wouldn't be good enough. Whoever the asshole was, he'd probably check behind Quinn. He'd have to apply at a few fire departments to back up his claims. Meanwhile he'd do what he could to protect Cassie. It never once occurred to him that he or anyone he held dear would be in danger because of a mission that went bad, but why would it? And what was the reason behind keeping track of his mediocre life? What did he know that made him a liability for some lowlife who lived in the shadow of the beam of right and wrong?

Just who the hell was the ass-wipe? Did he really care enough to reenter that fucked up world of deception and danger?

If it put Cassie at risk, then no. Hell no.

He elbowed the building's door open and trudged into the sunlight, the late-morning glare intensifying his headache. The middle of January and it was a balmy sixty-eight degrees. Man, he was going to miss the hell out of Florida. Life here had practically been a ceaseless vacation, even with the forty-eight hour shifts at the station. On days off he jogged on the beach with Cassie or went to beer parties or Buckaneers football games with other firemen. Often he rode his Harley, Cassie's arms and legs wrapped around him, across Dunedin Causeway to Honeymoon Island, a favorite snorkeling destination of theirs. Wolf and Jace included him in their jet ski races off Gulf Boulevard. Then there were picnics and beach-combing on Caladesi Island, also with Cassie.

He would miss it all—the weather, the beautiful scenery, his friends, the satisfaction of his job.

Cassie.

If sadness had a color, it would be navy blue, for damned if a severe case of blues wasn't settling in. He'd have so many memories of Clearwater, Florida, and almost every one would revolve around Cassie Wolford.

"Well, well, well…if it isn't Mr. Hot Lips Chicken Shit."

Fuck.

He plopped the boxes at the rear of the U-Haul trailer he'd backed into one of his two assigned parking spaces before unhitching it from his Wrangler. With a push of one hand, he slid open the retractable door. Meanwhile, he braced himself for the five-foot-five, dark-haired tirade barreling down on him, that infernal streak of red hair standing on end as if it were a battle flag flapping in the wind. By the murderous expression on her face, now probably wasn't the best time to mention the hairdo. What the hell made women do that to their hair anyway?

He lifted each box and swung at the waist, tossing them into the interior. Hopping in, he began arranging the boxes around his Harley he'd tied to the inner sides of the trailer. He wanted to create a second support system for the bike to secure it in place for the trip to wherever he'd end up going. After careful measuring, he knew how much room to leave for his bed, box springs, mattress and sofa. The rest of his furniture he'd donate to Goodwill.

The U-Haul bounced slightly when she scrambled in behind him. "I'm talking to you. Don't you dare ignore me!"

"I don't have time for your drama. And shouldn't you be in bed with a hangover?"

Her open hand fluttered like a crazed butterfly. "Pffft. It would take more than a hangover to keep me in bed. I want to know when you decided to move and why?"

He jumped out of the trailer, trudging for the building. God, he was bone-tired. "Since when do I have to report my comings and goings to you?" She was in a mood. If he invited her up so he could keep an eye on her, she'd no doubt refuse. Better to ignore her, so she'd storm up to the safety of his apartment to continue her rant.

"This discussion is not over."

"Yes, it is, peanut." The gauntlet had been thrown. She'd be pounding on his door within the minute.

The sound of a foot stomp behind him made him smile. "Don't call me peanut!" The woman was damn adorable when she was pissed. "I'm warning you, Quinn Gallagher, you don't want to make me blow a gasket. It's not a pretty sight. You have no idea the extents I'll go to."

"Yeah, yeah, I'm trembling in my shoes, little one. Go home. Leave me the hell alone." Yanking the door open, he charged inside and jogged up the steps to his second-floor apartment. With any luck he'd outrun her. Looking into her sad emerald eyes was more than he could handle right now. Her voice may have sounded angry, but her pinched expression cried sadness...and it tore at his soul.

He'd already packed up his closet and chest of drawers, stuffing enough clothes to wear his remaining four days in Clearwater into his duffle bag. Furball had quickly hopped into the open piece of luggage as if he wanted to make sure he wasn't left behind. Or maybe the cat instinctively knew his owner couldn't beat holes into the canvas. He'd gone into hiding as soon as Quinn took his first hit on the wooden door, raging at the world, and came out when his owner calmed down enough to place his fist into a sink full of ice cubes.

Quinn scratched under the grey feline's white chin and was rewarded with a loud purr. "Sorry I scared you earlier. We've got big changes ahead, buddy." He rolled over for his owner to rub his white belly. "Cat's aren't supposed to like this." His palm ruffled fur from the animal's neck to groin. "Besides, I've got work to do."

Furball nipped the edge of Quinn's hand. "You little grey bastard, and after the way I saved your ass too." This was an ongoing argument between the two since the night Quinn found him scratching frantically on the outside of his sliding glass doors in the living room, drenched, wild-eyed and scared all to hell and back. A category two hurricane was blowing through and, the best Quinn could decipher, the hundred-mile-per-hour winds had propelled the scrawny kitten onto his second-story balcony. How it had survived had been a miracle. He'd shown signs of malnutrition according to the veterinarian he'd taken him to as soon as the hurricane abated.

That stormy night back in September, when Quinn slid open the door, Furball teetered in on his last leg of energy and collapsed as if he'd finally found home. The man, who'd never been allowed to own a pet as a child, wrapped the sodden animal in a hand towel—hell he'd been too small for a bath towel—and laid him across his lap while he watched a New England Patriots football game. During halftime, he'd fed the weakened kitten by dipping his pinky finger into warmed milk and allowing its roughened tongue to lick it off. A few minutes later, the power went out, and both cat and new owner snoozed on the sofa.

Five months of constant feeding, deworming, flea dips and care had fattened the Furball. Someone had spoiled the feline, too, and Quinn had no clue who *that* bastard was. Surely not him. The trouble was the kitten's harrowing experience in the hurricane had left him traumatized. He trembled during storms, seeking refuge in the crook of Quinn's neck or in a pile of old beach towels he kept under the bed for the tomcat's sanctuary, along with a stuffed toy or two.

The cat also hated riding in the Jeep. Quinn wasn't so sure how he'd handle a long trek on some highway confined in his cat carrier. He'd have to call Furball's vet to see if he could prescribe some tranquilizers. Still, thank God he hadn't turned into one of those doting cat owners. His concern was merely...responsibility.

Pulling his extra towels and sheets from his linen closet, Quinn carried them into the kitchen to use as packing material. He shoved his toaster and blender into the interior of his microwave, jamming washcloths around them. After taping the bottom of a box, he set the appliance inside and shoved a sheet around it.

Any minute now Cassie would be pounding on his door.

Tape roller in hand, he put together four more boxes. He pulled containers and junk from his cabinets and drawers, packing everything but his coffee pot and one mug. How had he accumulated so much cooking stuff and plates? Reaching up on the wall, he snatched two roadside fruit signs he and Cassie had found at a church bizarre last spring. All of his cabinets were empty, except for one nosy cat who insisted on sniffing every corner. He'd keep the doors open a few inches so Furball could come and go as he pleased. The food in the pantry remained. He'd make more boxes and tackle that job next.

He stopped and frowned.

Still no Cassie.

Had she given up and gone home? He carried the box containing his microwave into the living room and peered out the sliding glass doors overlooking the parking lot.

Holy Mother of God!

How in the *fuck* had she gotten his Harley untied and out of the trailer? She'd pushed it onto the small patch of yard in front of the apartment building. All of his neckties flapped from the handlebars and what looked to be his jock strap was stretched across the back of its seat. Jammed into the ground at both ends of his bike were his water skis. The rope that *had* secured his bike upright in the U-Haul was now strung from one ski to the other with all of his damn boxers hanging from the rope. In a semicircle around the bike sat his high school and college football trophies.

His gas grill had also been dragged from the trailer, and hanging like dogs' ears from the closed chrome lid was every sock he owned. He narrowed his eyes as his blood pressure exploded through the stratosphere. Because there...*there*...in the midst of all his previously packed boxes was the object of his wrath, kicking each of the cartons, arms waving, mouth moving as if she were cussing someone out. And he had a damn good idea who that lucky son of a bitch was, especially when she scowled up at his balcony and shook her fist.

Just what the hell did she think all this chaos would do?

She stormed back to the trailer and crawled into its cavernous interior. He leaned toward the glass and cocked the box on his hip. Now what was she after? His gaze scanned his belongs scattered helter-skelter over the lawn. She'd already removed everything he'd worked so hard to pack. Except for his...oh no. Oh, *hell* no! A flurry of movement flashed in the corner of his eye, followed by an unholy sound, resembling a moose in heat. His narrowed gaze swung to Cassie standing below his window playing his treasured saxophone. If one could classify the metalized shrieking she produced as playing.

Jesus Christ, she's a dead woman. That horn's all I have left of Uncle Mat.

He slammed the box onto the sofa and barreled out of his apartment. By the time he sprinted down the steps and charged through the building's door, every damn dog in the complex was howling along with Cassie's demented saxophone caterwauling.

"What the hell are you doing?" He tried to grab the instrument from her hands, but she spun and hit a high note he'd never imagined an alto sax capable of reaching.

"If you don't stop that infernal racket, I'm calling the cops!" Milt Garland, the old coot who lived on the first floor, ambled out of the building, put-putting as he walked. The senior citizen had a terrible problem with gas and either his hearing was so bad he never heard it or he just didn't give a damn if everyone else did. "I had to turn down my hearing aid." He gestured to his trembling Chihuahua, snuggled between his arm and his chest. "Scared poor Killer so bad, he peed on the floor."

"I'm sorry, Milt. I'm trying to stop her."

Cassie slipped the mouthpiece from her lips. "I'm serenading the man I love. Don't tell me you're against romance, Milt—" She hip-bumped the old man and winked at him. "Not a stud muffin like you."

Milt's wire-framed glasses all but fogged up and a cheezy grin spread. "Well, no, I'm all for a little romance, sugarplum." His gaze shot to Quinn. "Don't know if this young whipper-snapper can deliver, though." He smirked and his pigeon chest puffed out. "Maybe you'd be better off with an older, more experienced gent."

Shit, as if this old man could be as experienced as I am.

She plucked a piece of toilet paper off Milt's chin. "Did you cut yourself shaving?"

"Yeah, I've got four electric razors tucked in a drawer somewhere that the kids got me over the years, but I like the close shave a sharp razorblade gives me." He rubbed his gnarled fingers over his cheek. "The wife always preferred a smooth face. Said it made kissin' nicer."

The neighborhood dogs quieted since Cassie had stopped frantically pounding the instrument's keys as if she were typing a letter to Santa.

She leaned against Milt's bony shoulder. "I'm going to marry this young whipper-snapper. I don't care how much facial hair he's got."

Milt narrowed his eyes and pursed his lips while he petted Killer. "Don't look like the marrying type to me."

Quinn folded his arms and widened his stance. "That's because I'm *not* the marrying type. I'm more the one-night stand type." This whole conversation was totally bizarre. He glared at Cassie. Thanks to her shenanigans, he'd have to repack everything.

"Oh, you can make book on this, Milt. Hot lips here is mine. His ass is grass and I'm the lawnmower." Cassie sucked a bucketful of air and blew four sour notes at one time.

Quinn jammed his index fingers into his ears and cursed.

Milt farted, jerking his hearing aid out of his ear.

And Killer pissed on Milt's shirt.

"Dammit, Cassie!" Quinn reached to snatch the saxophone from her grasp; she swung it out of his range and laughed. What he wouldn't give to lay her over his knees and paddle her ass. "Look, that horn belonged to my late Uncle Matisse. He used to play in jazz clubs in New Orleans. It's all I have left of him. Now give it here."

Although Quinn Matisse was not a blood relative, he had been someone very important in his life. Uncle Mat taught him how to throw a ball, to fish and toss rocks in a stream to make the most circular ripples. In short, the smiling man spent time with young Quinn until a bullet ended the musician's life.

"You know Matisse is a nice name. We'll name our first child in his honor. Matisse if it's a boy or Mattie if it's a girl." She placed the brass instrument in his outstretched hand. "I think it's time we take this conversation upstairs, don't you?" She smiled so sweetly it looked pure evil.

"First, you repack my belongings." He jerked his thumb over his shoulder. "When all my things are safely locked away, we'll talk."

Milt flapped his urine-soaked shirttail away from his body. His dog stood at his sandaled feet, his tail tucked between legs. "Go on inside, Quinn. Killer and me will pack up your stuff. Looks like you and Cassie have some things to work out." Milt shot a worried glance at Quinn's motorcycle. "Don't know if I want to move your Harley though."

"Don't worry about the bike. If you'll just cram my clothes and trophies in boxes and secure them away in the trailer, I'd appreciate it. I think the bike and grill will be safe enough sitting where they are for a few minutes." His gaze swept to the feminine pain in his ass standing next to him. "I'd like to say it won't take long to pound some sense into her head, but any woman who would dye a swath of her hair stoplight red can't be too bright."

"Hey!" She poked a finger in his side.

"Your hair was perfect before, peanut." He smirked at Milt. "See, that's the difference between men and women. Men don't diddle with their appearance. They know perfection when they see it. Am I right, Milt?"

The old guy extracted a small black comb from his back pocket and skimmed it over the seven grey hairs plastered to his scalp with some kind of hair goop. Nodding, he slipped the comb into place again. "That's exactly what I used to tell Louisa." He crossed himself. "God bless her soul." He hiked up his baggy khaki pants with the insides of his elbows tucked against his belt. "A man does *not* mess with perfection." He hip-wiggled a couple foxtrot steps and passed some gas as he hummed some ancient tune.

Cassie's jaw dropped and her gaze ricocheted from Milt to Quinn. "Let's state the facts correctly, shall we?" She planted her hands on her narrow hips and swayed her shoulders one at a time for some kind of goofy feminine emphasis. "Women like change. We have no fear of experimentation the way you men do."

"Fear?" Was she calling him a coward?

"When was the last time you tried a new kind of food? Or a micro-brew beer?" She spun toward Milt. "When was the last time you wore navy blue pants? Every time I see you, you're wearing khakis." Turning her harangue back on Quinn, she pointed to his comfy Nikes. "You need new sneakers. You've been wearing those raggedy things for the three years I've known you."

She poked a fingernail through a hole in his beloved Puddle of Mudd t-shirt. Using some of his college expense money to buy a concert ticket to go hear them with a group of Harvard freshmen had been one of the highlights of his life. How great to be out from under the condemning, watchful eye of his father.

"And this faded, tattered rag belongs in the trash bin!" One swift tug and the hole grew from the circumference of a dime to fist-size. "See? It's like tissue paper!"

Quinn couldn't believe she'd torn his favorite shirt. Hell, the thing was barely ten years old. His gaze slowly swept from his ravaged, quality rock and roll wear to her green eyes, snapping with righteous indignation.

"Women also like variation in our sexual positions while, according to ninety percent of my female customers, their men do it the same way over and over."

Something in him snapped. Control? Anger? The need to shut her up? Who the fuck knew? "You mouthy little brat." He coiled his fingers around her bicep and charged them toward the building's entrance. "Milt, we're going to be a while." He yanked the aqua door open so hard it banged against the front of the yellow stucco structure as he hauled her ass up the steps.

CHAPTER EIGHT

"What the hell's wrong with you?" Cassie jogged to keep up with Quinn's furious movements.

"I'm warning you. Shut. The hell. Up. I've had enough of your nonsense. We are *not* getting married. We are *not* having children. And I'm about to show you more ways to have sex than your stupid-ass, gossipy customers ever dreamed of." He pushed his apartment door open and shoved her inside before kicking it shut. "You have an evil heart, Cassie Wolford. You may look like an angel, but deep inside you are one hellacious monster."

He pivoted to turn the lock and when he looked at her again, she grabbed the hem of the yellow cotton top she wore, jerked it over her head and tossed it aside. One flip-flop flew over his shoulder and he ducked. Furball, who'd come out to greet her, scampered for the kitchen and the safety of the empty cabinets. A flick of her other ankle and the second flip-flop landed on top of his boxed microwave.

Cassie's thumbs tucked into the elastic of her navy capris.

"What the hell are you doing?"

"Getting naked so we can have sex." She shimmied out of the capris and twirled them on her index finger. "You're falling behind, big guy." Her head dipped in his direction. "Come on. Show me some skin." She reached behind her to unhook her bra and stopped after it hit the floor. "Wait, you want me to undress you, don't you? Cool. I can handle that."

What the fuck? His cock voiced the same sentiment, throbbing the words in a sensual Morse code as the traitorous appendage filled with blood and lengthened. He shook his head. "No. Now Cassie, we are not doing this." He focused on that silly swath of red hair because if his eyes devoured her firm naked breasts one more time, he was a goner.

Hell, this was why he'd resigned from a job he loved and was leaving a life he totally enjoyed. Getting into a physical relationship with her was wrong on so many levels. She was seven years younger than he was and his best friend's baby sister. And he was emotionally damaged by Renata's betrayal of his team, his heart and his manhood. He had nothing good to offer Cassie. Nothing but raw physicality.

"If we have sex, there will be no emotion to it. Just two adults seeking release. Hell, if all you need is a good climax or two, I'm game. Just don't expect me to cuddle you afterwards or wax poetically about how grand it was. Because that's not how I operate."

His little Pollyanna ran on emotion. Maybe his crude remarks would be enough to cool her mood.

She stalked toward him, her tongue moistening the evil grin stretching across her full lips. "Oh, but we *are* doing this. You said so just a minute ago when you dragged me up the steps. And you always do what you say." She lifted a shoulder. "Besides, I could go for a good release right about now." She fisted his t-shirt and ripped it from neckband to hem. Leaning in, she rubbed her breasts across his chest, her erect nipples tearing apart any self-control he frantically held onto.

Sweat beaded on his forehead. Dear God, he would die.

Her tongue circled his areola and his cock hardened more—if that were possible. She bit his nipple before taking it into her mouth and sucking it. Her fingertips fondled the ring in his other nipple and tugged the piercing, sending the combined shocks of pain and pleasure he so enjoyed to his nerve endings. His hands fisted in her hair. Another tug on his nipple ring and he groaned. *Sweet mother of God.* He'd gone to nirvana with the girl of his dreams.

While her frantic kisses covered his body, her busy hands traveled to his jeans to pull the button through the denim and unzip his fly. His cock sprung free, and she dropped to her knees.

"Oh, hot lips, I love a man who goes commando."

Jealous rage rudely snatched him from his state of bliss, and he jerked her head back. "How many damn men have you seen who go commando?" His voice was harsh, his breathing ragged. "How many, Cassie?"

The tip of her pink tongue touched the head of his pecker and swirled around it once. Her emerald gaze remained locked on his and the corners of her mouth lifted. "Guess." Her hand wrapped around his cock, stroking him from balls to crown while her tongue circled the head.

His aroused nerve endings warred with his male ego. She was his angel. *His, dammit.* How many men had there been before him? Did it matter? He'd certainly had more than his fair share of women. Okay, so he wouldn't be her first, but he damn sure would be the one she remembered. The one she measured all others against from this point forward.

But, dear God, she sure as hell knew how to give fantastic head. Shivers skied down his spine and his balls ached for release. All the while she tortured him with licking and sucking designed to send any man to the edge of sexual madness.

"Enough." Quinn bent and scooped her into his arms. "Let's move this to the bed." He kicked the bedroom door shut behind them. The last thing he needed was Furball watching and pouncing.

She wrapped her arms around his neck and bit his earlobe. "How many?"

"How many what?" He laid her on his rumpled sheets and toed off his sneakers before removing his tattered shirt.

"How many positions are we going to do? Four? Six?" She

burrowed into his pillow and bedclothes, her face flushed with excitement and her eyes shadowed with something. Was it fear? Surely not.

He shucked his jeans, opened the drawer of his nightstand and grabbed a fistful of condoms, shaking them at her. "Guess."

Her eyes widened for a beat. "What do you do? Buy them by the box?"

The bed dipped when he pressed his knee into the mattress, spreading her legs so he could settle between her hips. Her question seemed a little naïve, but then maybe her other lovers were the type to tuck a singular rubber in their wallets. Damn fools.

Visions of young, horny guys stretched over her, in her, forming the double-backed beast, twisted into an unfamiliar bitter rage of jealous possessiveness. He wanted to kill every male who had ever touched her—and he knew more than fifty ways to do the deed.

"Quinn, what happened to your closet door?"

"Temper tantrum." *I was mentally killing the bastard who dared threaten you.*

A smile brightened her features and orneriness twinkled in her green eyes. "I'm glad I never have temper tantrums."

He laughed. "Me, too, angel." Kissing a trail from her temple to her ear, he struggled for control. He had no right to such emotions. Once he left the boundaries of Clearwater, he'd lose contact with her. His life would be sterile again, cold and damn lonely. But for now, with her arms draped around his neck, her breasts against his pecs and the backs of her calves restlessly moving over his, she belonged to him.

"How many?" He bit her neck and she gasped. "How many lovers have you had?" His male ego had put forth the question before his mind had a chance to censor it.

"We're not doing this, Quinn. I'm not telling you how many men I've had and I sure as hell don't want to know how many women you've been with." She kissed his jaw and nuzzled closer. "Let's just enjoy the moment."

His lips feathered kisses down her neck and met the delicate gold chain. Pleasure rippled through him. "You're wearing my necklace."

"I'll wear it forever. Thank you. It means more to me than you can ever imagine. It's the most beautiful necklace I've ever seen."

Her sentiments touched him deeper than he wanted to acknowledge. "Another guy will replace it with something better."

She made an annoyed sound in the back of her throat. "I can't imagine who. Not when my heart will always belong to you." Her sweet lips made contact and his mouth opened to touch her tongue with his. For several seconds, as the kiss deepened, the world faded. There was no botched mission, no dead comrades, no Renata with her devious feminine ruses—only his sweet angel. And in her arms, he was pure again. He was worthy.

Be honest with yourself, man.

He wrapped his hands around her head and pressed his forehead to hers. "Are you going to be okay with this? I never took you for a one-time only type of woman. I'm leaving, Cassie. This is sex. Nothing more. Sex between friends."

Tears pooled, and she blinked rapidly as if she were willing them away. "I don't want you to leave. You're the best friend I've ever had. I don't understand why…"

He kissed her with just the barest joining of lips. "I feel the same about you, but sometimes…" Sometimes what? How could he possibly explain to her why he had to leave when, right now, with her naked beneath him, his thinking made zero motherfucking-sense?

****

Cassie waited for Quinn to finish his sentence. His forehead was furrowed as if he were deep in thought; he shook his head a couple of times and forced out a ragged sigh, saying nothing. Something had him in turmoil. Should she ask?

Hillary, her steady Friday shampoo and style, always insisted the best time to worm information out of a man was after sex. Which was why Cassie was where she was, damn near naked, lying beneath a totally naked and aroused Quinn Gallagher. Once they did the deed, she planned on getting some answers, like why he was suddenly intent on leaving Clearwater.

After all, Hillary had been right about the jealousy thing. "Mention the possibility of other men and the guy will go all possessive on you," or so Hillary claimed as she doled out advice on how to snare and keep a man. As for how to give oral, Cassie had absorbed the graphic lesson Eva Mae, her Saturday morning regular, demonstrated using a bottle of conditioner as a cock prop.

Ninety percent of what Cassie knew about sex, she'd learned from her customers. And, as a virgin waiting three years for the man she loved to come on to her, she had no qualms about asking questions. So, here she was, beneath the man she adored, armed with second-hand knowledge, waiting for him to take her virginity and hoping she didn't make a complete fool of herself in the process.

For if he laughed at her inexperience, she didn't think she'd ever recover.

"Raise your arms over your head, angel." Quinn wrapped his large hand around both of her wrists and held them in place even as he shifted off her onto his side. The warm fingertips of his other hand trailed down the side of her face. "You are so beautiful, even with that patch of red hair I dislike. What color was it the other week? Silver?"

"Yes. Something sparkly for New Year's Eve." She almost told him she'd dye her hair any color he wanted if he'd stay, but she'd not do that for any man. Even him. If he couldn't accept her as she was, as much as it would destroy her, they really had no chance for a future. Hadn't both of her brothers preached the importance of respect and acceptance between a man and a woman?

Quinn's fingertips moved down her neck and slowly, almost

reverently, continued over her collarbone, his gaze intent on where he was touching. "Your skin is so soft." He leaned in, his nose brushing across her neck and chest, inhaling deeply. "And your perpetual smell of peaches and cream is so embedded in my male psyche. God, I love it." The sweeping trace of his fingertips on her breasts was so light she quivered and arched into his hand.

"Like that, do you?" He leaned over her and covered the mounds of her breasts with feather-light kisses, moving ever closer to her nipples. His woodsy cologne and male musk smelled like her heart's home, for this hunky man was indeed her heart and had been since she laid eyes on him at her eighteenth birthday party.

So often in the past, she'd watched his sensual lips while he talked or laughed, and fanaticized about the sensations his mouth would evoke when it drew one of her nipples inside to suck. In mere seconds, she'd find out. Her toes curled in anticipation.

His tongue circled her beaded nipple before he claimed it.

The pull of his mouth spiraled an arrow of need directly to her core and wetness pooled between the folds. *Oh. My. God. More. I need more.*

"Quinn!" She squirmed and trembled as he sucked harder. A deep throbbing she'd never experienced threatened to toss her over some precipice.

He stopped and gazed at her. "You really like it when I do that." His fabulous lips upturned at the corners. "Can you climax when a man does this to you? Hmm?" His mouth sought her other breast and she was swept once more into a miasma of novel sensations.

"Let go of my hands. I need to touch you." She tugged against the hold he had on her.

He released her wrists, his eyes darkened with what she hoped was passion. Slipping his arm under her shoulders and turning her slightly toward him, their legs tangled even as his hand slid down her back where he slipped his fingers under the elastic of her thong. "I want this off. I plan on biting and kissing every inch of your beautiful body." He squeezed one of her ass cheeks.

"When you go back to your other lovers, you're going to find them lacking. Because no man will ever love you the way I do." He bit the tender flesh where her neck joined her shoulder and she trembled. "No one, baby."

He enveloped her in his arms and kissed her as if he had all the time in the world to break her heart, which was what he was doing—loving her and breaking her heart at the same time.

The man was hell-bent on leaving and this was his goodbye. If his crass remarks to her at the station yesterday were hurtful, they held little power compared to this excruciating sweetly sensual parting.

Her chest constricted, trapping her breath in a body too aching to operate in a normal pattern. It was as if her heartbeat morphed from *lub-dub...lub-dub* to *Quinn's leaving...Quinn's leaving.* Tears burned the back of her throat, and she fought to keep her mind on his kiss.

Passionate, yet painful.

Tender, yet torturous.

Seducing, yet sad.

Finally, he released her lips and kissed a slow journey down her torso. To hide her tears, she laid her arm across her eyes and sighed, hoping he'd take her action as someone lost in the moment, instead of a woman falling apart and dying in his arms.

Focus, dammit. You will never have this again. You will never feel his lips and hands on you if he leaves. And he's right, every other man will pale in comparison.

"Feel how I touch you. Remember this, baby." He pushed her thighs farther apart, holding them as he dipped his head and swiped his tongue along her slit.

Her eyes crossed beneath her forearm.

"Damn, you taste so sweet." His tongue played a slow pattern over her as if she were a violin and he a virtuoso, plucking music from sensitive areas she'd only heard other women mention during their sex talks in her beauty shop. Now she understood the fascination. The yearning for more. The sexual addiction.

Quinn Gallagher could so quickly become her drug of choice.

The muscles low in her stomach tensed as if preparing for some magical leap. A quivering began deep within, and her thighs trembled under his hands. His tongue danced around her button of need, closer yet never touching it. She squirmed, raising her hips to entice him to pay attention to the aching spot.

"Patience, angel." Finally, Quinn covered that button with his lips and sucked.

Her eyes popped open as waves of desire undulated from every nerve ending in her body. The world spun and flipped before she pinched her eyes shut to concentrate on each nuance of pleasure surging through her system. The moan that started low in her chest quickly developed into a screaming chant of his name. Tears flowed, and she gasped for air.

He pressed kisses to her abdomen. "God, you're breathtaking when you come. I will never forget how you cried my name over and over."

Cassie kept her arm over her eyes, hoping to hide the tears that flowed freely. Dear God, how would she ever get over the beauty of his lovemaking and her body's reaction to it?

She sensed movement when he reached toward the nightstand, followed by the tearing of a foil packet. "Hold on." Latex snapped, and Quinn's body covered hers again. His hand positioned the head of his cock at her entrance. "We'll do missionary first. Mainly because I can't wait to get inside of you."

Desire blended with apprehension urged her forward in her quest to give him as much pleasure as he'd given her, to bring him satisfaction too. Her arms floated over his shoulders and she wrapped her legs around his hips. He pushed in and she took a deep breath, preparing for the pain.

He stilled, his wide eyes searching her face. "Cassie, what the hell?"

"Don't stop!" She used the strength of her thighs to force him in. The tearing sensation burned, but only for an instant. Getting accustomed to the fullness of him inside her would take a little longer. Instinct had her needing to push him back out, but love made her want to keep him there forever.

His hands cradled her head and his lips brushed hers. "Angel, why didn't you tell me this was your first time? I'd have made it better for you."

"And I'd have died."

He kissed her again, his hips moving in a slow rhythm. "You made me believe there'd been others."

"Did I?" Her palms swept up his muscular back as she recalled how he'd looked earlier when she'd alluded to other guys. The anger and passion that darkened his features were priceless.

He slowly pulled out until just the head of his cock remained. "Hell, yes. I nearly went insane with jealousy." His hips angled and he slid in to the hilt.

This stroke didn't hurt as much as the first one. Pleasure sparked along her nerve endings now that her body recognized and accepted the fullness of his size, the totality of his possession. "Why, Quinn? Why do you care when you're leaving?" She had to get him to come to grips with how his fear of what might grow between them was in direct opposition to his actions.

"Don't." He settled into a slow, sensual rhythm that caused her pelvic muscles to undulate and coil again. "Don't question. Just feel. Enjoy." He trembled in her arms. "You are so damn tight, baby. I've never felt anything like this. Like you." His strokes grew stronger, faster. "Only you."

"I love you." He needed to hear this, whether he wanted to or not. There'd been times in the past when she'd felt unworthy of love and yet her siblings had told her repeatedly, if she stood a chance at helping him, she had to bare her heart to him, regardless of whether or not he handed it back to her in tattered pieces.

"Don't say that. I don't want to hear it." Pain etched his features. His dark eyebrows dipped and his blue-grey eyes turned steely.

Those sensual lips thinned in determination.

"And you care for me." She fingered her necklace. "This proves it."

His forehead touched hers and their eyes locked. "Yes, I care, but I still have to leave. There's too much in my past. Things I can't tell you. I'm not worthy of your love."

"No one's ever worthy, Quinn. Love is freely given because it hurts too much to hold it inside. Love me. Love me and let out some of the pain."

They melded, folded into each other as if they were magnetic halves of each other's souls. Their breaths mingled as their muscles moved in unison toward the release they both sought.

"I have to go," he whispered as if it pained him to hear his own words.

"No, Quinn. I won't allow it. I can't live without you." She held him tighter.

"I can't live without you either, love. I'll only exist. My heart will beat, but it won't feel." His movement intensified and his grasp on her grew stronger.

"Stay, Quinn. Stay with me and learn how to love again." Tears spilled down her cheeks. Her climax approached, a sharp knife that would surely cleave her soul in two. "Please, love me."

He entwined his fingers with hers and pushed their hands into the pillow, his movements growing faster. Sweat beaded on his forehead and moisture grew in his eyes. "Baby, don't you know? Can't you tell?"

Her climax hit and, for an instant, she couldn't breathe. The bittersweet beauty of it turned her tears to sobs. She had to convince him to give up this insane idea of leaving, because she needed him more than her next breath.

Quinn tensed and his head reared back, the muscles in his neck corded and bulging. He cried her name as he convulsed in climax. Tucking his head against her neck, he struggled for air and his finger twirled around a curl. "Angel, I would rather have had one breath of your hair, one taste of your lips, one touch of your silky skin than a lifetime of never knowing it." Then, forehead to forehead, lips to lips, they shed their tears of farewell.

CHAPTER NINE

Quinn's palms were planted against the white tiles in the shower, his chin touching his chest and hot water sluicing over his fatigued muscles. His mind trudged and stumbled on the damn-me-to-hell treadmill. He was a bastard. A cold-hearted motha. The ass-wipe of Florida. Hell, the entire world. He'd taken Cassie's virginity and then sent her on her way, her heart obviously shattered. The edge of his fist hit the tile. He was one self-centered son of a bitch. How could he do that to her?

Why couldn't he get beyond the pain of his past and open his heart to love? Lord knew he wanted to. He wanted Cassie, needed her. Yet with all his baggage, he'd never be good enough, free enough for her. She deserved better than he'd ever be. Hell, his angel deserved the moon and seven stars, not a man with scars so cavernous he couldn't climb out of their depths no matter how hard he tried.

Added to this was the very real possibility he'd put her life in danger. He had to get as far away from her as he could and had to prove to everyone he'd contacted in DC that he'd changed his mind about returning to government work. God, his life was such a hellacious mess.

The nightmare he'd suffered for over three years surfaced to pay him a daytime visit. He angled his cheek against the tile, fighting the rising horror of the night his life had tumbled headlong into hell.

His descent hadn't been a split-second event, but a gradual one born of ego and ambition. Fresh out of college, he'd gone to work for the State Department in the huge Harry S. Truman Building on C Street in Foggy Bottom, not far from the White House, determined to prove he deserved the position despite his father's influence.

He'd been such an eager beaver shit, a pain in everyone's ass. So much so, when the department needed a patsy, a dispensable bastard to send over to the DEA for a temporary long-term assignment, they gladly chose him. Not overtly, of course, but covertly—and he'd been too drunk on self-importance to realize it.

Department heads included him in a meeting about drug trafficking from Bolivia into Chile. The DEA, in tandem with the State Department, wanted to plant someone in Arica, a city in northern Chile, to watch the Indian runners carrying drugs across the borders on their backs. From there, whatever agent they assigned, along with his team, was to follow the cars taking the cocaine to southern Chile for refining. The biggest part of the job, though, was to find which parts of the country's thousand miles of coastline was used to ship the product abroad.

Superiors played on his ambitious ego like a cheap saxophone. After the brass laid out the bare bones of the mission, they tossed around names of guys to send, no doubt knowing he'd see it as a golden career opportunity and volunteer. And he'd eagerly swallowed their bait. With supervisory experience overseeing a team of four Americans and two Chileans, he was sure a promotion would be waiting at the end of the assignment.

What he hadn't counted on was Renata—one of the Chileans. Against his better judgment, he'd gotten involved with the dark-eyed beauty. Blinded by her sexuality, he'd been careless with his computer passwords and phone calls.

One night, on a recon run to Puerto Montt, to where one of his men had discovered a boat bound for the States tied to a small pier, everything went south in a hurry.

Someone had tipped off the drug cartel—not just Renata, the woman he'd loved, but someone deep inside the agency, the organization he'd respected. Betrayal was a bloodsucking motherfucker. Nine chances out of ten, its victims were the innocents who paid the ultimate price. Those victims were his men: Andy, DeShawn, Skip and the Chilean, Vicente. He'd nearly lost Chris too.

Their mission that evening had been a total cluster-fuck from the time they exited their vehicles. Pandemonium reigned as gunfire pierced the night. His heart pounded as memories of explosions lighting up the sky brought forth sensations of the earth trembling beneath his feet. Dark smoke filled his nostrils and stung his eyes. There were screams and the stench of torn flesh. He lost four of his men and another was captured.

As those long-ago events flashed through his mind like a slideshow from hell, he struggled to keep his breathing from slipping into the frenetic category. Gasping for breath, his hands trembled as the shower droplets stung his face. *Man, get a fuckin' grip.* He willed his erratic breathing to slow as second by second, heartbeat by heartbeat, he got his shit together.

Damn the mole in the agency.

Damn his weakness.

Damn Renata.

But mostly, damn himself for falling in love. With force, he turned off the faucets and jerked a towel from the rack, rubbing the water from his hair and body before he stepped from the steam. Tossing the towel aside, he trudged into his bedroom and stopped.

Memories of Cassie lying tangled in his sheets was burned into his brain. He'd gone into the bathroom after they'd recovered from making love to dispose of the blood-speckled condom. When he'd returned, her expression wavered from expectation to devastation.

She'd patted the bed. "Come here, big guy. You still have a few positions to teach me."

He snatched his jeans from the floor and turned his back to

her before he stepped into them. "I think I've taught you enough already. You were a virgin when you came here."

"I waited on you, Quinn. I waited on you for three years. I gave my virginity to you freely. I have no regrets."

"Christ, don't say that." He didn't mind being a first-class heel with every other woman, but not with her.

The bedclothes rustled behind him. "What are you afraid of? Loving me or hurting me? Because I have to tell you, you're doing a damn fine job of tearing me apart." Her fingertips brushed his back before he made for the door.

"I'm going outside to check on my bike and grill. I think it's time you went home."

Five minutes later, when she'd stormed past him, all but running to get to her car, she was crying. He wanted to call out to her, but he knew it was for the best to let her go, to allow her anger for him to fester. They'd already said their goodbyes. It was over.

She's right. I am a chicken-shit bastard. The sweetest girl in the word hands me her innocence and I toss her a dose of fuckin' attitude so I don't have to deal with her heartache. Hell, I can barely deal with my own.

Reliving that scene was doing him no good. Hell, he'd treated her terribly before she left. Now that he'd re-secured his Harley to the inside of the U-Haul trailer, lugged his grill into the other corner, and rearranged his packed boxes, he'd come back to his apartment to shower. His flashback hadn't been part of the plan, nor was his ginormous dose of regret over Cassie.

He tugged a pair of navy sleep pants out of his duffel bag and yanked them on before he flopped across the bed, inhaled her peaches and cream fragrance that lingered on the pillows and groaned. She would always be a part of him, the happiest part, the best part.

Why hadn't she told him she was a virgin? He replayed their earlier conversation in the living room. When she'd talked about loving a man who went commando, he'd assumed... He shook his head and snorted. She'd been playing him and he fell for it. But damn if Miz Innocence hadn't given exceptional head. Jealousy churned in his gut again. Just where in the hell had she learned *that* fine talent?

He ran a palm over his face before locking his hands behind his head. What did it matter? He was leaving Clearwater. He'd pushed her away and ruined their friendship. One more thing to add to his list of unpardonable sins. Only this fiasco topped them all. But if he kept her safe, then that would be one plus against all the minuses of his life. The most important plus he could ask for.

Furball leaped onto the bed, landing like a whisper on the sheets. He flopped next to Quinn's side and began kneading his owner with his white front paws, his purring growing louder. In an absent-minded move, Quinn stroked the cat even as his thoughts remained on Cassie. Dammit to hell, the last person he ever wanted to hurt was his angel.

His cell rang and he snatched it from his nightstand. The caller ID showed Caller Unknown. "Gallagher."

There were a couple of clicks and a faint whir. "Hey, you ignorant ass son of a bitch, how's it hangin'?"

Quinn smiled for the first time in hours and rose to sit on the edge of his bed. "T-Bone? Hey, long time no hear, man." Hell, he hadn't heard from Chris "T-Bone" Mason in nearly a year. Even so, he recognized the deep, rasping voice, a result of barely surviving a hanging in Chile. The hiss of a lighter sounded and a long inhale followed.

"Thought you quit smoking." Quinn tried not to dwell on memories of finding T-Bone dangling from a chain looped around a rafter in an abandoned warehouse in Puerto Montt after everything went to shit. Two more men of his team, Andy and DeShawn, were discovered beaten and dead in the next room. Skip was out back, his fingers cut off and his throat slashed.

Quinn pressed the speaker button on his cell and laid it next to him so he could sink the heels of his palms against his eyes, hoping to block out the images of finding his tortured team. The large chain digging into T-Bone's bloody, swollen neck, his back scared with multiple tracks of a whip. He still had no clue how long his friend had hung there. As for Skip, Andy and DeShawn, their deaths had not come swiftly; signs of their suffering were gruesome. The cartel held no qualms against mutilating their enemies.

Cold sweat broke out on Quinn's body. The bile of guilt burned the back of his throat. If only he hadn't been so beguiled by Renata, so into her body, maybe none of the torture to his comrades would have happened.

T-Bone's gravelly voice ripped him from his thoughts. "I did quit smoking. Hell, it's bad for your health. Two weeks later, I got run over by a cigarette truck." He wheezed at his own joke. Then his voice turned serious. "Sent you an email, man. Did you read it?"

"Yeah. Just haven't had a chance to respond. I've been packing up my apartment." *And deflowering my best friend.*

"So?" T-Bone had patience the length of his pecker.

"So, I'm still thinking about it. Give me twelve hours to give you an answer." He'd have to make arrangements for Furball. Taking him to a shelter was out. The little devil deserved better, a hell of a lot better. Maybe he could convince Cassie to…then again, after the way he'd just treated her, maybe not.

"You got eight hours to decide, buddy. I need to know who's going to be on my team so I can line up training. Bet you're soft as a motherfucker. Bring warm clothes and snow boots. Montana can be a bitch in the winter, but I love the solitude. Got any skis?"

"Water skis."

"Hell man, the only water we got here is the frozen variety. Get yourself some snow skis and snow shoes. They'll help build up your legs for where we're going. How many miles a day are you running? Bet you can barely climb a flight of steps, you candy-assed-motherfucker."

Quinn chuckled. Spending time with T-Bone again would help ease the agony in his soul…or would it? Quinn had come out of the mission with two bullet holes that eventually healed, yet he was mentally crippled. He'd often questioned that fact in the darkness of night. Why him? Why had he survived?

T-Bone would bear the scars forever. Seeing them every day would be a constant reminder, but then maybe that's what he needed. A strong dose of facing up to what he'd done, what he'd allowed to happen because of his involvement with Renata.

"Hey, any of your team members have pets?"

"Pets? You mean like Dobermans and shit?" T-Bone took another drag on his cigarette.

"Any kind of pets. What do they do with them while everyone's out on a mission?" Furball could take a couple days of being alone with an automatic feeder and water supply, like he did when Quinn was on duty at the station for forty-eight hour shifts. Even so, Milt made it a practice of coming up twice a day to hold the cat and make over him, but Quinn wasn't sure how Furball would handle a week or more of being alone, with no human interaction. Nor could the territorial tomcat take being around big dogs. Even little Killer put him in a pissy-cat mood.

"Nah, we ain't got time for worrying about dumbass animals. Lots of time, we're gone within the hour heading for a new target."

Working for T-Bone would take some serious thought. "Eight hours and you'll have my answer. Later, man." He ended the call and eased back on the mattress. His gaze snagged on a small ribbon of dried blood on the sheet. *Cassie.*

Four steely pointed paws stomped up his chest until two beady copper-colored eyes glared at him and a warm nose barely touched his.

"Hungry?"

Furball responded with a loud meow.

Quinn stood and headed for the kitchen, the cat streaking around him as if he hadn't been fed earlier that day. He washed the feline's bowl and snapped open a can of Fancy Feast. Furball pounced onto the counter and headbutted Quinn's arm. "Oh, yeah, one smell of fish and I'm your BFF, you old food-hound." He sat the filled bowl on the floor on a plastic placemat emblazoned with the cat's name. Wouldn't T-Bone roll with laughter if he knew he'd taken a liking to a stray cat? But then weren't they alike in that regard? He and Furball, alone and doing their damnedest to survive in a world that concentrated too much on an emotion that eluded them both—love.

Opening the refrigerator, he snagged a bottle of beer and the makings for a chicken salad sandwich. By the time he opened his laptop on the coffee table, he was onto his second beer and halfway through the sandwich. Three unopened emails sat in his inbox. One was from Becca, trying to set up a time for a farewell party with family and co-workers. "Not gonna happen, sweetheart." Family meant Cassie. As far as he was concerned, they'd said their goodbyes. He wouldn't put her through any more emotional angst.

The second email was from Lance Blakewell, his old boss at the State Department. It was written in his typical short and succinct style: *Call me.*

The third was from his dad and practically emitted the smoke of an angry man when Quinn opened it. It hadn't taken long for news to circulate through the department grapevine that he'd been making inquiries. Nor had it taken long for his old man to voice his narrow-minded, hold-onto-a-grudge-forever mentality. Hudson "Buck" Gallagher, head of the Bureau of International Intelligence and Research within the State Department, had never forgiven his son for the failed mission, for leaving the agency and for inadvertently smudging his sterling thirty-four-year work record.

Quinn hit the delete button. Hell, he hadn't planned on screwing up everyone's life. The shit just happened. "Yeah, I love you, too, dad."

He did a search of fire and rescue companies advertising for personnel. He found two in Miami and Saint Augustine and filled out the online applications. He'd be far enough away from Cassie that she'd give up hope of a future with him, yet he'd be close enough if she needed him for any kind of emergency. Lynn Haven and Pensacola had openings too. So did Brunswick, Georgia. After applying at those stations, he made a list of everyone he'd emailed earlier in the day and composed a standard message stating he'd decided to stay closer to the water and warmer temperatures. Thanks for checking around for openings for him, but he planned to stick to fire and marine rescue. *Blah, blah, blah, have a nice, boring life. Kiss my ass and leave my woman the hell alone.*

His email to T-Bone was more personal. He mentioned the need to move on, yet stay near the ocean. Even joked about joining the navy or the coast guard if he were younger. T-Bone would get a charge out of that. Only one person remained to reply to—Buck "the man" Gallagher. While he told his father he was looking for another position as a fireman, he also stated he was not considering government work ever again. He asked about his mom and Grandpa Hudson.

Once he finished that email, he went into his bedroom and stripped the sheets and tossed them in the washer. Sleeping with Cassie's fragrance on his bedclothes was more torture than he could handle. For now, his focus had to be keeping her safe.

CHAPTER TEN

Cassie rotated her shoulders after settling on a stool at Ryder's Healthy Café and tried to ignore the aches in her leg muscles and feet. It had been a long day at the beauty shop with next to zero time to sit. The manager wielded a pair of scissors in one hand and a whip in the other, too often forgetting the stylists were human beings with legs and backs that throbbed if they didn't have a chance to rest. Just five minutes with one's feet propped up worked wonders.

Working for someone else wasn't as rewarding as having her own business; thank goodness it was only temporary. Repairs to the strip mall where a fire had gutted Cassie's Wolf Den salon ten days after her grand opening were progressing. The debris was finally cleaned out. The rafters and roofing replaced. Exterior walls and insulation were to go in this week and then electricians would come to install new wiring—a welcome upgrade since faulty wiring had been the cause of the blaze.

She'd found some cool shampoo and station chairs on eBay at a fraction of the cost of new. Mirrors and counters were on order, as were myriad small, yet essential items. If all went according to her timeline, she'd be cutting hair in her own shop in less than sixty days.

Time seemed to control all facets of her life right now. Her business. Quinn.

"Want your usual, baby doll?" Ryder leaned his muscled forearms on the counter. Fluorescent lighting glistened on his bald head, glinted off the gold ring in his brown earlobe. She nodded and he reached for the blender to fill the pitcher with ingredients for a strawberry-blueberry smoothie.

"Yes, something to calm me down. Some moron driving a black crotch-rocket nearly ran me down in the mall's parking lot."

"You don't say."

"I think he followed me here. Whizzed past me when I got out of my car, stared at me through his dark helmet. Gave me the willies." She jerked her thumb toward the street. "I think he pulled into the parking lot of Gulfside Treasures."

"Jest a sec, while I have a look-see." Ryder stalked toward the door and opened it, stepping out onto the sidewalk. The drone of the bike whined up the street, showing off. Ryder chuckled when he came back inside. "Probably just some young buck, checkin' you out. Quinn joinin' you?"

"No. He's packing to move."

Ryder scooped in blueberries. "No shit? Really? He buy a condo? A house?"

She shook her head, wishing that were true. A house for both of them to go with a set of wedding rings and bridal china. "No, he turned in his notice at the fire station. He's leaving Clearwater."

"What?" The café owner's dark eyes widened. He pressed the lid on the pitcher before crossing his arms. "Why?"

"Me." She lifted a shoulder and yanked a paper napkin from the chrome holder. "Us." She wrapped the napkin tightly around her index finger. "Our friendship took a turn and he got spooked." The napkin remained coiled when she slid it off her finger.

"So, he finally admitted to his feelings where you're concerned." Ryder's remark was a statement, not a question. He set the pitcher in the power unit of the blender and depressed a button.

A brash whirring assaulted her ears for a few seconds. Ryder made a skewer of orange, lemon and strawberry slices, shaking his head as he worked. Once the blender quieted, he poured the concoction into a large glass and plopped in the fruit garnish. After setting the drink in front of her, he wiped his hands on a white rag. "Never figured him to run like some scared virginal bitch. Got to be somethin' else goin' on, baby doll. Gots to be."

"He won't really give me a reason why." She ripped the napkin in half. "Generalities. Vague bullshit." The napkin was torn again and again. "He claims he's not worthy of me." Her nervous fingers flayed the pieces into finer ones, much like Quinn had shredded her heart. She blinked back tears and reached for her drink, the cold fruity mixture soothing the burn at the back of her throat. *I will not cry. I won't.*

"Hold on a sec." Ryder called to his waitress and made some hand signals she seemed to understand, then strode around the bar and sat on the stool next to Cassie. "Business is slow today. My main girl can handle the place while we talk. Looks to me like you need a shoulder." He tucked her hair behind her ear. "You're in a world of hurt, aren't you, baby doll?"

Wolf had introduced her to this gentle giant soon after her brother left the SEALs. Ryder was an ex-SEAL, too, trained in surveillance, yet for all the menace his rough exterior implied, the man was gooey chocolate on the inside.

"He's the only man I've ever loved. I don't know what I'll do after he leaves."

"Bad thing is you two have been datin' for years and were too damn dumb to realize it. Hell, you went everywhere together."

"We're best friends. Or were. Now that I all but forced myself on him, he won't even look at me." She wiped her tears and laughed at the same time. "Guess that was TMI, huh?"

Ryder snatched some napkins from the holder and blotted her face. "I see how he looks at you. Better yet, I see how he scowls at any man who looks your way. He's damn possessive where you're concerned. I can't get over his leavin'." He waved the waitress over.

"Hand me a bottle of water, sweetness, and fix us a plate of cheese and nuts. My friend, here, and I have some heavy talkin' to do. Can you handle the place for thirty minutes or so? I'll let you off early."

"Sure." The blonde beamed a smile and passed him a cold bottle of Evian.

"Let's move to someplace more private." Ryder led her to the empty booth in the corner, sat and snapped off the lid before he guzzled a long drink. "Okay. Tell me what you feel comfortable sharin'. Maybe together we can figure out what's promptin' him to leave town. Cause this is the last mother-effing thing I expected."

While they sipped their drinks and nibbled from the food tray the waitress set on their table, Cassie shared the major points that had happened since her birthday between her and the man she loved. Talking to someone who knew Quinn was a great relief. She could have never told Wolf or Jace she'd given her virginity to Quinn. Never. Her brothers, especially Wolf, would have torn Quinn apart, limb from muscled limb.

Ryder ran a wide palm over his bald head. "Somethin' else is goin' on here." He curled his hand into a fist and tapped his stomach. "This whole leavin' town business just ain't sittin' right. It unsettles my gut." His head tilted to the side. "What was Quinn before he came here? He's not ex-military, but he's got a wariness about him. Tries too hard to be a funny guy. Not that his ass isn't comical as hell at times."

"How can you tell if someone was or wasn't in the military?" She stuck the skewer into her mouth and pulled off the succulent fruit.

Ryder gave a wave of his open hand. "By the way they hold themselves. Their walk. The habits the military drills into you." He popped a cube of cheese in his mouth and chewed. "No, he's more the CIA type or FBI. Maybe he's on some kinda long-term undercover assignment."

She'd just taken a sip of her smoothie and choked. "CIA? Undercover? Not Quinn. That's nuts." Wasn't it? The thought took hold and niggled at her gut. "What if he has a wife somewhere?

What if I'm in love with a married man?" *My god, what if I had a married man's cock in my mouth...or inside me?*

Ryder's hand covered hers. "Calm down, baby doll. Don't go borrowing trouble. He's been here for three years. That's a long time to be away from a wife and family. Did he ever take long vacations? Or wasn't where he told you he'd be?"

She shook her head. "No. He's constantly been open in that regard. We were often in and out of each other's apartments and usually without advance notice."

He scooped a handful of nuts in his big palm and gestured toward her with his hand. "Then I'd venture a guess he doesn't have a wife or another woman stashed somewhere. I'm just curious as to what kind of work he did before he moved here."

"I always figured he was a fireman wherever he'd lived before. He graduated from Harvard. I've seen the diploma hanging on his wall. I know his parents live in DC." What else did she know about his past? Not much. He was an only child, which was why he claimed to enjoy the loud madness of her family. His mother taught music at American University, and he spoke of her with great fondness. Mentions of his father were sparse and cold, as if there were strong tensions between them. But, beyond those few things, she knew nothing.

"See?" Ryder's eyes narrowed. "A Harvard grad workin' as a fireman? Don't compute." Both hands rose in an openly defensive move. "Not that there's a damn thing wrong with bein' a fireman. God bless em all, but Harvard doesn't exactly offer Firefightin' 101, if you catch my drift." He leaned toward her. "So what happened between his college graduation and the day he rolled into Clearwater? We find that out and we find out what's makin' him hightail his ass outta here, cause, baby doll, it ain't you."

His words made her cry in relief and tense up with concern at the same time. "You don't think it's me? Really?" She swiped at her tears.

"Hell, no. That man would kill for you. Would lay down his

life for you." He stared at her for a few seconds. "You got anything that belongs to him? At your apartment or in your car? Things you oughta return before he leaves?"

"Ah…I have a pair of his swim fins and an old Madonna CD. Why?"

Ryder laughed. "Let me make a quick call. Is he off duty tonight?"

"Yeah." She placed her hand over his cell phone. "Who are you calling? What are you up to?" He fought a smile that tugged at the corners of his mouth, and it didn't exactly give her the warm and fuzzies. Maybe because pure evil glinted in his gaze.

"Was just thinkin' you oughta have an escort when you return his stuff." A chuckle bubbled forth. "An escort every bit as macho and good lookin' as Quinn. Yup, more I think on it, the better I like the idea. Man, I'd love to be a fly on the wall to see this. I'm callin' my godson, Micah. He was Green Berets. Runs his own gym now." He expelled laughter and shook his head. "Hell, Quinn's gonna be so damn pissed. Meanwhile, you think of the sexiest outfit you've got to wear."

"Are you kidding? The last time I wore my red leather skirt, Quinn nearly went bonkers."

"Then that's the one to wear tonight, baby doll. Cause he's gonna be all over you. Got some fuck-me heels?" His forehead wrinkled and quirked where there should have been an eyebrow. "Better still. Any thigh-high leather boots? The ones with stiletto heels? Man, they are instant boner-birthers for a guy." He cleared his throat and winked. "Got a pair?"

"My roommate has a pair, but her shoe size is bigger than mine."

"Don't matter. Stuff em with tissues or newspapers or somethin'."

She slipped her purple mobile from her purse and started composing a can-I-borrow-your-boots text. Meanwhile, nervousness churned in her stomach like the surf with a hurricane approaching. "I'm not so sure I like this idea. I'm not one for playing games."

Ryder held his black cell to his ear with one beefy hand and waved the other as if to erase her objections. "Hell, all of life is a game, baby doll. I'm tellin' you, that man of yours will be like a man possessed when he sees you with my godson. Quinn'll drag you off, caveman style." Ryder winked. "Trust me." He turned his attention to his phone. "Micah? Got an hour you can spare your Uncle Ryder tonight?"

Two hours later, Micah eased his black Escalade into Quinn's apartment complex, slowing to coast over the traffic bumps. The firecracker nerves that had moved into Cassie's stomach hadn't ceased their quivering and sparking since the second she left Ryder's Café. She glanced at the handsome man next to her, his thick wrist draped nonchalantly over the steering wheel. His head was shaved bald like Ryder's and sported a tribal tattoo over half of his scalp. More ink decorated his arms. The tense set of his jaw said he was ready for battle if the situation called for it.

Oh, this was so not good.

More pyrotechnics exploded in her stomach, sending acid up her throat and tingles down her limbs to her tissue-stuffed, booted feet.

Damn the fireworks!

They'd sizzled and made her tremble as she'd shaved in the shower. Had she known what lay ahead of her tonight, she'd have undergone a Brazilian bikini wax at the shop. But how was she to know Ryder would talk her into pushing Quinn a little closer to the ledge? If things worked out the way Ryder claimed, and Quinn took her to bed, she wanted to give him a little surprise. One of her clients claimed her honey loved a bald hootchie. Would Quinn? By damn she'd soon find out. With his foolhardy plans to leave, this might be her last chance to convince him to stay. She had to give tonight her best effort—it would be balls to the wall seduction.

Once she'd blotted her skin dry from her shower, she slathered on her signature peaches and cream body lotion as the emotional fireworks continued to pop and detonate. The only soothing thing she had to apply over her freshly shaven labia was fuchsia-infused aloe gel.

Pinwheels of excitement lit up her system as she'd slithered into her red leather skirt and buttoned her black blouse, shoving the tails beneath the waistband with trembling hands. She was going to deliberately make Quinn jealous and then seduce him with her sexiest black lingerie and her bald "hootchie". *Oh God, this better work.*

Her doorbell rang just as she'd zipped up what Ryder called "boner-birther boots".

Micah's expression when she'd opened the door had been priceless—pure flattery, yet predatory. "Damn. Uncle Ryder's talked about Baby Doll for years, but I had no clue what a baby doll you'd be."

"And I had no clue you'd be Irish and full of blarney." She winked and he laughed. "Hold on, let me grab Quinn's things I'm returning." She bent over to retrieve the yellow flippers and CD from the sofa. Out of the corner of her eye, she saw Micah adjust himself. *Gee, maybe I should invest in a pair of these boner-birther boots.*

"Which building is his, *bébé*?"

His question as he drove through Quinn's apartment complex jarred her out of her reverie. Cassie unbuttoned the top three buttons on her blouse for the second time. "The second unit on the right. See the U-Haul trailer backed into the parking space?" Making Quinn jealous on purpose was such a high school tactic; she was beyond that. Besides, what if it didn't work? Did she want his last memory of her to be one of her making a complete fool of herself? Her fingers rose to re-button her top.

"Leave them open," Micah growled, his eyes obliterated by the dark shades he wore. "I'd demand my woman show me some skin."

She fiddled with the button at the front clasp of her bra. "Yeah, but I'm not your woman. Quinn won't know what your preferences are."

He shoved the car into Park and turned off the engine. "He will as soon as he sees me. I'll make sure of it. I'll have him so damn jealous he'll charge at me like an Angus bull." He unsnapped the seat belt, and the leather squeaked when he angled toward her. "I'll be doing little things to make him jealous. Nothing overt, *bébé*. Just enough to send him over the edge."

"I doubt it'll make any difference." Her insecurities were fighting with her sensual bravado.

His hand curled around her thigh. "You really are naïve, aren't you? Don't you know how hot you are? How you still radiate innocence even if he's already tapped that?" He dipped his head in the direction of her crotch.

Is "lost my virginity yesterday" engraved on my forehead, or what?

"He'll be able to tell if I've touched you. If we've kissed." He leaned toward her, one hand slipped under her hair to cup the back of her neck and his other drifted from her thigh to open two more of her buttons.

"Hey!" She knocked his hand away. What a macho creep. "If you don't keep your hands off my buttons and my leg, the only thing he'll be able to tell about you is that you talk funny. High-pitched. Like a soprano."

Quinn's head peeked out from the back of the moving trailer, his ball cap pulled low over his eyes. Even so, by the set of his square jaw and the scorching glare he aimed their way, he'd zeroed in on Micah's hand inching up her leg.

Oh hell.

CHAPTER ELEVEN

Who the hell was Cassie with and what the fuck was his hand doing on her damn thigh?

Quinn stepped away from the U-Haul, assessing his options while his blood pressure ratcheted into the stroke zone. Even though he didn't want to spend time with her, he sure as hell didn't want to see her with another guy. He pressed the heel of his palm to his heart and rubbed, trying to ease the pain. *Christ, this hurts.*

The driver's door opened and six-foot-four of muscled mass hopped out and sauntered around the hood of his highly waxed Escalade to lift Cassie out of his SUV. Where in God's name had she met this bald, inked son of a bitch? Quinn's hands curled into fists. Was this bastard the one who'd taught her how to give such incredible, enthusiastic head?

A jealous rage, cavernous and foul, bubbled in his soul as if it were a gigantic cauldron holding all his negative emotions. This stranger was not the kind of man he'd choose for his angel. He'd pick some knock-kneed, hollow-chested paper-pusher. A nice man, for she deserved to be treated with gentleness and respect, but not someone she could care for more than she did Quinn. No, he was a selfish bastard; he wanted to be the one she yearned for, dreamed of, thought about—for she'd damn sure be the one invading his thoughts forever.

The stranger bent to kiss Cassie's neck before he backed away. Quinn's heart stopped. Her blouse was unbuttoned to her navel and she was wearing that damned red leather skirt again. And, God help him, she wore black leather, over-the-knee, stiletto boots. Blood rushed from his brain to his cock. Possessiveness took hold. She was his, dammit. He'd been her first. A part of her would always belong to him. Always.

"Hi Quinn. Sorry to drop by unannounced, but I wanted to return these things of yours." She extended his flippers and an old CD he didn't give a good rat's ass about.

He snatched the items from her hands and tossed them in the back of the trailer. His hands on his hips, his narrow-eyed gaze raked her from head to toe. This woman—his angel with the heart-shaped face—who he'd made love to yesterday, was all dressed up for a date with another man. A man who would inhale her sweet essence, taste her lips, trail his fingers over her soft skin, hear her needy moans and sink into her wet tightness. His gaze shifted to the man poised in a military "at ease" stance behind her. Damn the motherfucker all to hell. Quinn's scrutiny settled on her again.

A blush kissed her cheeks. They knew each other so well they could almost read each other's thoughts. She retreated a couple of steps.

The stranger's large hands enveloped her waist, pulling her to his chest. "Easy, *bébé*, I don't want you to fall." His hand shifted to splay over the juncture of her thighs. A slow smile of ownership spread like muddy water over a beautiful garden as his middle finger circled an area that, up until today, only Quinn had touched.

Cassie squirmed in embarrassment. "Don't."

"You should know I don't take orders from any woman I date." His hold on her tightened.

She elbowed him and spun away.

Quinn lunged and shoved the slimeball against his vehicle. Two quick jabs to his firm stomach, a punch to his jaw and a couple of karate chops to his neck, and the bastard crumbled down the side of his Caddy.

"You've hurt him!" Cassie scurried to kneel over the man shaking his head, no doubt wondering which direction the truck had gone that had run him down.

"I'll be okay, *bébé*." His hand rose to cup her cheek.

Quinn grabbed her wrist and hauled her to him. "I'll kill him if he ever touches you again." He leaned close until he was nearly nose to nose with Cassie. "I will fucking kill him," he enunciated through clenched jaws.

"How? You'll be gone." Her green eyes, smoking hot with all the make-up she'd applied, bore into him. Possessiveness, the likes of which he'd never thought possible, burned in his gut. That heart-shaped face of hers was so beautiful, it nearly stole the breath from his lungs. And, dammit, she was his.

"Until I cross Courtney Campbell Causeway, you belong to me and I'll be damned if I'll share you with the likes of that lowlife bastard, or anyone else." His fingers coiled around her bicep, and he marched her toward the door to his building. "I mean, what the hell, Cassie? After what passed between us yesterday?" He jerked open the door and ushered her inside. "The next freaking day, you want to move on to someone else?"

She jerked her arm out of his grasp and rounded on him, her dark hair flying about her head like a dusky storm cloud. His Cassie was never one to back down from an argument. "Oh, you're a fine one to talk. You all but kicked me out of your apartment once you got your rocks off, so don't hand me some song and dance about how much it all meant to you." She jabbed her finger in his chest. "Because it didn't mean diddly." The strap of her handbag slipped off her shoulder and she yanked on it, wrapping the leather around her wrist a couple of times before swinging her purse to belt him across his arm. "You are such a cold-hearted bastard. I gave you everything…*everything*…and you gave me the boot."

She'd zeroed onto the heart of the guilt ripping at him the last twenty-four hours, and he didn't like it.

He shook his finger under her nose. "You want me to give you something? I'll give you more than you can freaking handle."

She bit his finger.

He tossed her over his shoulder in a fireman's carry and marched up the steps. She yelled and cursed, beating his back, but he was so agitated he didn't give a flying fuck. His fingertips slid into the front pocket of his Levis for his keys, and he unlocked the door. As soon as he'd closed it behind him, he slid her down his body into the corner between the entrance to the foyer and the coat closet.

"Cassie, you better settle your ass down!"

"And you better go to hell!" Her disheveled hair billowed away from her face when she screeched.

A streak of grey fur charged back down the hallway toward Quinn's bedroom. "Hush, angel, you've scared Furball."

He brushed her tumbled curls back only to find two big pearly tears glistening on her lower eyelashes. God, he hated seeing her cry. Knowing he was the cause of her distress wounded him far more than he'd expected. He forked his fingers into her hair and made slow, comforting circles on her scalp. He lowered his head. "Angel." His lips found hers as if they were a part of him he needed to connect with in order to live.

On a moan, she opened her mouth to his and their tongues met and mated, swirled and seduced, touched and tortured. He leaned into her as if she were the other half of his being and, for a few minutes, he feared she was. How would he exist without his angel? Yet staying with her would only bring her pain, for, in his soul, he lugged around deep agony and an innate ability to hurt others, while she carried goodness and light and happiness in hers. Added to all that was this new threat he hoped he'd averted with all those emails, because, frankly, when it came to Cassie's safety, he didn't trust anyone.

A moan of feminine need pulled him from his dark thoughts. He nuzzled her neck and swept a hand down her back to cup her sweet behind, bringing her against his erection, rubbing and easing the pain for a few blessed seconds before the ache grew so powerful he thought he'd lose his mind. He bit her jaw and soothed it with his tongue. "Sweetheart." His teeth grazed the column of her slender neck, and she shivered before tilting her head to grant him access.

There was no way to measure how much he needed her. She was the only good thing God had set on the path of his obscure, emotionless, desolate existence. A glowing daisy in the dark miasma of his guilt, bending and tilting with the winds of life.

His glorious, glowing daisy tugged on his t-shirt. "I want you naked. I need to touch you." Her breathless plea turned him on even more.

His hand fisted in her hair and he jerked her head back so her gaze focused on his. "You are mine, Cassie. Mine and no one else's. From now until the moment I leave, you belong to me. Do I make myself clear?"

Her hand rose to cup his cheek. "I've always belonged to you."

He wrapped his fingers around her wrist and brought her hand to his lips, placing a kiss in her palm. He'd give anything if his life was different, if his history hadn't destroyed the young man he'd once been. "Don't ask for what I can't give."

She pulled her hand back. "But I want more. I need more." She swiped at a falling tear. "I want you now and tomorrow and next week." A wobbly grin tried to form and failed. "I want you next month and all summer long. I don't understand why you're leaving and you're determined not to tell me." Her green eyes regarded him for a few beats, and then, as if a decision had been made, she trailed a finger up his arm. "I want you naked. Now. If this is all you're prepared to give me then, by damn, I'm taking it."

Swooping her into his arms, he carried her into his bedroom. She wanted to see him naked, did she? Oh she would, but he'd not let her touch. Not until he was damn good and ready.

He laid her on the bed. "Stay. You want my clothes off?" She nodded, her eyebrows waggling in delight. He toed off his ratty sneakers and, with one hand over his shoulder, tugged off his t-shirt. His cock nearly sighed in relief when he unbuttoned his jeans, the rasping of the zipper echoing in the silent bedroom. He shucked them and his boxers to the floor in one swift motion.

Cassie's gaze shone with passion and hunger when it traveled down his chest and abdomen, snagging on his erection. It was the kind of visual inspection, laced with appreciation, men dreamed of, and his cock grew and stiffened in response, a wonderment given how hard he'd had been minutes earlier.

Her manicured hand reached for him. "Let me touch you."

"Not yet." He strode to her side of the bed and sat. Yanking the edges of her black shirt together, he quickly buttoned them all.

"What are you doing?"

"A little trick. Wait and see." He unbuttoned the cuffs and tugged her shirttails from her skirt. To raise her upper torso off the bed, he slid one arm under her and pulled her shirttails over her head. Then he laid her back down, her head covered by her shirt.

"If you wanted to take it off my—" her voice got muffled when her shirt covered her mouth. "You thoulda left the buttonth open."

He tied the cuffs of her sleeves around one of the posts of his brass headboard.

She wiggled and kicked, pulling on her arms. "What did you do?"

Furball hopped onto the bed and sniffed at her covered head.

"I tied you to the bed. Don't. Stop flailing around or you'll tear your shirt. Can you breathe?"

Her mouth drew the cotton material in and out with each frantic breath. The material's movement snagged the kitten's attention and he pounced on her mouth. Cassie shrieked. The cat sat back, tilting his head to watch his prey. "Behave, Furball."

Quinn fought the urge to laugh. God, he was going to enjoy this. He worked to open the button through the fabric near her nose so she could take in air. "Can you breathe better now?" He kissed the tip of her nose. The cat moved in and sniffed it before he bit it.

No response.

He shifted the material so he could see her one eye.

Narrowed in anger, it all but exploded fiery daggers at him.

"Just checking to see if you're still awake. Looks like kitty-cat wants to play while I undress you."

She made an annoyed sound in the back of her throat and, when he pulled the opening over her mouth, she stuck out her tongue at him. God, she was so much fun. He was going to miss her temper and the teasing banter he'd enjoyed these last three years. Sadness squeezed his heart with sharp, frigid tentacles, so intensely he could barely breathe. *How can I leave her?*

He willed away the pain and doubt to bring himself back into the moment, back to enjoying her. He moved the hole over her nose again. "This is a bit of punishment for hooking up with that bald bastard. I'm going to undress you and kiss your soft skin, and all the while you won't be able to touch me in return.

"I don't want to touch you, you bossy asshole." She squirmed on the bed as if she wanted desperately to get her hands on him—no doubt around his throat.

He smiled against her one bare shoulder and tsked a few times. "Is that any way for an angel to talk?" He bit her freckled flesh until she inhaled in shock, or arousal. Then he soothed it with the tip of his tongue and solid kisses. "I love these freckles. I might play connect the dots with a Sharpie and send you home with my brand all over you."

She mentioned an uncomfortable place he could shove his Sharpie pen and he smirked. God, she was a vocal piece of work when she was pissed.

With a well-practiced flick of his thumb and index finger, he unsnapped her black lacy bra. Furball dove in to claim the under-wired cups. Quinn shoved him away. "I do love your choice in lingerie, but I think I want to see you naked again." He cupped her breasts and, bestowing kisses on each one, thought of something else to make her mad. "I'm thinking of a tat above each one of these beauties. Above the right one, you need the word 'Quinn's' and above the left one 'tits'. He rolled off her in self-preservation.

She kicked air with her boots, no doubt hoping to make contact. If he didn't get this leather footwear off her, he'd have one stiletto in his ankle and the other rammed into his knee.

"Easy, now." He leaned across her thighs, grasping the decorative pull on one zipper. "Are these new?"

"No."

"I don't recall you wearing them." He tugged one long boot off, his fingertips trailing the soft skin on her legs as he exposed it. Four crumpled tissues floated onto his sheet once he removed the footwear. The cat dove for white paper butterflies. "Let me guess. These are Sarah's boots. She's got damn big feet. Hold on while I put the cat in the hallway. He's liable to use my cock for a scratching post."

"Huh, he'd need a pair of glasses to find it first."

"Now is that any way to talk?" He scooped the kitten in his arm, set him out in the hallway and threw down the tissues to attract the feline's attention. Quinn quickly closed the door. When he returned to the bed, he removed her other boot as slowly as he'd slipped off the first. Yes, slow and deliberate would be the modus operandi for the evening. He'd slowly drive his angel insane with need.

One by one, he drew a toe into his mouth and swirled his tongue around it. At first she jerked. Then she stilled. He feathered kisses along the arch of her foot and over her ankle, and heard what he hoped was a sigh. Moving from leg to leg, the smooth skin of her calves enticed him. Each received meticulous attention of nibbles, soothed by kisses. He inhaled her peaches and cream fragrance, knowing he'd never be able to taste of the sweet fruit again without thinking of his Cassie. His hands stroked her toned thighs, while his mind recalled how tightly they'd squeezed around him to push him through her barrier, breaking her cherry. She was his first virgin. He'd been her first man. Three years and they'd shared so much.

"Roll, angel." He tilted her to the side so he could unzip her leather skirt and slid it over her hips, dropping it onto the floor. She wore a tiny swath of black lace attached to a narrow black elastic band. "Your ass has been my fantasy for years."

"Yours, too."

Delighted by her two-word confession, he smacked one of her ass cheeks. "Like my tight bubble butt, do you?" She giggled and he pressed kisses to each cheek of her most delectable behind. He slipped his thumbs under the warm ebony silk and tugged her thong off, tossing it over his shoulder.

The aroma of fuchsias, a wild flower that grew abundantly in Chile, reached his nose, conveying his thoughts back to the lush, green countryside. Renata used to bathe in fuchsia water. He shook his head to clear his mind.

And spied Cassie's shaven pussy.

He stilled. Anger, hot and unforgiving, rolled through him. He ran a finger between the folds of her labia. "What the hell is this?" The tone of his voice deepened to a dangerous level.

"I shaved tonight."

"You shaved for him? Does that bald motherfucker like his women bald as well as obedient?"

"No. No, it's not like that at all. Untie me, Quinn. I need to see your face."

Strong emotions of betrayal and fear of losing Cassie overtook him. She was the continual beam, the bright ray of sunshine in his world of obsidian emotions. God, she was everything of value in his life. Confusion muddled his cognizance. His familiar bedroom faded away and the opulent coastline of Chile shimmered into his consciousness. The labyrinth of inlets, canals and twisting peninsulas lined with magnificent greenery and dotted with occasional waterfalls and lakes, once a place of beauty to him, was now a memorial of death. Bouquets of exotic blooms and humid earth replaced the delicate fragrance of the peaches and cream lotion Cassie wore. His fingers curled into fists. *Damn*

Renata for her treachery.

A red haze of fury covered his vision, or was it the spilled blood of his team members? He trembled as memories of gunfire rang in his ears. The acrid smell of gunpowder and the coppery stench of blood filled his nostrils. He'd been deceived. His whole team had been betrayed, set-up and damn near destroyed. Only two people knew about their mission that night—Renata and his contact in the State Department. And only one had confessed.

"You used me. Filled my mind with lies." He forced air into lungs constricted with resentment and revenge.

"What? You're not making any sense." She pulled at her restraints. "Get this shirt off me so we can talk sensibly. Enough games."

"Oh, you like playing games, don't you, Renata? You move from me to the next guy as quickly and easily as you change underwear. The cartel paid you well for your loyalty, didn't they?" He rolled off the bed and stormed out of the bedroom. Renata's cries—no, Cassie's—followed him. Jealousy and anger had him so damned confused. He needed space, time to think and a cold beer. Maybe two.

Twisting off the bottle top, he guzzled a long drink. He shook so badly, beer dribbled down his chin and chest. He slammed the brew on the counter and reached for some paper towels to hold under running water to wipe his face and upper torso. Sweat poured out of him, and he gulped deep breaths of air to calm the shakes. His first assessment had been correct. He was too emotionally damaged for Cassie. One whiff of Renata's favorite exotic flower and he'd had a full-blown flashback. What had he said to Cassie? He couldn't recall.

She was so precious to him. If he hurt her, he'd never forgive himself. Yet someone had to talk to her about the choices she was making. Hell, next thing she knew she'd be saddled with some loser like him…or worse, if that were possible. He took another pull off his beer. Maybe if he talked to Becca, explained how reckless

Cassie was behaving of late. Asked Becca to keep an eye on his angel. He upended the bottle to his lips. Lord knew, someone needed to explain the consequences of her actions to her.

Furball jumped onto the counter and headbutted Quinn's arm, meowing his I-need-a-treat plea. "You're eating me out of house and apartment, cat. And let me tell you one damn thing. Lucky for your sorry ass, you're a male and not female. Cause, just between us, I suck at relationships with women." He stroked Furball's head twice before holding a snack triangle for him to eat. "Easy now, don't mistake my skin for a piece of salmon." He glanced toward the hallway leading to the bedroom. "I'm more the ass type than the fish variety." Quinn drained his beer, tossed the empty container in the trash and trudged back to the bedroom to face Cassie.

Why in the hell did I let myself fall in love with her? Who the hell am I kidding? One dose of her sassy sunlight and I was fuckin' toast.

CHAPTER TWELVE

If she didn't stop struggling, she was going to suffocate under her own blouse. Cassie laid still and breathed slowly. God, this thing was hot and drawn tight. Who was the idiotic expert who claimed cotton breathed? Once she got out from the humiliating position of her shirt pulled over her head while she lay completely naked on an empty, *deserted* bed, she was going on a feminine rampage.

Men. Not a single one of them had a lick of sense. Ryder and his bright idea of making Quinn jealous. Micah and his touchy-feely tactics. Quinn with his hot-and-cold affections and spontaneous temper tantrums. All of them deserved a good old-fashioned ass-whooping and she was just the pissed off woman to deliver.

What soured her mood even more was that her body still hummed with desire for more of Quinn's touch. Being stroked and kissed during the temporary loss of her sight was a real turn-on. Every cell in her system honed in on whatever part of her body he worked. The man certainly knew his way around the female form, how to arouse and whip into a sensual frenzy.

Which brought to mind another question that deserved answering in a damn big hurry: just who the *hell* was Renata? Some other woman Quinn was seeing? He would pay big-time if he was having sex with both her and someone else.

Footsteps sounded in the hallway. She ground her molars

together and tensed. Victim number one in her feminine retribution approached.

The bed shifted and dipped when he sat, his naked hip warmed her waist. "Are you all right, angel? I shouldn't have left you tied up like this." Oh, so he was back to being Mr. Nice Guy now. His lips pressed a kiss to her navel and around the mounds of both breasts. "I'm sorry for the way I acted." His tongue flicked across her beaded nipples, already straining for his attention.

Her eyes narrowed beneath the fabric of her shirt. What made him think he could kiss her so casually? After all he'd accused her of? After calling her by another woman's name? A simple "I'm sorry" was supposed to erase leaving her tied up like this? *Not on your freaking life, bucko.*

The material pulled her arms while he untied the knots in her sleeves around the posts of the headboard. "I'll rub your shoulders to get the circulation going again. I should never have left you tied up while I walked out to cool off."

Her fingers curled into her palms. *Oh look at how nice and concerned Mr. Moody Ass is now.*

Once her arms were freed, pain rushed in. Her nerve endings pinged and pronged throughout her shoulders and arms as blood flow returned. She gasped to swallow the aching while a couple of moans eked out from her throat.

"You okay?" Quinn tugged her blouse off her head and arranged it around her body, gently and with tenderness, as if he really cared. His fingers massaged her shoulders and arms, while steam built inside her like a teapot without a release valve. Mr. Moody Ass had the nerve to smile, as if his charm would just melt away his offensive behavior. "Although, I gotta admit, you looked damned appealing laying there in the middle of my bed, naked with your face covered up like that."

She belted him.

Her fingers were curled so tightly when she gave him an uppercut to the jaw, she wasn't sure she'd ever be able to cut or comb hair again. "You ignorant asshole! How dare you say I looked good with my face covered up? Were you referring to the adolescent joke about putting a bag over every woman's head so we'd all look alike? How dare you?"

He flopped onto his back, his hand to his chin. "Ow! You made me bite my tongue."

She straddled him, shaking her fist under his nose. "You're lucky I didn't hit you in the balls, then you could bite on those for a while. You had no right to leave me tied up like that and then to make that stupid-ass remark."

"Look, I'm sorry. Okay? I had a bit of a flashback." He blinked and then winced at his uncustomary admission. "I got jealous when I saw you'd shaved."

"Flashback? Of what? A parade of bald hootchies!"

His eyes narrowed. "I think it's time you calmed down. You're overreacting."

"Overreacting, my ass. I went through all these preparations for you tonight, you big, unappreciative jerk. I even suffered the advances of Ryder's godson. And let me tell you, he was one touchy-feely prick."

He rolled her over, tucking her beneath him. "Calm. The Fuck. Down. Did I ask you to get mixed up with someone else?"

His thick thighs encased her legs, the dark hairs setting off her nerve endings from her scalp to her soles. Why, oh why, did a touch from any part of his body always excite, bringing her sensuality to life? Not that she would think about that now—or pay attention to his cock growing long and thick against her abdomen—not when she was so damn angry with the man inside the firm mound of muscle embracing her.

"Yes, you did. You told me to leave your apartment yesterday and forget about you. So, that's what I did." She hiked her chin, hoping to hell she pissed him off half as much as he'd done to her. *Paybacks are hell, Quinn Gallagher.*

His teeth grazed her chin. "I think you may have misunderstood, *bébé*." His accent imitated Micah's.

Okay, she'd play the game. She knew just the buttons to push. "Oh," she cooed, inserting a breathy quality to her voice, "you sound just like Micah. I just adore how possessive he is. He's *all* man. Not afraid to show his attraction to a woman in the slightest."

Quinn's head slowly rose from her neck where he'd been nuzzling and nibbling, his whiskered stubble sending delightful shivers through her system. The grey overtook the blue of his narrowed eyes as they fixated on hers. "You little green-eyed pain in my ass. You want to see possessive?"

His fingers clenched the lapels of her blouse and rent it open. One or two buttons zinged against the wall over her head. He practically vibrated with anger. Even the ink of his tattoo shone darker in the dusky light of his bedroom. "I'll show you more possession than you ever imagined. Because no one touches you, but me. Do you understand?" His finger slipped into the moisture of her folds. "No one makes you wet like this, but me." His thumb circled her clit while he repeatedly chanted she was his and no one else's.

Demanding lips covered hers in a passionate, almost frantic kiss. One hand cupped the back of her neck while the thumb of his other hand continued its slow, torturous odyssey around her clit, moving closer with each pass. His tongue invaded her mouth and stroked every surface, which somehow soothed the burning sensations created by his thumb nearing her core of need. He had her emotions ricocheting from searing desire to sweet appeasement. All she could do was anchor her arms around his massive shoulders and hope she'd survive the whirligig ride he had her on.

He released her lips and pulled back far enough to stare into her eyes. "I've been fighting possessiveness for you like a four-alarm fire. Half the time when you're around me, I'm so damn horny, I can't think straight. I keep telling myself you're off limits. Hell, you're my superior's sister, for Christ's sake. And being seven years behind me, you're too damn young. You entice me like no one I've ever met. I adore your combination of fun nature and feistiness." He lowered his head to kiss her breasts. "God, how I love your sweetness."

Her hands swept across his straight dark hair, holding him to her breasts for he knew how to do the most fabulous things with his tongue and lips. And, as angry as she was with his earlier behavior, his mouth on her was like a powerful, sensual eraser. "Don't stop. Take me to that place only you can take me, Quinn."

Two of his fingers entered her and began a slow rhythm; her hips rose to match every stroke. He released her nipple and laved his tongue over the beaded point. "I have yet to figure out what it is about you that appeases my savage beast. You have a way of soothing my soul, even when I'm in a dark place where I don't think anyone can reach me."

So her brother was right. Something had hurt Quinn—ruthlessly, extremely, irrevocably. She'd gladly give him everything she had to get him to open up. He needed to strip off that scab of protectiveness covering the deep wound. Once he did, the poison he so carefully guarded could channel out of his soul. Because she suspected it was slowly eating him alive.

She'd have to proceed with caution. Hadn't her years of counseling taught her that? Weren't her biggest breakthroughs a result of unbridled high spirits from something totally unrelated? Would making love give him the same healing euphoria?

"Show me, big guy. Show me how possessive you can be. Make me cry out your name when I climax."

"You need proof, do you? Proof you belong to me and no one else?"

I guess now isn't the time to remind him of his nearly packed U-Haul out front.

His lips and hands were like multiple entities, touching her everywhere at once. Her skin scorched from his touch, stung from his gentle biting and succumbed to his kisses. For a fraction of time, it was as if she levitated from the bed, so seduced was she by his agitated, wild lovemaking. Whispered words and promises were shared. Pleas were uttered and surcease offered to ease immediate desires.

When he finally pressed his thumb upon her clit, she trembled and shuddered as his name exploded from her lungs. He held her to him until the tremors eased and all the while he feathered kisses over her face and neck, whispering words of praise and love. At least she thought that's what they were. She wasn't quite sure since the buzzing in her mind obliterated part of her hearing. Slowly, she slid from disorientation to reality again. The burning in her lungs eased and her heart rate returned to normal.

On a stretch, Quinn reached to open the drawer of his nightstand and palmed a foil packet. He settled on his back. "Want me to teach you the proper way to put on a condom?"

"There's a wrong way?"

He smirked as he shifted on the sheet, folding and shoving a pillow under his head to raise it. "Well, there's the ordinary way to put a rubber on and then there's the exceptional way." A slow, sexy-as-hell smile spread. "And, baby, we don't do anything ordinary." He passed her the pack. "Straddle my thighs and tear open the wrapper."

She eyed his cock standing tall and proud like a soldier ready to conquer anyone who came close. Her gaze swept back to his. "Straddle your thighs?"

The blue was back in his mesmerizing eyes. "Do what I tell you, angel."

After sliding back to straddle his thick, muscular legs, the hairs tickling her bare bottom, she tore the edge off the foil. "The wrapper says the condom's flavored."

"Yeah, I bought strawberry, your favorite." Quinn extended his palm. "Put the edge you just tore off here and slide the condom out without unrolling it. Then give me the rest of the wrapper. See the opening band? You'll place that in your mouth after you squeeze the tip to get the air out so the condom doesn't break.

Then you'll basically push against the rolled up rubber ridge until it covers my cock."

She glanced at the fragrant strawberry latex in her palm and then at him. "So I'm putting this thing on you with my mouth?"

"Damn straight." Now there was a pun if ever she'd heard one.

She put the ribbed edge in her mouth, leaned over him and positioned it over the end of his pecker and rolled it on with her lips. The groans from Quinn indicated her technique was to his liking. She sat back, quite pleased with the strawberry-covered cock. "Condoms do stretch. Right?" She pointed. "Because I swear you just got bigger."

Male laughter, deep and rich, caressed her. "Straddle me, sweetheart. Take all you want. Fuck me hard or easy. Any way you want it, that's how I'll give it to you. Take tops this time so I can watch your beautiful breasts."

His hands encased them while she slowly eased onto his shaft, his thumb and forefinger pulling and twirling her nipples. "That's it, go slow so I can enjoy every sweet inch of your tightness. God, it's like squeezing into a snug glove of heat and moisture." He could charm her any day with that deep, sexy voice of his.

She moved her hips in a leisurely pattern. "You know I'm still kinda pissed at you. Gigantic orgasm, or not." His hands settled at her hips and he winked. No doubt he didn't give a shit as long as she kept riding him. "And just wait until I see Ryder again. Don't think I won't give him a good going over for his stupid-assed ideas to get you in bed."

A fine sheen of sweat beaded Quinn's forehead. "Ryder was part of this…" He waved an open hand, the corners of his mouth quirking upward. "Seduction?"

"Hell yes. I stopped at his place for a smoothie after work and he asked where you were. I told him you were moving to get away from me, because you hate me."

He pulled her toward him and kissed her. "I don't hate you, angel. Nothing could be farther from the truth. Trust me."

She increased her movements a little more and decided to face his changing temperament head-on. "Trust you? Mr. Mood Shifter? First you're jealous, then you're all over me like you can't get enough of me, and then you storm out like I'm damn repulsive. You've got me raw inside. So emotionally raw, I don't think I can take much more."

"Hell, baby, I don't mean to hurt you. I'm just not good enough—"

She shook her fist under his nose and his eyes widened. "If you give me that stupid song and dance again about how you're not good enough for me, I'm going to send you out of Clearwater with two black eyes." She leaned in until they were nose to nose. "Do you hear me, Quinn Hudson Gallagher?"

The man had the audacity to smile. "Yes, ma'am."

"I'm trying to be nice here, but I've gotta tell you, I'm tired of listening to men. I don't think a single one of you knows what the hell you're talking about." But, oh how nice they felt when they were inside you—at least this particular annoying man. The muscles in her lower abdomen started to coil with the silent promise of an approaching release.

His dark eyebrow quirked.

"'Wear sexy clothes,' Ryder said." She jerked her hips faster. "'Wear boner-birther boots,' he said." Tremors started low in her belly and, against her will, she flexed harder against him. "'Make Quinn jealous,' he said. And what did I get out of it? I got tied to the bed with my shirt pulled over my head and left there while you went off to fantazize about some bitch named Renata." Her climax started overtaking her. "And now, dammit all to hell, I'm going to come with another woman's name on my mind. Damn you for that."

The tears started, and he pulled her down into an embrace. "Don't, baby. Don't think of anyone but us. Of this minute." He rolled her over and positioned her legs on top of his shoulders. "This is just you and me. All that matters is us."

He braced himself on his elbows. "You and me, angel." His lips locked on where her neck joined her shoulder, while his hips pistoned into hers, his balls slapping her ass. His eyes pinched closed and his head reared back as he shuddered his orgasm in tandem with hers.

After a minute of rasping breaths filling the air, Quinn kissed her forehead. "Let me go dispose of this condom."

"The last time you did that, you came back a different man and told me to leave. To never come back."

"I was scared. Making love to you had shaken me to my core. The only way I knew how to handle it was to act the ass. I'm more in control now. It won't happen again." He rolled off the bed and strolled out of the bedroom, turning the corner into the bathroom.

So I've had two orgasms and no answers about who the hell Renata is. Quinn Gallagher, you're a helluva lot of work.

When he stepped back into the bedroom, he was smiling. "Cold, baby?" He tugged the sheet and light blanket over her before he crawled under the bedclothes with her, sliding his arm under her neck to pull her closer. His other hand slipped between them, his index finger stroking between her folds. "You never did tell me who told you to shave your cunt."

"My customers at the shop, and don't think I'm not giving them a piece of my mind too. 'Shave your hootchie,' they said. 'It'll drive your man wild.'"

Quinn threw his head back and laughed, long and loud. "You… you're taking sex advice from women while you do their hair?" He wiped his eyes. "God, angel, you're priceless. And stop calling it a hootchie. It's a cunt. Say it. I shaved my cunt for you."

"I'm not using that word. Men use it as an insult when they want to belittle a woman. I'm not saying it, so get used to hearing hootchie. So, tell me, if I'm so priceless, why are you so insistent on leaving Clearwater and me?" She placed her palms on his cheeks and leaned close to peer into his eyes. "And who the *hell* is Renata?"

The steely grey of his eyes overtook the blue and his lips formed a thin line. He was pulling away from her, not physically, but emotionally. This time she wasn't having it.

She grabbed his ears and tugged. "Stay with me. Don't you dare go to that dark place."

His eyes narrowed to slits. "How the fuck would you know about dark places?" He lifted a shoulder. "If I was going to one, which I'm not."

Classic avoidance.

"Haven't you ever noticed?" She shoved the insides of her arms close to his face to show him the faint scars and leaned closer as she lifted her boobs to display the white lines on the swells of her breasts. "I'm a cutter. Or was."

Quinn grabbed her arms and studied them, ran a fingertip over her chest. "Cassie, what the hell? I noticed some of them and figured they were just normal childhood scars or recent scratches. Furball always has me ripped to hell. But..." his eyes pinned her. "Cutting?"

She blotted tears that moistened her cheeks. "It's the family's dark secret. Not the kind of thing we share, you know? I carried a great deal of guilt after Mom and Dad's death in that horrible fire."

"Hell, baby, you didn't set the fire. Some sick arsonist did."

"True. But I'd lied to my parents. I told them I was staying at Renee's house for a pajama party when, in reality, we'd gone to a party held by some senior high kids." Her fingertips trailed across the whitish lines the razor blades had made several years ago. "If I'd stayed home where I belonged, maybe I'd have smelled the smoke and gotten them out.

"After their deaths, I went into such a dark place, I couldn't even cry at their funeral. I had emotionally shut down. The last thing I'd said to my parents, my final words to them, were lies. What kind of person did that make me? The only time I could feel, could shed tears of grief was to take a razor blade to bleed out the pain."

"Angel, I never knew." His forehead wrinkled as if he were

deep in thought.

"More females than males are cutters, or so my counselor told me. Men act out. Yell, curse, beat a fist against a wall. Women go inward. We often hold our pain inside, seeking unhealthy outlets for it. Eating disorders for some. For others, especially teens, it's cutting." She bent to kiss his collarbone. "Some men distance themselves from people. They act like a fool to hide the pain."

"Yeah, like the words of the old blues song Uncle Mat used to sing. 'I laugh. Laugh just to keep from crying.'"

Maybe she had him to the point of opening up. Wolf claimed if anyone could reach Quinn, it would be her. She pressed kisses to his forehead and eyelids. "I shared with you. I shared how hard I worked to seduce you tonight and how humiliated you made me feel." His whisker stubble scratched her lips when she kissed both of his cheeks.

"You never told me where the hell you learned to give such great head." His lower jaw pushed out like a little boy ready to throw a tantrum.

She slid on top of him and wiggled closer. His eyes drifted shut when she rubbed against his semi-hard cock. "Cassie." A thrill leaped for joy at his warning tone.

"You'll laugh at me again."

"Somehow, I doubt it. Now who the hell taught you to lick and suck cock like that? Because, baby, that was the best I've ever had."

Her lips quirked. "Eva Mae, my Saturday morning regular, demonstrated using a bottle of conditioner as a cock prop. There's this new brand that has a round top shaped like a...like the head of a man's penis, and she showed me her technique."

"You gotta be fucking kidding me!" His eyes shot open as if he'd seen an elephant walk across his ceiling or something.

She shook her head. "No. Ninety percent of what I know about sex I learned from my customers. The other ten percent I learned from you yesterday and today. Although, I have to admit, your ten percent was more fun." She winked.

"So no other man showed you. Micah didn't teach you…"

"Oh Quinn, you've been my first in every way. If only you'd be my first in trusting me." She kissed him, her tongue sweeping across his lips. "If only you'd be the first man who ever trusted me enough to open up and show me what lies inside."

He exhaled a harsh bark of laughter. "Oh, angel, you don't even want to see the darkness inside me." He glanced away, closing off again.

She reached for his earlobes, applying gentle pressure. "I'm wise to you, buster. All these little tricks of avoidance, of transference, of acting like a sanctimonious victim." She made a loose fist, pointing a thumb at her own chest. "I've done them all. Many times, in fact, and quite well. Wolf fought me every step of the way."

She leaned in until their noses touched and her eyes bore into those mesmerizing blue-grey orbs of his. "And now I'm going to show you how a Wolford does combat against all that scared crap. Because that's all it is, you know. At least, that's all it was with me. I was too scared to open up and talk about it. Too afraid the people I loved would walk away. Love doesn't work that way, big guy." She lowered her head a couple of inches and bit his lower lip, pulling it out to run her tongue over and inside it.

He moaned as his hands swept up her back.

"Love stays. Through good and bad times, love stays. Especially for us. We can be damned determined. At least I can." She slithered down his body and ran her tongue around the nipple with the piercing, taking it into her mouth before she tugged on the silver ring, giving him that blend of pleasure and pain he evidently needed.

He groaned her name and his cock rose as if to announce it was ready to party again.

"I can be ruthless too." Her palm slid down his erection and wrapped around it for the return journey upward. Just to punish him some more, her hand made several long, slow strokes. "Think how good it'll feel to open up and share some of the pain. When two people share, the agony lessens and they grow closer."

"Christ, all I can think about is how damn good that feels." He narrowed his eyes and glared at her. "You play damn dirty."

"When the occasion calls for it, yes I do. When the person means everything to me, then hell to the yeah, I'll do whatever it takes to reach them." She smirked. "Hell, I've even been known to shave my hootchie for the cause."

Furball took that moment to make a flying leap onto the bed. Quinn covered his cock with both hands to protect his most cherished possession. Cassie stroked the cat for a few seconds and laid him next to Quinn's head.

He lifted the sheet and light blanket. "Come up here, angel. Lay on my shoulder." Once she was in place and they lay on their sides facing each other, he covered them. "When a rowdy kitten's in bed with you, it's best to keep protected." The cat wormed its way under the bedclothes between them and turned so just his grey and white face peeked out. He licked Quinn's bicep.

Cassie fought a smile. "I think the cat's spoiled."

"I agree, and if I find out who the son of a bitch was who spoiled him like this, I'll tan his hide. I hate a spoiled animal."

"Well, the cat lives with you. Maybe it was you who spoiled him."

Furball inched upward until he could rest his face on Quinn's shoulder, his white paws laying next to his owner's neck. Soon he started to purr and Quinn pretended to scowl.

She kissed Quinn's collarbone and slipped her leg between his thick thighs. "It's hard for you to admit you care for animals and other humans, isn't it? Love isn't a sign of weakness. It takes a strong man to love, to make himself vulnerable. Tell me, big guy. Tell me why you fight loving so much."

CHAPTER THIRTEEN

"I care for you, angel. I know I can't fight that anymore. Though God knows I've tried." He kissed her forehead and face, enveloping her in his arms.

He cares for me. He used the word care, not love. Don't get hung up, Cassie. Pay attention.

"I don't know if I can share my past, even if I feel I should. I've carried this ugliness inside since the day I resigned from the State Department over four years ago."

Quinn worked for the State Department? So Ryder's suspicions about him were right. She'd have to be very careful how she reacted, or he'd close up again. She would not put pressure on him by being all nosy, though Lord knew her nosy gene was in full what-the-hell questioning mode.

She ran a hand up his chest. Firm and strong, with developed muscles she suspected were produced by frequent trips to the gym and long hours running to purge some of the pain in his heart rather than maintain a hot physique, though he was vain enough to give into the "my body is a temple" philosophy.

A gentle tug to his nipple piercing got his attention. "This will be hard for you then. Take your time. By the looks of Furball's positioning, we've got all night." She pressed her lips to the dip between his pecs.

He inhaled a deep breath and expelled it slowly. "I went to work at the State Department a week after I graduated from Harvard. My old man was a legend there." His other hand settled in the small of her back as if he needed her securely in his arms. "At the State Department, Buck Gallagher heads the Bureau of International Intelligence and Research, so he carries a lot of clout. No doubt his influence helped get me the job.

"My admittance at Harvard, his alma-mater, was a cinch, too, although I'd rather have gone to MIT. But, even at Harvard, Buck was a damn hard act to follow. He'd been captain of the basketball team, a game I hated and refused to play. I was more into football and fencing, but never made captain of either team, which was why he never came to watch me participate in either sport. Buck graduated with a four-point-oh, while all I could manage was a three-point-nine-three."

Buck. He called his father "Buck," not dad or pops. She was beginning to understand the cause for the cold dynamics between the two and a defensive anger against good old Buck bubbled in her soul. "Well, it's easy to get that four-point-oh when you're taking ceramics and coloring inside the lines. What was your major, Quinn?"

"I took what Harvard calls a double concentration, similar to a double major at other universities. I studied Statistics as well as Engineering Sciences. Took extra classes in Spanish and Portuguese."

"That's a heavy load."

"True that, but I always loved learning. What you put into your mind no one can take from you out of anger or if you didn't measure up to their standards, which I never could. Knowledge is yours forever. But that can be a blessing and a curse. Sometimes bad experiences invade your mind and refuse to leave."

She nodded into his chest. "Yes, I agree. I know exactly what you mean." What things had his demanding father taken from him because he wasn't a mini-Buck? The image of a younger Quinn having things he loved confiscated by his severe father hurt her deeply. She wanted to reach out and ease all his past hurts, to kiss and love them away.

His hold on her tightened and he kissed her with slow, seducing, sipping kisses. "If anyone would understand, it would be you."

"Did you like working at the State Department?" Or had he gone to work there, like he'd gone to Harvard instead of MIT, because Buck demanded it? Frankly, she couldn't imagine any one making Quinn do anything. Was he still that little boy trying to win his dad's approval?

"A job is a job in today's economy. Government positions like I had paid well. But with office politics being what they are, it didn't take long for word to spread that I was big Buck's only son and probably lacked both the brains and the work ethic to land and keep the job on my own merits."

"Huh. Bet that stung."

He entwined his fingers with hers and brought their joined hands to his lips to kiss her knuckles. "Oh yeah. Big time. So I worked harder. Put in more hours. Did whatever I could to get noticed for me, Quinn Hudson Gallagher, and not Buck's boy."

"I can so see you doing that. Wolf has always bragged about your strong work ethic."

"Basically, I was doing anything to get ahead. To get a promotion. And the State Department used my ambition as a tool."

"How so?"

"I was invited to take part in a planning meeting, which should have clued me in since I only had a mid-level security clearance." He stopped talking and leaned back to scowl at Furball who had crawled next to Quinn's head to knead his hair, purring louder with each stroke. "Damn cat." Even with the annoyed exclamation, he allowed Furball to continue the head massage.

Cassie petted the cat's soft fur. "Then how were you allowed in this private meeting?"

"I'd been granted a temporary higher level security authorization for the project, but I was too flattered to think there were ulterior motives. My ego overrode my analytical skills. Details of the State Department joining forces with the DEA were revealed. The object was to curtail drug trafficking from Bolivia into Chile and up the coast to the United States. They wanted to plant an agent in Arica, a city near the Bolivian border, to observe Indian runners carrying drugs to members of the cartel, who had armed vehicles to transport the raw cocaine to southern Chile for refining. The biggest part of the job, though, was to find which parts of the country's coastline were used to ship the product abroad."

She tugged gently on his nipple ring. "And you volunteered?"

"You got it, angel. I saw it as a prime career opportunity to move into a supervisory position once the long-term assignment was over. I was given a team of four Americans and two Chileans to provide local intel. One of the Chileans was an exotic beauty named Renata."

Cassie's stomach dropped and she tensed. Hell, the last thing she wanted to hear tumble from his lips were compliments about another woman. Still, if it helped him, she'd tolerate it. Wasn't there something in the Bible about love enduring all things?

"I'd spent so much of my earlier years studying and playing sports that my experience with the opposite sex was quick and shallow. Until I met her. In my limited knowledge of games women could play, I had no clue I was being set up and used. I was too into her fabulous body to suspect she was working for the cartel."

God, this was killing her. "You...you loved her?"

"Like I'd never loved anything before in my whole life. That's what caused my flashback earlier. You're wearing fuchsia, aren't you?"

"A little, yes." No way was she telling him she'd lathered it on her labia to keep her skin from breaking out after shaving."

"They were Renata's favorite flower and I used to gather them for her bathwater."

I don't know if I can take hearing about this. Quinn's never so much as picked me a dandelion or a palm frond but he picked fuchsias to scent her bathwater?

"I was careless with my passwords and text messages. To cut a long story short, she informed the cartel about a small pier we'd found in an inlet with a boat moored to it bound for America. We'd planned a raid, but she'd warned them and they were waiting. I lost four of my men. They were tortured before death mercifully claimed them. I found my fifth man hanging with a chain embedded in his swollen neck and his back whipped."

She pressed her palm over Quinn's heart. "Dear God, no. How awful."

"So naturally I was frantic to find Renata. As soon as I was sure Chris, who we all called T-Bone, my team member I'd found hanging, was going to survive, I went looking for her. I nearly went insane during my desperate search. She meant everything to me."

Some emotional ogre was shredding Cassie's heart with a machete, laughing with maniacal glee at her foolishness while he carved away. After all, she was the ordinary girl-next-door while Renata was the experienced beauty with the exotic name and looks. "Yes, you would, loving her the way you did." Spiderwebs of emotionlessness spread outward from her heart, their frigid fingers numbing everything they enclosed their steely tentacles around. He'd never love her to the depths he'd loved Renata.

"When I found her unharmed in her apartment and finally took a look at the furnishings beyond the big bed where we'd spent so much time, I began to put things together. I interrogated her until she confessed."

"What did you do?" Could he have arrested her?

"I told her I loved her and then I put a bullet between her eyes." He rolled over and sat on the edge of the bed, his head between his hands. "Because of my sexual bungling, four of my men were dead and one severely injured."

Reaching out to him was more an act of humanity than love, for she doubted now he could ever love her to the degree he'd loved

Renata—and she'd accept no less. Her palm rested on his back. "You're not the first man to be taken in by a scheming woman. Granted your judgment may have been wrong, but your aim, your purpose, was true to your country and to your mission."

"Four men died, Cassie. Four. Another was severely tortured. I resigned from my job, and my fa—Buck told me I could never call him father or dad again. That he'd disowned me."

Which hurt him most? The betrayal of his lover, the loss of his men or the denial of his father's love? Or was it the overwhelming combination that ate at his soul?

She rose to her knees and wrapped her arms around his, placing her hands on his pecs and her face against his back. "None of this was your fault. You hear me? None. Being careless with confidential information would have been no problem with an honest person, but Renata wasn't honest. She used you for the position you held, for the way it would help her standing in the drug cartel."

He jerked from her consoling embrace, reached for his boxers and stepped into them when he stood. The muscles of his back shifted and bunched under his tanned skin as he strode for the window. "I should have known. Been more committed to the mission. Love makes us weak. It's a deceptive emotion."

Pain, every bit as deep and destructive as when she'd lost her parents, fractured her soul. "Love makes us hope for things that can never be." She rummaged around on the floor for her clothes. Finding her bra and thong, she slipped them on, a sarcastic laugh stumbling from her throat. "I mean, look at me. I've loved you for three years and all that time you've mourned the loss of the woman you loved more than anything." She scooped her skirt off the floor and wiggled into it before snatching her blouse from the footboard of the bed.

His hands bracketed the wood trim around his window. "Renata, my dark-eyed, exotic beauty." His chin reached his chest. "I loved her. I loved her with all my heart, yet to avenge my men, I put a bullet in her forehead."

"I'm leaving now." Cassie had to get out before she broke down and cried.

"Now I've got you to worry about."

She exhaled a short burst of laughter. "Quinn Gallagher, the last person you have to worry about is me." One by one, she felt the coldness and emptiness of her emotions shutting down. Hopes, dreams, plans were all over and done. Only emptiness remained.

Had he even heard her? He'd turned silent, lost to her again, vanished into the dark place where he could relive his time with perfect Renata. "God, how I adored that woman. She'd wake up every morning singing before she'd roll over on top of me and… Renata…"

If Cassie had to hear this woman's name one more time, she would reach for the next razor blade she saw. God, how she needed to cut herself right now. She sat on the opposite edge of the bed and quickly put on the boots. Tears flooded her eyes when she removed her angel necklace and laid it on the nightstand. "None of what happened in Chile was your fault. You need to stop blaming yourself or you'll never find happiness."

Lord knew, she never would. Not without his love.

CHAPTER FOURTEEN

Someone pounding on Quinn's door wrenched his mind from replaying the continual loop of the gruesome details from the disastrous night in Chile. Furball wove in and out between his feet, meowing to be fed. What time was it? The room had darkened. His forefinger depressed the Indiglo light on his wristwatch—eleven-twenty. He released his firm grasp on the wooden frame of the window and straightened, rotating his head and neck to work out the kinks from his previous tense posture.

"Cassie?" Except for the ceaseless racket at the door, the apartment seemed eerily quiet. How long had he vanished into his own world?

The knocking continued, and Quinn scooped Furball into his arms. Had Cassie gone out for something to eat and couldn't get back in? He turned on a few lights as he strode out of the hallway, flipped the lock and opened the door. "Sweetheart, did you—" The sight before him froze his thoughts before they had a chance to form into words.

Milt, his downstairs neighbor, in all his scrawny maleness, face creased into a scowl and fists cocked, bounced into Quinn's foyer, weaving and bobbing, wearing purple shorts, white tube socks and black sandals. "Put em up, you miserable lout."

"What the hell's wrong with you?" Quinn set the cat down on

the sofa and backed up, palms outstretched to show he wasn't going to fight the old man. "What the hell's got your drawers in a twist?"

"You destroyed that sweet woman. Sent her off without a care for her heart. Had sex with her and then bragged about how much you loved someone else, that you gathered flowers for her bathwater and how she woke you every morning with a song." Milt swung a couple wild punches. "My God, man, where the hell did you learn how to treat a woman? Assholes-R-Us?"

Hell, had he said that stuff to Cassie? He'd shared working for the State Department and his assignment in Chile, but, beyond that, their conversation was a blur. "Where is she?" He started to charge around the combatant man.

Milt swung at him a couple of times, never making contact, but halting him in his steps nonetheless.

"Good thing Killer's got excellent hearing. He heard Cassie crying in the vestibule and alerted me. When I opened the door, she all but collapsed into my arms. I took her in to try to calm her." He shook his head. "Ain't seen a woman bawl like that since my wife lost our first baby. Poor little thing cried her heart out until she asked to use the bathroom to freshen up."

A chill skittered through Quinn's body. Surely she hadn't resorted to cutting. "How long was she in the bathroom?" He started to pass Milt. "Dammit, man, is she still in there?"

Tears filled Milt's eyes. "No. When she came out she was dazed and bleeding down both arms."

Fuck, no. What have I done to her?

"And you didn't think to come get me?" Anger curled Quinn's fingers into fists, not with Milt, but with his own thoughtless treatment of Cassie. Disgust with himself made his stomach drop and shame extend its sticky antennae to catch it.

He had to reach her, talk some sense into her and reassure her how important she was to him. God help his angel, he'd driven her back to cutting. Of all the people in the world he never wanted to hurt, Cassie was at the top of the list, his mom second and this irascible old coot in front of him was third.

"I used her cell to call her brother, the big one. Wolf." Milt collapsed onto a chair. "I did my best to stop the bleeding. It was coming from her chest and down her arms. When her brother got there, he took one look at her, cursed a blue streak and carried her to his truck." Milt wiped his eyes. "He mentioned the hospital, if you care enough to go."

"If I care enough—hell, man, I love that woman." Quinn grabbed his wallet off the bar at the kitchen and glanced at his feet. "Need shoes."

"Might do with a pair of pants and a shirt too. You get dressed proper and meet me at my apartment. I'll throw on a shirt, let Killer out to water the grass and drive us to the hospital. You're not fit to be behind the wheel of a car. You don't seem too steady on your feet. What all went on up here? You been smokin' weed, son?"

"Weed? Hell, no! I had a flashback. I don't even recall all of what I said to Cassie."

"Flashbacks? Holy shit. My baby brother had them after he got back from Nam. Ranted about killing Charlie and went into a world of his own, wild-eyed, almost feral. Is that what you've been living with, son? Is that why you're okay some days and moody as hell on the others?"

Quinn scrubbed his hands over his eyes. "Yeah." He pushed the word from a throat rusted shut with regret. Whatever he'd said to Cassie had driven her to cut herself again. Damn his worthless life to hell.

Milt eased out of the chair as if every bone in his body ached. "Meet me in ten minutes." He turned and ambled out. His gnarled fingers grasped the edge of the door, and he stopped. "I never saw anyone disintegrate like that. Cassie is always the sweetest blend of sugar and vinegar. Lord, you never know what that girl's gonna say next, but her heart is pure gold. To see her bleed like that…" The old man shook his head, exhaled a long, pained sigh and closed the door behind him.

What the hell did I say to her to push her over the edge?

Quinn tried his best to replay their earlier conversation as he hurried into his bedroom, but all he could focus on was her cutting. He snagged his jeans off the floor and stepped into them. Grabbed a clean t-shirt from his packed duffle bag and jerked it over his head. When he sat on the edge of his bed to yank on his sneakers, something golden sparkled under the light—Cassie's angel necklace.

She loved that piece of jewelry. Why would she take it off? He picked it up; was the clasp broken? He rested his elbows on his thighs and fingered the chain. What had he said to her to make her take it off?

He'd told her about college, his job at the State Department, volunteering for the assignment in Chile. Milt's words socked him in the solar plexus. You "had sex with her and then bragged about how much you loved another woman, that you gathered flowers for her bathwater and how she woke you every morning with a song."

Fuck me blind. I have got to be the world's biggest asshole.

He palmed the necklace into his pocket and strode through the hallway, grabbing his keys and ball cap off the bar between the kitchen and the living area. He sat Furball's automatic feeders and water container on the kitchen floor before charging out the door.

Milt was waiting for him in the building's vestibule. Quinn tossed him his keys. "Here. You drive my Jeep."

The old man tossed them right back. "Don't need em, son, my car's got a V-8. Don't make engines like that anymore. Got a little duct tape here and there but, other than that, she's in prime condition."

The back bumper was duct-taped to the body of the orange vehicle that was probably once red. From the four-inch height of the landau roof, Milt evidently had been adding a layer of duct tape twice a year over the vinyl top since Reagan was elected president.

"Can't this piece of shit go any faster?" Hell, Quinn could run to the hospital quicker than Milt was driving. *I need to see Cassie.*

I need to apologize.

"Watch it now. This is a classic seventy-six Cutlass Supreme."

"Yeah, well, looks like the supreme part wore out. Can't this heap pick up some speed? Or are you afraid the duct tape won't hold under the wind velocity?" *I have to get to Cassie.*

"Speed limit's thirty-five. Besides, this baby hasn't gone over the speed limit since ninety-eight when I was late for my proctologist exam. Driving at a sensible speed saves wear and tear on the engine." The narrow-shouldered man, hunched over the steering wheel, braked for a red light.

"Name me one person who drives the damn speed limit." Quinn's nerves jittered so badly he was ready to crawl out of his skin. He had to see Cassie, had to find out if she was all right. She must have bled something fierce if Milt had all that blood on his shirt.

"Yeah, well, douchebag." Milt aimed a disgusted expression Quinn's way. "Name me one man who screws a woman and then brags about how much he loves another. Never known you to bring a woman to your place, except for Cassie."

Quinn never had. Going to the woman's place kept things on a more impersonal level and made it easier to go home once the itch was scratched for both of them. Saved him the embarrassment of having one of them showing up on his doorstep whenever Cassie was there. His home was for him and her; it was their place to hang out, even though nothing sexual ever happened until yesterday.

God, he had to see her, make sure she was okay. "How damn long is this freaking light going to stay red?" He wanted to punch his fist against Milt's dash in frustration.

"Stay calm, son. Everything happens in its own time." Finally, the light turned green and the old man stomped a sandaled foot on the accelerator. The car sputtered forward on a cloud of blue smoke and Milt farted some noxious fumes of his own.

"Hell man, what crawled up your ass and died?" Quinn depressed the window button for some fresh air, but it didn't open.

"Those automatic window-operating buttons stopped working in oh-one."

"And you never paid to get them fixed? Cheap bastard." He tried to turn the old-style window crank, and the chrome handle snapped off in his hand. In a fit of desperation, he flung it over his shoulder onto the back seat. "If you don't soon get me to the hospital, you stingy-assed old coot, medical personnel will have to pry my hands from your throat."

"No need to keep bitching at me. We both know it's you you're damned mad at."

Quinn grunted and tugged the bib of his ball cap lower.

"Years back, when my wife and I owned our house, she asked me to replace a few basement steps she claimed were getting weak. I was drinking pretty heavily back then. Stopping at the corner bar after work, staying too long. Was just too tired and drunk to fix the steps once I got home."

Milt turned a corner at five freakin' miles an hour while Quinn gnashed his back molars together. *What the hell do I care about your damn steps? I need to see Cassie. Don't you get it?*

"I kept putting her off. Then one day, when she was carrying a basket of dirty laundry down the steps, one of the boards snapped in two and she fell. Broke her leg. Messed her other ankle up pretty bad. 'An accident,' they called it. But I knew deep in my soul that I'd caused it. I loved that woman to pieces, but I loved the taste of liquor too. Even to an idiot like me, it was clear I had to make a choice. While she was in the hospital, I took my self-hate out on those basement steps, beat them to hell and back. Sometimes a man needs a physical outlet to get his pain out."

"I don't think there are enough things for me to tear apart to ease the way I'm feeling right now."

Milt eased the old car into the hospital's parking lot. "I had to decide which I loved more—my woman or the booze. You gotta do the same thing. Which means the most to you? Cassie or the memory of that woman from your past?"

"Hell, that's an easy decision to make. Cassie."

"Glad to hear that, son. I hope you got a strong apology lined up. One that will win her heart back. And I hope you get a chance to spit it out before her brother tears you apart. You gotta be expecting that."

"I can handle whatever Wolf dishes out." Quinn deserved every cuss word, every threat, every punch Cassie's protective oldest brother threw at him. My God, what had he been thinking to tell Cassie about Renata? As soon as the car came to a stop, he tried to unlatch his seatbelt. It wouldn't release. Quinn shot the old man a murderous look while he pulled and tugged and cursed.

"Ain't no use carrying on like that. Seatbelt hasn't worked since oh-four."

Quinn jammed his fingers into a pocket of his jeans, coiling them around his Huskie emergency knife he'd been using earlier to cut packing rope. He snapped open the largest blade and began sawing away at the seatbelt. Sweat beaded on his face from the combination of his efforts and frantic nerves. If he didn't soon see Cassie, he'd lose his damn mind. "How in the fucking hell does this deathtrap pass inspection? You wanna tell me that? Huh?" His knife finally cut through the tight weave of the seatbelt.

Milt grinned. "I've got this cousin…"

"Well, damn your cousin to hell and back." When Quinn pulled on the door handle, Milt coughed and farted. Quinn slowly turned his head to scowl at the old man. "So help me God, if you tell me this goddamn door doesn't work, I will rip off the handle and jam it up your skinny, flatulent ass."

Milt farted again. "No need to get so testy, son. Life is full of little inconveniences. You'll have to get out on my side. The passenger door stopped opening from the inside in oh-seven. Still opens great from the outside though."

Quinn shifted in his seat and, with one solid kick, forced open the door. "Well, I just gave your cousin some more fuckin' work." He took off running for the emergency room entrance. Milt wheezed behind him, his sandals slapping on the pavement.

Once Quinn inquired about Cassie Wolford, the receptionist pointed them in the direction of the waiting area on the fringes of the emergency room. Cassie's older twin sisters, April and Jenna, were there. So was Jace—one of her brothers and Quinn's friend and fellow firefighter— who sat with his arm around his wife, Wendy Anne. Her baby bump was growing bigger every time Quinn saw her. Not sure whom to address, he simply asked how Cassie was doing.

Becca, who walked into the waiting area with a cardboard container full of coffee cups and a couple bottles of juice, evidently overheard his question. "Wolf's in the examining room with her. She's had a few stitches. They've called in the psychiatrist she hasn't seen in several years, to talk to her. I'd think it's safe to say the three of them are battling it out now."

Quinn's gaze swept to the curtained cubicles. "But she's all right. I mean...hell, she's *not* all right, is she?"

"Take a deep breath, son. You've been on an emotional tear since I told you what happened to her." Milt wrapped his gnarled hand around Quinn's bicep.

"It should never have happened, Milt. I should never have told her all I did."

Jace stood, jerked his hand from Wendy Anne's firm grasp, and advanced on Quinn. "It took us over two years of counseling and constant reinforcement to get our baby sister beyond her self-destructive behavior, and in a couple of days you've got her cutting again."

Stars exploded when Jace's fist made contact with Quinn's eye. He'd been expecting it from Wolf, the protective older brother, but not from jovial, gentle Jace. The power of the impact forced Quinn back a couple of steps. Cassie's family crowded around in one collective gasp of support, and he doubted any of it was for him. Milt's support backed against the wall along with his bloody shirt, his hand over his bony chest and his eyes wide.

"I had that coming." Quinn straightened. "And more. I'll grant you another shot before I start standing my ground. Because you have to believe me when I say I want to rip something apart so badly right now, I can barely see straight. We've been friends. Good friends. I'd rather it not be you I tear into."

Jace landed another blow, this time to Quinn's stomach.

"That's two." The hit barely hurt his hardened abs.

Jace shook his fist as if to relieve the sting. "Well, damn if you don't take the fun out of revenge. You're supposed to fight back."

"No way in hell! I'm not staying!"

Everyone's heads swiveled in the direction of the cubicle from where Cassie's shrieking emanated.

A female's response was too low to completely distinguish, although Quinn caught a couple of terms like "overnight observation" and "possible treatment".

Quinn made a few steps toward Cassie's cubicle when Becca's hand touched his arm. "Not yet. Not until they get her under control."

His gaze swept to her cool hand resting on his forearm and then to the concern in her eyes. "Don't try to stop me. I'm the only one who can help her."

"Look, it was just a temporary relapse." Cassie's voice stopped Quinn in his tracks. "Like...like an alcoholic tossing back a shot after learning someone he loved had just died. I am not going to cut myself again. And I, for damn sure, am not spending a couple of nights in the psychiatric ward. Wolf, either you take me home or I'm calling one of my sisters."

April and Jenna groaned and shook their heads. Their arms were wrapped around each other's waists, their expressions mirror images of each other.

"She needs *me*." Why was it so hard for everyone to understand? "I'll talk to her. Apologize."

"Apologize?" April scoffed. "Wolf said you'd upset her to the point of cutting again. No. Let family deal with this like we've always done."

"Megan gets off her nursing shift in four hours. Let her handle Cassie's temper." Jenna fiddled with her rows of bangle bracelets. "Remember what it was like dealing with her before when she was cutting?" She covered both eyes with her hands and sobbed. "I...I can't bear seeing her go through this again."

April enveloped her sister in her arms while giving Quinn the evil eye.

"That little girl's got herself worked into a state. That's for sure." Milt scratched his neck and tweaked a bit of gas.

There had been fear in Cassie's voice, and Quinn's urge to go to her was greater than he expected. She was his. His to protect.

His demeanor must have telegraphed his thoughts because Jace waved his index finger under Quinn's nose. "Don't even think about it, Gallagher. The last person she needs to see right now is you."

Something in him clicked. It clicked so soundly it felt right, damned right. Maybe it was the sound of distress in her voice, or his hunger to be needed by her, or his rebellious nature resenting what anyone said he could and couldn't do. But, in that instant, surrounded by the antiseptic smells of the hospital, the squeaking of crepe soles and the almost constant squawking of some doctor's name over the intercom, he knew he'd crawl through hell and back for this woman. He had to tell her how much he cared for her, that Renata's shallow, exotic beauty was nothing compared to the complex mixture of sass and sweetness that lined the preciousness of Cassie Wolford's soul.

He switched his attentions to Becca. "I said some shit to her I never meant for her to hear. Things from my past. Cassie kept telling me we needed to learn to trust each other with everything and so I communicated with her in a bungling, foolish way."

She pursed her lips and blinked a couple times. "You finally opened up and told her about the woman who hurt you so badly?"

He removed his ball cap, twisted it in his hands and then slapped it once against his thigh before resettling it on his head. "Yeah," he glanced toward the curtained space that held the woman he loved.

"It had been so many years since I'd talked about it, my words were clumsy, and I hurt Cassie like hell in the bargain. I need to make things right. I need to tell her how much more important she is to me than that other woman ever was."

Becca removed the plastic top from a coffee container and blew on its contents. "Wolf will pound the heck out of you, you know. He's very protective of his sisters."

Quinn exhaled a harsh bark of laughter. "Hell, won't be anything I don't deserve. I just need to do whatever I can to stop Cassie from hurting so much. A few days ago I decided to leave Clearwater to keep from screwing up her life. Now I'm not sure if I can leave until I know she's over this depression I put her in." He glanced at Becca. "Until I'm sure she's safe."

April, the most outgoing of the twins, got right in his face. "You think your leaving for good won't put her into a deeper depression? You're the only man she's talked about in, like, forever. She sees you as some Greek god or something. When we went shopping for my wedding gown, she picked one out for herself. One she thought you'd like."

"Please, tell me she didn't buy it." Marriage to him would be disastrous with his baggage and ghosts.

April lifted a shoulder and huffed her annoyance. "She put it on layaway."

"Veil, too," Jenna chimed in.

"I'm telling you, I'm not staying and you can't make me!" Everyone's head whipped around at Cassie's threat. The green curtain shook as if she were climbing the fabric walls.

"Cassie, I'll get a court order and admit you myself." Wolf returned his own warning.

Like hell! No one makes her do what she doesn't want.

"I'll never forgive you if…" A sob rose above the rings of the curtain and tumbled over the connecting rod. Her words choked, ripping Quinn's heart in two.

He stormed in the direction of the examining area, hell-bent on doing something, *anything*, to protect her, even if it meant putting his private emotions out there. When he yanked back the curtain, three pairs of eyes pivoted in his direction.

CHAPTER FIFTEEN

A familiar pair of brown orbs darkened and narrowed. Wolf practically shoved the older woman in the white coat out of his way to get to Quinn. "I will fucking kill you for what you did to her!"

"Ten minutes, buddy, and I'm all yours. That's a promise. Jace already took a couple shots. Looks like you'll have to be happy with what's left."

Quinn's gaze settled on Cassie, who had her bandaged arms over her eyes, as if by doing so she could pretend he wasn't there. Seeing her like this erased all the pain, the agonizing pain of finding his men dead in Chile. At this definitive moment, one thing became flawlessly clear—the depth of his love for Cassie Wolford. The urge to scoop her into his arms and cradle her to him, to take on her agony, was so powerful, he wasn't so sure he could keep his hands off her.

"Take a good look at her, Gallagher. This is all your handiwork." Wolf pointed to his sister.

The two men glared at each other. Quinn could see love and fear mirrored in Wolf's eyes. How could he blame Wolf for caring about the woman Quinn adored? He could understand her brother's snarling. Damn if he didn't want to snarl and tear apart every piece of equipment in the narrow cubicle, himself.

"Ten minutes, Wolf."

Protective brother stepped between Quinn and Cassie. "No way in hell."

Quinn shoved Wolf aside and placed his hands on Cassie's thighs. "Baby, give me ten minutes to explain why I had no clue what I was doing." He gently stroked her legs. "Once I started talking about the past, all the ugly poison of it came flowing out. Honest to God, Cassie, I don't even remember all of what I said."

She shook her head and her shoulders trembled from crying. The urge to embrace her was so pronounced he could barely inhale his next breath. He had to ease the agony of what he'd done to her, the frailty of what she'd become. "Angel?"

"No. Not your angel anymore." She kept her hands over her eyes, refusing to look at him.

Oh, but she was his angel and would be until he took his last breath. Even if she moved on to another man, which she might well do after the way he'd bungled things today. His awkward words must have hurt her deeply to put her here—cut, bandaged, sobbing from the depths of her wounded soul. His hand reached to touch her hair.

Wolf got between them. "Not on your freakin' life, pal. Can't you see how delicate she is right now?"

Quinn could see it. Hell, his heart could comprehend it. He looked at the middle-aged therapist. Maybe there was another way. He stepped back and directed his plea to the doctor. "Would you listen, please, and help us through this? Cassie trusts you. If you've earned her respect, then you have mine too."

The woman's grey eyebrows rose for a second, and she edged next to Cassie, wrapping her arm around her patient's shoulders. "Can you handle this? Do you want me to do some joint counseling here…today? Or would you rather I made him leave? You're in charge here."

"I'm not talking to him. Let him talk. Let him tell you how much he still loves a dead woman. How he loves her more than… more than…"

He had to reach her somehow. "Cassie, if you don't listen to what I have to say, won't you always wonder?" His voice was low and, he hoped, calming. "Give yourself the gift of knowledge before you order me to walk out of this cubicle."

"I hate how you always make sense." She turned her back and reached for the box of tissues on the bedside table. "Wolf, you'll have to leave."

"Are you kidding me?" Her brother's hands fisted at his hips and his scowl skewered Quinn to the spot. The man cared deeply for his family. No one could fault him for that.

"Couple's counseling is best done in private, Mr. Wolford." The doctor pulled back the curtain as a sign for him to leave.

Always one to deliver the last word, Wolf pointed at Quinn. "Ten minutes and your ass is mine."

"Twenty minutes." The psychologist made it a point to look at her watch and note the time on her chart. Wolf stormed around the edges of the curtain and she thrust out her hand, a charm bracelet jangling with her movement. "I don't think we've been formally introduced. I'm Dr. Paxwell."

Quinn shook her hand and noted its warmth. "Pleasure meeting you, ma'am, if you're the person who helped Cassie in the past, you have my eternal gratitude. I'm Quinn Gallagher."

"I've heard your name mentioned a time or two today. I will demand you leave your macho attitude outside this curtain." She pointed her pen over her shoulder.

"Anything for Cassie. Just so you realize, sharing with you won't be easy, but I'll do anything to help the woman I love."

Cassie gave her typical smart-ass "huh" and he fought the smile it always brought.

Dr. Paxwell nodded once. "I appreciate that, Mr. Gallagher."

"It took me a long time to build up enough trust with Cassie to tell her what happened in Chile, so—" He took off his hat and ran a hand through his hair. "No doubt I'll bungle it up with you the same as I did with her. She was the first person I told in four years and...shit..." He socked his hat back on, pulling it low over his eyes. "I said everything wrong. Look at what I did to her." He stepped closer, needing to touch her. Without thinking, he fingered her long hair. "I adore everything about this woman, even the fiery part of her personality that drives me crazy insane at times." He smiled at Dr. Paxwell. "If she only knew how her rants make me laugh deep down inside where no one else can reach."

Cassie sobbed, covering her eyes with tissues, still refusing to look at him.

"Take your time, Mr. Gallagher. Cassie, any time this gets to be too much for you, you have the power to stop it. Do you both understand this rule? Cassie's feelings must come first. Her relapse, however temporary, is of great concern to me. It was so unexpected. She was doing so well."

"I'm to blame for her setback." Hell, he was always to blame for whatever went wrong.

"I don't want him to...to...see me like...this."

Her sobbing was killing him, unmanning him. "Angel, I'll turn my back." He shifted and leaned against the foot of the gurney. "I won't look at you. I promise. Will that be okay with you, baby?"

The sheets rustled behind him. "I suppose."

"I don't know how to start this, except at the beginning." He sighed and gathered his thoughts, jamming his fingertips into the front pockets of his jeans. "Four years ago I was on a clandestine mission for the government."

"Covert ops?" Dr. Paxwell's grey eyebrows furrowed.

He nodded. "Yes, in Chile, hunting drug traffickers. I headed a team of four Americans and two Chileans. One of the natives was a woman. Beautiful. Willing. Charming. I wasn't experienced in long-term relationships. I'd always been more of a one-night stand kind of guy and, for the first time in my life, I allowed myself to get emotionally involved. What I didn't know was she was working for the cartel I was investigating, and, because of her, I lost three of my American team and the other Chilean. The fourth man on my team was badly hurt."

"I'm sorry to hear that." The concern in the doctor's hazel eyes was genuine. "You must carry a great deal of guilt."

He nodded. "You have no idea. It's changed my whole life."

"Guilt often does."

"When Renata, she's the woman I was fu...ah...seeing, confessed she was working for the cartel and had given them information that caused my men to die, I was so enraged, I shot her between the eyes." He glanced at the psychologist, who stared at him, her expression unreadable. "I resigned from the agency and started a new life, here, in Florida. Tried my best to keep to myself, but the guys at the station were the best. Friendly. Outgoing. And then there was Cassie."

"How do you feel about Cassie?"

"I've never shared this with anyone." He crossed his arms and glanced at his crossed feet. Several seconds passed as he gathered courage. "But right now, seeing her like this, I'd tell you every secret I have. I fell in love with her the moment I saw her at her eighteenth birthday party."

There was a gasp behind him. He wanted to turn to make sure Cassie was okay, but he'd promised he wouldn't look at her. He gaged the doctor's reaction to make sure all was well with his angel before he continued.

"I knew she was too young for me. She's still too young. There's a seven year difference in our ages. So we hung out as friends."

"We dated without the sex. That's what Ryder said."

The therapist glanced at Cassie. "And who is Ryder?"

"A friend who runs a health bar. He makes the best fruit smoothies. Quinn and I stop in once or twice a week."

"I see. Do you and Quinn do other things together?"

Cassie blew her nose again. "We jog a couple days a week. Scuba-dive. Go to movies."

"The two of you alone or do you do these things in a group?" The doctor scratched her grey hair with the blunt end of her pen.

"Usually we go alone. Sometimes her family has picnics or holiday meals, and I'm always invited." It was the only time he felt part of a real family, with all the noise and teasing and caring.

"Do you enjoy family functions, Quinn?"

He nodded. "As long as Cassie's around, I enjoy most anything. Hell, she's even gotten me to go to a few church bazaars and yard sales."

"And you've dragged me along to a few Buccaneers football games."

Quinn chuckled. "Come on, you love the tailgating parties."

Her soft laughter alleviated the edge of tightness in his muscles. "Yeah, guess I do. All that yummy food you grill."

"Cassie, how do you feel about him?"

"You'll never believe this. I fell in love with Quinn at my eighteenth birthday party—the same night he says he fell in love with me."

Dr. Paxwell tucked her pen behind her ear and then wrapped her arms around the chart she'd been making notes on, holding it to her chest. "So you two fell in love at first sight and have dated without the intimacy of sex for three years?" It did sound kind of incredulous the way she put it.

"I chased him and he treated me like I was his annoying little sister. The man wouldn't even kiss me."

"Why did you do that, Mr. Gallagher? Why hold her off, when you obviously care so much for her? To spend so much time with the same woman with no physical release isn't healthy."

He shrugged. "I'm bad news. Thanks to me, four men lost their lives, another was badly scarred and I shot a woman I cared about." He exhaled a shuddering breath. "Even my own father disowned me. What did I have to offer someone sweet like Cassie?"

"Have you had counseling for PTSD?"

"Yeah, for a month."

Dr. Paxwell made an annoyed sound in her throat. "That's hardly enough to scratch the surface. Are you having nightmares?

Flashbacks?"

He nodded. "Memory lapses."

"So you kept all this hidden for nearly four years? What was the impetus for telling Cassie now?"

He stalled in responding. Would Cassie want her therapist to know they'd become intimate?

"We had sex. His attraction to me scares him so badly he's resigned as a fireman and is leaving Clearwater. Leaving me. I gave him my virginity and he gave me the boot."

"Dammit, Cassie. I tried telling you I'm damaged inside. What if I hurt you?"

The sheets rustled before her slap landed across the back of his head, knocking off his ball cap. She moved on her knees until they were eye to eye. "Hurt me? Hurt me! You self-centered, self-pitying, control freak." The tears started flowing again.

He swept her into his arms and stood. She wrapped her bandaged arms around his neck, snuggled her head against his shoulder and sobbed. "Angel," he whispered as he carried her to the other side of the small room, hoping they'd gain some semblance of privacy. "I hurt you, baby, and I'm so sorry." He kissed her forehead. "I never meant to imply I loved Renata more than I love you." He kissed her cheek. "I meant to show you what it did to me to shoot someone I cared about. I mean, hell, what kind of person does that?" He kissed her jaw. "My feelings for her were real, but not nearly as deep, as all-consuming, as they are for you." His lips barely touched hers. "The way I felt about her wasn't even close to how intensely I love you. You're everything to me. *Everything.*" Then his lips covered hers, and he breathed in the sunshine from her soul.

****

Could she trust him? He pulled her closer to his chest as if he couldn't bear to let her go. His muscles flexed to tighten his hold on her and his lips—dear Lord, his lips wrought some kind of sensual magic on her whole body.

Quinn finally pulled back from the kiss and leaned his forehead against hers. "I love you, angel." He leaned her against the bed, shoved his hand into the back pocket of his jeans and removed something. "Open your hand." When she did, he poured the gold chain onto her palm. "Put this back on and promise me you won't ever take it off. Whether you're able to sense it just yet, things between us have changed. I can't fight how I feel for you anymore. My love for you has changed me."

The angel with the diamond-encrusted wings stared back at her, almost forlorn in her solitude. "I don't know." She'd been in so much pain when she removed it.

She hadn't wanted Quinn to see her like this, weakened to the point of cutting, something she hadn't resorted to since the summer between her sophomore and junior years of high school. Her siblings had gathered around her that night, several years ago, and embraced her as they cried. Seeing Wolf, Jace, her three sisters and Jace's wife, Wendy Anne, in tears was akin to electric shock treatment. She finally realized she wasn't just hurting herself; she was punishing them all. Her love for her family became her healing focus.

Now, here she was again. Cutting and punishing those she loved because a man she adored had affections for someone else. She was here because she felt "less than" what he normally desired in a woman. This wasn't one of her proudest moments.

"Put it on, sweetheart…for me." He picked her up again, setting her properly on the bed, and tried to tug the chain from her grasp. "Hold your hair up so I can place the angel back where she belongs. And, once I've got my necklace back on you, I'm going to give you hell for scaring me like you did tonight. Don't you ever resort to cutting yourself. Shit, I'd rather you chased me down with a razor blade and sliced me to shreds."

The corners of her lips lifted. "Now there's an appealing thought, but, for now, I'm not ready to wear this." Before she put the piece of jewelry back on, she had to be sure of his feelings toward her. Right now, she was more confused than positive.

"If you two are through, we have some important issues to discuss." Dr. Paxwell slid the pen from its resting place on top of her ear and jotted on some cards. "I want to see each of you separately for a month." She handed an ivory card to Cassie: "I'll see you once a week." She shook an appointment card filled with lots of writing at Quinn: "You, I'll want in my office twice a week. We have a lot of post-traumatic stress issues to resolve."

He extended an open hand in a stop gesture. "I don't need counseling."

"Typical man," the doctor quipped. "The only things he'll confess to needing are cold beer, more food and a hot woman." Dr. Paxwell's eyebrow quirked in challenge. "Do you want Cassie in your life? If you do, then you'll go through counseling."

He snatched the card from her outstretched hand and slid it into his wallet. "I know when I'm being manipulated, and I don't like it."

His wide hand, warm and strong, swept up Cassie's spine, a caressing yet possessive move. "I want her more than anything. I'd planned on leaving Clearwater because I was afraid of the passion we had for each other, given our age difference, but we've already crossed that line. I can't walk away from her now. Even though I have job applications at other fire companies in the state, I might talk to my current boss about staying on here."

Cassie gulped her next few breaths of air. This sudden transformation in him was certainly unexpected. Was he thinking of staying because of guilt over her cutting or because he really couldn't bear to leave her? "Why the change of heart?" She had to know.

He cupped her chin in his hand and lifted her face for a quick kiss. "Sometimes it takes a man a while to admit what or who is really important in his life. For me, it's you. It will always be you."

He glanced at Dr. Paxwell. "You've scheduled the appointments. I'll be there, but I'm warning you, I won't be an easy patient."

"You government, military-damaged men never are. If I could survive Wolf, believe me, I can take on your issues and help you whip them."

Cassie's head popped up. "Wolf was a patient of yours?"

"That's between me and him. Now, I want the two of you to stop seeing each other as friends *and* lovers for a month. Will you agree to that?"

Quinn's gaze swept over Cassie. "I can't see her for a month?" He crossed his arms, his square jaw jutted in that pugnacious way he had. "Tell me why, in a way that makes one damn bit of sense."

"You two need to learn to operate independently of each other. To lead your own lives. I might even suggest you date others."

"Oh no. Oh, *hell* no!" His hand gently fisted in Cassie's hair. "This woman is mine."

Dr. Paxwell stepped closer until she was almost nose to nose with Quinn. "She's not a dog or a cat. She's a grown female. You cannot think of her as an object you own but as an equal."

"As an equal?" Those three words exploded through his clenched jaws. The expressions that played across his face were priceless as his index finger pointed in the doctor's face. "Just one fucking moment. I may have thought of her as too young. For damn sure, I have always thought her too good for me. But make no mistake about this, I have always thought of her as my equal. She can do the crossword puzzle in the Sunday papers with a pen. Not using a pencil so she can erase her mistakes, but in ink because she makes none. This young woman can make her point known in the most bizarre and maddening way. Try running ten miles with her or scuba-diving for hours. I don't think of her as an object, but as someone I'm not sure I can live without."

His simple, honest admission brought tears to Cassie's eyes. Quinn cupped her face in his large hands and gently kissed each one away. With one hand, she lifted her hair from her neck. She extended the other one that held the necklace. Understanding her silent request, he stepped closer and, with their gazes locked on each other, he fastened the clasp and cuddled a long kiss where the clasp met her spine. Something in his tender kiss opened the door to her heart and allowed hope to skip right on in. He admired her. He respected her. He cared.

"I love you, angel. You might be my sex toy, but, hell, I'll never think of you as an object. I don't think love's supposed to work that way."

"I love you, too, and I love that you're *my* sex object." She gave him a saucy wink.

Sober-faced Dr. Paxwell seemed to fight a smile so hard a blush crept across her cheeks. "Looks like you two have reached an amicable agreement."

"How many times a day can I call her?" Quinn sounded hopeful when he fired the question at the doctor.

"None. Zero contact." The therapist glanced at both of them. "That applies to texts too."

Quinn aimed his dimpled smile at no-nonsense Dr. Paxwell. "I'm guessing Skype is out of the question."

"As are smoke signals, Mr. Gallagher."

CHAPTER SIXTEEN

"Well?" Wolf was waiting on Quinn before he made it inside the waiting area. Talk about a dark squall ready to break. The air in that wing of the hospital fairly crackled with the static electricity of brooding storm Dan "Wolf" Wolford.

"Cassie's agreed to spend three days here for observation. We're not seeing each other for a month, but during that time we'll both be meeting with Dr. Paxwell for individual counseling. Cassie, once a week. I'll go twice. Seems I come with more baggage than she does."

Wolf's head swiveled to the curtained area. "But she agreed to stay?" His narrow-eyed gaze settled on Quinn. "How did you manage that, because believe me, the doc and I were having zero luck in that department."

"I got her to agree on the one condition that means the most to her. She wants someone from the family to stay with her all the time. Preferably you, but she understands you have to report to the station too."

The self-proclaimed family patriarch seemed to appreciate Quinn's efforts. "Well, okay, then. Looks like you might get to live. At least until I hear your side of the story."

"Can we go outside for a walk? I'd like to talk to you in private. I'm dealing with some things I could use your help with."

Wolf stared at him for a few beats, his dark eyes assessing. "Becca, can you go sit with Cassie while Quinn and I have a private chat?"

The redhead hurried over, her eyes wary. "Sure. Will you two need a referee?"

"No, but I'd like Jace to come along too, if that's all right with you, Wolf." He might as well get both brothers out of the way at once. During his time in Clearwater, they'd befriended him and he'd rewarded their kindness with half-truths. Now there was also the element of Cassie's safety. It would serve him right if they both beat him into low-grade hamburger.

After grabbing a cup of coffee-to-go at an all-night café across from the hospital, they meandered through the large parking lot while Quinn shared his long story, beginning with growing up with a strict, demanding father. During the verbal unfolding process, Wolf asked questions, while Jace mostly added an emotional "*Jesus*" to the telling of Quinn's tale.

He eventually led Wolf and Jace in the direction of Milt's car and leaned against it to finish.

"So, because you dipped your pen in company ink, your team lost their lives while your pecker had a good time." He should have figured Wolf, the ex-SEAL, would give him the most grief.

"That about sums it up. Although, technically, she wasn't our company. She was local support."

Wolf tilted his head to the side for a second or two. "So this is what's been eating at you?"

"Yeah." He gulped the rest of his coffee and crunched the insulated cup in his hand.

"But to shoot the woman you were screwing between the eyes, Quinn." Jace leaned in. "Damn, that's cold."

"Not as cold as having my men tortured and killed." He went on to explain resigning from his government job, being ostracized from his family and coming here to start a new life.

"Your old man really disowned you? Man, when Wendy Anne has this baby, I can't imagine turning my back on him or her for any reason." Jace shook his head.

"You know, I always hoped Buck Gallagher wasn't my real father." Quinn rubbed a hand over his forehead to help ease the headache hammering there. "Over the years, I heard snippets of arguments. Not much. Just enough to make me wonder. There was a man my mother was good friends with and my dad hated. His first name was Quinn, too, and I adored spending time with him."

"Where is he now?" Wolf wanted to know.

"Someone shot him outside a jazz club in New Orleans. My mother nearly had a nervous breakdown over it."

"Do you still have contact with your mother?" Jace drank more of his coffee.

"I call her every Wednesday while Buck's at work, usually between eight and eleven in the morning. She knows fires can happen at any time and accepts the irregularity of my calls."

"You refer to your dad as Buck?" Wolf leaned a shoulder against Milt's car beside Quinn and waited for his answer.

"He told me never to call him dad or father ever again. That only leaves his nickname or his first name, which happens to be my middle name. My grandpa's name too." He took a steadying breath. "I'll be damned if he's getting that."

The three stood silent for a minute, and Quinn took that time to compose himself. "There's more. And it concerns Cassie." Both of her brothers angled toward him.

"The same morning I turned in my notice at the station, I emailed some old co-workers at the State Department and the DEA, putting out feelers for job openings. In less than three hours, I got this text." He tugged his cell from his pocket and thumbed through until he found the text that threatened Cassie, holding it out so both men could read it.

"Jesus H. Christ!" Wolf went fucking ballistic and Jace wasn't too far behind on the crazy brother track.

"Yeah, my freakin' feelings exactly. Some bastard's been watching me for the last three years. Why? I haven't a clue. Obviously, whoever's been observing my comings and goings—or hired some feckless asshole to spy on me—was the mole within one of my old departments."

Wolf snapped his own cell from his belt and thumbed a number. "Arlo, sorry to wake you, but I've got an emergency situation. My youngest sister's life has been threatened. Is it possible to trace a text? A threatening text." Wolf paced while the man on the other end of the call talked. "Well, can we check it out anyhow? Just in case? I'll drop the cell off at your office shortly after eight tomorrow morning. Thanks, man." He disconnected the call and clipped his phone to its holder again. "Arlo's a detective in the police department. If the person sending the text used a burner—a cheap phone used once and then tossed—his team won't be able to trace it, but it's still worth a try."

Quinn gave Wolf his cell. "Might as well hand it over. Doctor Get-in-your-head has prohibited Cassie and me from seeing each other for a month. Or calling, or texting. Can't skype. Basically, we're cut off from each other." *Yeah, like that'll keep me from sneaking in to see her. And God help the poor son of a bitch who tries to stop me.*

Jace stepped closer and shoulder-bumped him. "A smart man could find his way around all that."

Even in the dim parking lot security lighting, Quinn could detect Wolf rolling his eyes. "Here we go. The expert on women is about to impart some of his sexual wisdom."

"Hey, make fun all you want, but the day you can make your woman climax on command, then you'll have the right to scoff at me."

Wolf did scoff. "Hell, squirt, where would you learn shit like that?"

"Not from those cheap-ass BDSM movies you guys like to watch at the station, that's for damn sure." Jace effectively cut off any more questions from his brother by pivoting toward Quinn. "You can *still* send Cassie flowers, write her notes, poetry, get her little gifts that hold sentimental value. She's not one for showy stuff. You know that. She responds to presents from a person's heart." He tapped Quinn's shoulder, "Hell send her a calendar and a fancy pen. Tell her to circle a date." He chuckled and shook his head. "It'll drive her freaking nuts until she finds out what that means. You know, for a weekend get-away or something special. Ya gotta learn it's the small things in a relationship that keep a man and a woman close."

"Got ya. But I have to admit, her safety is uppermost on my mind right now. I'll send her gifts so she knows I'm thinking about her, but I have to know she's safe. That knowing me won't bring her harm."

"The big question remains." Wolf shook his finger as he talked. "What or who do you know that makes you a liability? Why waste government resources to put you under surveillance? I'm thinking this is a private endeavor. A classic CYA mode, although an expensive one. Who would have the funds to hire people to watch you day and night?"

"And what lowlife would use my woman's safety to force me to do what they want. The only thing I want to do right now is rip that bastard apart, inch by rotten inch."

"I feel you," Wolf said. "Someone's hiding something and it has to be something big, or why bother? Ever had your apartment swept for bugs or hidden cameras?"

"Bugs?" Chills beat a fast path up and down Quinn's spine.

Wolf stopped in front of him and pinned him with a glare. "You don't have any military experience, do you?"

"No. Which made me a bit of an oddity at the State Department. I mean, not all the men and women have a military background, but most do. I went there straight out of college. I've got a fourth degree black belt and training in fencing and sharpshooting, but they don't count for much in that world."

"So why did they put you in charge of an important mission like that? Usually one department sends a top-notch agent on temporary duty within another department. They like one of their top dawgs pissin' in someone else's yard. Just for the showing-off effect."

"Sounds like they wanted our boy here to fail." Jace clasped Quinn's shoulder.

Wolf folded his arms. "But you weren't failing, were you? Your team was digging up some important shit. Finding some good, solid intel. Did you turn over all your records to your superiors once you got back to the States?"

"Except for my zip drive. That I kept. It's in my lockbox at the bank."

"Bingo!" Wolf chuckled. "Always hold onto that special ace and keep it well hidden. First thing, we need Ryder to sweep your place for bugs and cameras. He's top-notch at that shit and he can be trusted. Have you talked to anyone about the hidden zip drive?"

"No one. Unless I rambled about it when I was having a flashback. I do some weird shit then." One time he'd trashed his apartment. Another, he'd stood in the shower until he'd used all the hot water and it had turned icy cold. Then there was the time he came into awareness, crouched in the corner of his closet, naked and grasping one of his water skis like a spear.

"Those things are a bitch, but Dr. Paxwell will get you through it. Teach you ways to manage them. She's the best, in my opinion. Now, back to this damn text."

"I sent a message to everyone I'd emailed originally and told them I'd decided against moving back to the land of cold and snow. That I'd applied at some other fire departments in Florida. Thanked them for whatever they'd done in trying to find me a job in the Truman Building or at the Pentagon. Then, in case any of them checked, I applied at six companies here in Florida, northern Gulfside and Oceanside, and also a few cities in Georgia, along the ocean."

Wolf nodded. "Good. That's good. You're showing them you want to be near the water in year-round warm weather. That should go a long way toward keeping Cassie safe. I gotta ask, man. Those two bullet scars you've got. The one in your back under the tat and the one in your thigh. When did you get those?"

"That night in Chile, when everything went to hell."

"And you still went looking for Renata?"

Quinn nodded. "By then I had a strong mother-effing inkling. I didn't want to believe it, but I had to know. I have to admit she looked mighty surprised when I showed up at her place, bleeding and hobbling."

"She figured you were already dead." Wolf chuckled. "I do like a man stubborn enough to cheat death. Makes us stronger than the average motherfucker. I'm taking personal time tomorrow to stay with Cassie. I'd rather none of the women find out about the threatening text."

"I agree," Jace chimed in. "I'll try to behave normally. I don't want Wendy Anne worrying any more than she has already tonight."

"Any chance you can surprise her with a short trip? Go away for a couple of days and shop for the baby? Might help her relax. You know how easily she picks up on everyone's vibes. We don't want another miscarriage."

Jace stopped and glared at his brother. "You don't trust me, do you? You want me out of town so I don't let it slip to Cassie about the text."

"You know you've always been the talkative one in the family, you dumb shit."

Quinn grabbed the opportunity, now that Wolf was more in a teasing mood. "I'd like to talk to Noah and you about rescinding my resignation. There's no way I can leave Cassie now."

Wolf crossed his thick arms. "Why? Do you think you're the only one who can keep her safe?"

"Because he's in love with her. Has been for a long time. You know how Cassie feels about him." Jace ran a hand over the multiple layers of duct tape on the top of the Cutlass Supreme.

"I wonder whose piece of junk this heap is?"

"It's Milt's and it's not worth the powder and keg it would take to blow it up. When I found out Cassie was hurt, I shook too bad to drive. He offered to bring me. Hell, I'd have been better off jogging here than riding with that old coot."

Quinn focused his attention on Wolf again. "I know you think I'm not good enough for your sister, and you're probably damn right, but I love her more than I've ever loved anyone in my entire life. I plan on asking her to marry me, unless you beat me to a pulp first."

Jace elbowed his older brother. "Well, there is that wedding dress she's got on layaway."

Wolf pinched the bridge of his nose with his thumb and forefinger. "And the damn veil. Let's not forget the veil. How many times have I heard every stupid detail of that dress and veil? I've got April's wedding in April. Becca and I are getting hitched in May. I'm giving you 'til June to find out who's threatening my baby sister or there's no wedding. Am I clear? Now are we through with this male bonding shit?"

Jace rocked back on his heels. "Well, we didn't sing 'Kum-Ba-Ya' yet."

Wolf cuffed him on the back of the head. "Smart-ass."

CHAPTER SEVENTEEN

Cassie and Dr. Paxwell were just beginning their session when a nurse's aide carried in a huge arrangement of red roses and calla lilies. Wolf stood from his sentinel position on a padded chair by the window, took the flowers from the young woman and, if Cassie didn't know better, she'd have sworn he removed the gift card envelope from the plastic holder. Yet a card remained when he set the bouquet on the stand by her bed.

Her gaze bounced from the card to her brother and he winked. She reached for the printed "sent with love" card that merely had the initial "Q" scrawled on it. A smile spread and her heart rate kicked up. The roses and calla lilies were from Quinn.

Dr. Paxwell's cell chimed and, while she walked toward the window to talk, Wolf slipped the envelope he'd purloined from the arrangement, under Cassie's pillow. He leaned over and kissed her forehead before he whispered in her ear, "Something for you to read later. I'm going to the cafeteria for a soda and something to eat. Want me to bring you back anything?"

"No, I'm good. Well, maybe a candy bar. After what the good doctor will put me through, I'm sure I'll need some chocolate." She'd also be better once she was alone so she could read the mystery note.

Wolf winked and sauntered out of her private room. Now what

was he up to? How did he know there would be an extra card with her flowers? She reached to run a fingertip over the velvety softness of the rose petals. She might not be able to see Quinn, but she would certainly enjoy the blooms he'd sent her.

Dr. Paxwell, in her typical low-key fashion, was able to get Cassie to talk about all the things that preyed on her mind. Even Cassie was surprised when she listed them: the fire at her recently opened hair boutique and the stress of scheduling all the work to reopen her business as soon as possible, living with two older friends who, at times, acted more immature than she did, listening to both April and Becca plan their weddings and wondering if she'd ever have one herself, and the thought of Quinn's leaving Clearwater. No wonder she teetered on the edge of stress, or so Dr. Paxwell insisted.

Their long discussion drained Cassie's emotions so badly she nearly fell asleep as soon as the door to her room whispered shut after the doctor left for her next appointment. Then her hand slipped under her pillow and paper crinkled.

Quinn's note.

She slid the envelope from beneath the pillow and tugged out the card. Quinn wrote with a slanted hand. *Angel...Dr. Dragon never said I couldn't write you notes or send you little gifts. I miss you already. Please work hard at getting your feet stable under you again. I promise to put twice as much effort into dealing with my issues so I can make you a happier woman. I love you more than I love the next sunset over the Gulf. I need you more than my next breath. You are as soft and sweet as these roses and as strong as the tiger lilies. Q.*

She glanced at the bouquet and chuckled. Poor man didn't know the difference between calla lilies and tiger lilies. She pressed a kiss to the card. He was perfect. Keeping the card curled within her grasp, she cuddled under the blanket as the medicine Dr. Paxwell had prescribed pulled her under.

Someone stirring around Cassie's room woke her. "Jenna? Why aren't you at work?" She struggled to sit up while Jenna played with the buttons on the bed. First her feet were raised higher than her head. Then her shoulders nearly touched her stomach. "You're doing this on purpose!"

After Jenna quit laughing and positioned the bed in a more comfortable situation, she pressed a kiss to Cassie's forehead. "I'm on lunch break. Where's Wolf?"

"He went to the cafeteria." Her gaze went to the gaily wrapped box Jenna waved back and forth in her hand. "Is that a present? For me?" She wagged her eyebrows.

"A handsome man showed up at my office this morning and told me what he wanted. He was very specific. I'm not so sure it's your style, but his face lit up when he saw it. He claimed it was perfect. There's a card inside you're to read first." She plopped the box on Cassie's lap, pulled over the chair and unwrapped a tuna sandwich.

"You're going to watch while I read the card?"

Jenna grinned. "Yup. Looks like I have to get my romantic fix vicariously through everyone else. Ain't nothing happenin' in mine."

"You haven't met the right man yet." Cassie lifted the wrapped lid to find a pale yellow envelope. The card inside was covered with a field of yellow daisies with one white one standing out in its purity and beauty. Inside, scrawled on the blank card, was more of Quinn's slanted writing. *Angel... You have always been the sunshine in my world of emotional darkness. What happened in Chile scarred my heart and soul. Losing my team made me feel inept as a leader. Having our mission explode in front of us affirmed that someone within our government as well as one of the local team members were cronies with the drug cartel. The fact that I was literally in bed with one of our enemies has been a guilt almost too heavy to bear. Then there was you. The sunshine in the obsidian of my soul. You were like a daisy, bringing purity and incandescence to my black soul where the bitter winds of culpability continually blow. Is it any wonder I adore you? Q.*

She swiped away tears and snatched a tissue from the bedside box. *Oh, Quinn. I adore you too.* Jenna reached for the card and Cassie snatched it back. "Sorry, sis, this is much too private." Cassie shoved the card under her pillow. Quinn had poured out his heart to her. It wasn't her place to share his words with anyone. Even her beloved sister.

The tissue paper crinkled when Cassie folded it back. Inside was a soft cotton negligee. The yellow robe had white daisies embroidered at the neckline, down the buttoned front and at the sleeve edges, while the yellow gown was covered with white daisies and edged at the neckline and hem with embroidered white lace. Beneath them were yellow bedroom slippers with a white daisy centered across the top.

"Quinn picked these out?"

"In a way. He told me what he wanted. 'A peignoir set with white daisies on it and slippers to match.' I showed him some sexy things and he turned up his nose. Claimed you didn't need clothes to make you sexy, that you just *were*." Jenna's eyes narrowed. "I won't even ask what he meant by *that*. I thought you were saving yourself for the right man."

"He is the right man." Cassie sat on the edge of the bed. "Help me into this before Wolf gets back. I can't wait to get it on. Then I want you to do a bit of shopping for me." A smile spread as an ornery thought grew. "I want you to deliver it to the fire station and make sure he opens it in front of all the guys."

Jenna laughed. "Oh, little one, I *know* that look."

****

To Quinn's great relief, Noah was content to ignore what he referred to as Quinn's moment of madness a few days earlier when he'd turned in his resignation. While he was talking to his superior, he told him about the failed operation in Chile, his emails to those he still knew within the State Department and the DEA and, finally, the threatening text regarding Cassie.

Except for the twitch in Noah's eye and his continual straightening and re-twisting of a large paperclip, he stared silently during Quinn's recanting of the whole goddamned mess. He didn't mention Cassie's cutting, simply that she'd gotten ill. He told Noah how he'd emailed everyone back, telling them he'd decided to stay in the fire and rescue business, hoping that would help ensure Cassie's safety.

Noah stood and rounded his desk. Once he had the door opened, he barked for Jace and Barclay Gray, one of the marine rescue divers, and known to the unit as Ice Man. "I want you two to follow Quinn to his place and help him unpack his U-Haul trailer. Quinn, return that damn trailer to wherever you rented it from. You guys have two hours to complete that job and get back here."

Quinn stood and, as he passed his captain, he stopped. "Thanks, sir."

"We need to reinforce all appearances that you're staying. Wait a couple days and then contact all the places you applied. Tell them you were offered a promotion to stay. I'll put in the necessary paperwork here on my end today in case someone does some deep investigating. I doubt it'll be approved, but it'll be in your file for any snooping son of a bitch to see. Keep me in the loop. I take care of my men. Simple as that."

By the time Quinn, Jace and Barclay reached his apartment, Ryder and his "assistant" had already swept the entire apartment, except for the kitchen. His right-hand man, aka Milt from downstairs, couldn't wait to give a full report. Ryder, his jaw tensed and eyes narrowed, appeared ready to snap the man's scrawny neck.

"We found two bugs in every room. That's listening devices for you uneducated folks." Milt extended a handful of tiny wired objects.

Ryder rolled his eyes and, behind Milt's back, mimicked someone jabbing the old coot with a knife.

Milt, apparently thrilled with his self-important role, kept on with his report. "Man must be a pervert is all I can say. A total, frenzied pervert. Had a camera mounted next to your showerhead, over your bed's headboard, at your desk so he could watch whatever you did on your laptop *and*...get this...beside the cat's litter box. He's been watching your cat take a crap." Milt scratched his balls and tweaked a fart. "What kinda demented fool wants to see that?"

Quinn, Jace and Barclay just stood there, dumbfounded. Furball climbed Quinn's jean-clad leg until he bent to scoop the cat into his arms and scratch his chin.

Jace was the first to speak. "I need a beer to wash that image from my mind."

Barclay glanced at Quinn. "Got any bleach we can use as eyewash? Damn, what the hell did he expect to see coming out of a cat's ass?"

Milt expelled a long string of gas and hiked up his khakis with the insides of his arms. "I'll lay you odds he probably made videos of everything and sold em on the Internet. Lot of sick perverts out there."

The memory of Cassie's first time having sex being shown online nearly drove Quinn out of his mind. An act that private, that special, was not to be shared. He'd kill the bastard once he found out who he was.

"Hey, I just found another camera attached to the top of the freezer's handle." Ryder carried it in from the kitchen. "While I've got you, Quinn, there's somethin' I need to tell you."

Quinn took the bug and examined it, trying his best to keep it away from the nosy cat's paw. Something in the tone of Ryder's voice alerted him. "What?"

"A couple days ago, when baby doll was in the café, she mentioned some guy on a black crotch bike nearly runnin' her down in the parkin' lot of the mall. Claimed at one point, he stared at her through the dark glass of his helmet."

"Son of a bitch! Why didn't she mention him to me?" *Because I was too busy being jealous and then caught up in a flashback.* Could the guy have been the same one who sent the warning text? If he was, she was in more danger than any of them suspected. Quinn looked at Ryder and instinctively knew there was more. "What else?"

"She said he followed her to my place and parked across the street at Gulfside Treasures Gift Shop. I walked out front to see if he was still there and he drove off. Black Kawasaki Ninja. Florida plates. First two numbers were three-seven. That's all I caught before he zoomed into traffic. Fella even did a wheelie to show off, like he wanted me to know he wasn't scared. I'm sorry I didn't pay more attention. I just figured it was some guy interested in her, you know?"

Quinn patted Ryder's back. "How were you to know? All this has happened so fast."

Jace tugged his cell from the scabbard on his belt. "I'm calling Wolf." He turned and leaned his elbows on the snack bar.

Ryder asked Milt for all the bugs so he could check them out to see if they were manufactured or homemade. "I'm goin' to make one more sweep through the apartment, check in the weirdest places I can think of. Milt, why don't you take a break? Go downstairs and spend some quality time with Killer. Bet he's been missin' you something fierce."

"You sure you don't need me? All this excitement, I am getting kind of tired."

"Maybe on my next job. Now that you're experienced and all…"

Milt's eyes lit up. "Hey, anytime, Roger."

"Ryder." The irritated man repeated for probably the umpteenth time.

"Whatever." Milt reached for a slip of paper and jotted some information. "Here's my landline and cell phone numbers. You need me, just call."

Ryder took the paper Milt extended. "Thanks. Gettin' good help is hard these days."

Quinn glanced at Milt. "I'd appreciate it if you kept an eye out for a black crotch bike. Kawasaki with Florida plates. Call me as soon as you see anything. I've got a new phone, but the number's the same."

"You got it, buddy. Me and Killer will keep an eye out. Don't you worry about a thing."

Milt pinched a smidgen of gas and bustled out the door.

Jace ended his call and slipped his cell into its holder. "Wolf wants to hold a meeting at the station in the meeting room. He's calling Noah now to arrange it. He'll also contact his friend at the police department. Ryder, can you come too?"

"For an ex-SEAL? You bet. Look, there was no camera near the litter box. I just told the old guy that to watch him go off. It got him out of my way for a while as he pranced back and forth, rantin' and ravin'. I found it in the light above this snack bar. The other cameras were where he told you."

"Even so, the son of a bitch saw some intimate shit." All the special private moments between Cassie and him came to Quinn's mind.

Jace held up an open hand. "As Cassie's brother, I don't even want to know. Let's get your U-Haul unloaded while Ryder does his thing in peace. By then, Wolf will have the meeting set up. He was one pissed off person."

"Yea, well, I'm not so jolly myself right about now. Someone's been watching and following my woman. This shit is damned serious. Look, Ryder, when I left a set of keys with Milt to give to you, it never occurred to me he'd stick to you like glue. I'm sorry if he got on your nerves." Quinn carried Furball into the kitchen and hand-fed him two treats.

"Yeah, well, that man needs his ass checked. Needs his diet changed or somethin'." Ryder shook his head and went back to work.

The guys made it to the fire station ten minutes over the two-hour limit the Captain had allowed them. The remaining members of the squad were situated around the dining table, their eyes glued on Jenna who held a wrapped box.

Jace kissed her forehead before aiming a scowl at the guys. "What are you lowlifes doing ogling my sister?"

"Oh, it's not me that has them wound up, although I wish it was." She spared them all a wink and they laughed. "I have a gift for Quinn from Cassie."

So, she was thinking of him too. "How did she like the neg…" he cleared his throat. "My present?" *God, I want to be with her now more than anything. I want to keep her safe.*

"She loved it. She put it on right away and told me to tell you it felt sensual against her skin."

The guys hooted and elbowed each other.

"She sent me on a shopping trip with explicit instructions on what to buy." Jenna extended a box wrapped in shiny black paper and tied with a bright red ribbon.

"Looks like something sexy, Quinn." Noah glanced away, his shoulders shaking with laughter. "Might help you up your game a little bit."

Quinn stared at the box as if it were a snake. Knowing Cassie's sense of humor, he wouldn't be surprised if a python crawled out. "Ain't a damn thing wrong with my game." Hadn't he been nice to her? Hadn't he laid his emotions on the line? He took the box from Jenna. Once he knew his Cassie was safe, he would paddle that pretty ass of hers and then kiss every inch of it. But for now? He wasn't in the fucking mood. "Thanks. I'll open it later. Is Wolf here?"

"He's picking up tacos for everyone. Said he'd be here shortly." Jenna shook her head and held up her cell phone. "Go ahead and open the box. I'm under orders here. Cassie's exact words were, 'Pictures, big guy.'"

CHAPTER EIGHTEEN

With everyone's eyes trained on Quinn, what choice did he have? He set the box on the table, and they all leaned in as he tore off the ribbon and black paper. He gingerly folded back the black tissue paper and examined the contents. What the hell? He picked up the first item, a black satin male thong with a red-lace stretchy pocket and a damn bell where his pecker should go.

"The bell's to help you find that tiny thing you call a cock," one of the guys chimed in. *Oh, I am definitely going to paddle her ass.*

Of course, every person on the squad, including the new female in their unit, Ivy Jo, who Ryder couldn't seem to keep his eyes off, laughed over his new underwear, especially when he turned it around to examine the strip no wider than dental floss that was to slip between his ass cheeks. *Cold day in hell, angel, when I put these sons of bitches on.* The second thong nestled in the tissue paper was leopard print. He held it up for one and all to see. Hell, he might as well get this show over with so he could move onto more important things, like finding out who was threatening the woman he loved. The gorgeous female with the heart-shaped face who was going to get her sweet ass smacked. Dear God, were those movable eyes at the end of the cock holder?

"Wait!" One of the guys, Eduardo, reached for his cell. "Let me take a picture for my wife. She's always dishing on Quinn's ass anyhow." He snapped a couple shots. "She will love these. Look, it's got eyes on the pecker pocket!" Eduardo pointed.

"That's so the little leopard can see to find the pussy." Barclay's face mottled red. "Sorry, ladies. Sometimes we guys forget our manners." He glanced at Ivy Jo. "I meant no offense. We're still getting used to having women in the unit."

"Don't feel you have to change the way you normally talk on my account. I knew coming into a typically male environment, I'd have some adjustments to make." She smiled and shifted a shoulder. "Besides, it's no worse than what I hear around my brothers and cousins." She turned to Quinn. "Will you be modeling them for us?"

"Hell, no!" He wasn't even sure he'd put them on for Cassie.

Beneath the two pairs of thongs was a book, *One Hundred and One Ways to Make Your Woman Beg for More.* Quinn's gaze rose to meet Jenna's. "Tell my woman she won't need to beg. She'll have more than she can handle."

The entire force was in a raucous when Wolf sauntered in carrying an armful of taco boxes. Another man beside him, wearing a suit, carried a carton of soda. "Captain, Jace, Barclay, Ryder and…" with an amused glance at the leopard underwear in Quinn's hands, the corners of Wolf's mouth twitched before he added, "*thong-man*, let's assemble in the conference room. The top three boxes are for us. The bottom five are for the rest of you worthless bums and our new 'bummette.' Jenna, you staying? We've got plenty of tacos, if you want to join in."

"No, I'm heading back to stay with Cassie and show her the video I just took of thong man and his goodies.

Ryder reached in one of the pockets of his black cargo pants and extracted a wad of business cards. He started passing them out. "I own a health food café on Sunset Dreams Boulevard. And I'm not too shy to say I make the best smoothies in Clearwater. This card entitles you to one free smoothie. Stop by." He paused in front of Ivy Jo and pressed several cards in her outstretched hand. "Anytime."

Quinn checked the blush spreading across the new recruit's chubby cheeks. Had Ryder just hit on her? That sly dog, passing out free smoothie cards to the entire squad just so he could give her his name and work address. Quinn needed to learn some flirting techniques too. Ways to make his angel blush and charm her so she was confident in the extent to which he loved her.

Once the unofficial team was settled around the table in the conference room, ground beef, chicken and steak tacos were slapped on paper plates and cans of soda opened. Wolf introduced Detective Arlo Jacobs, a man he met years back when Wolf had given a couple of courses on boat safety. Arlo Jacobs was one of his first students.

The detective took off his jacket and loosened his tie. "So, everyone here has had military and/or tactical training?"

Wolf glanced at his brother. "Everyone except Jace, but he's got one of those minds that sees things differently. Zeroes in on what ought to be obvious to everyone else but isn't for some stupid reason. Besides, I need my brother here. End of discussion."

Everyone nodded their assent and Arlo made no objection.

"Okay. Let's make a list of what we know. See what ties into what. Or maybe nothing fits just yet." He pointed to the men, his eyebrow arched. "But the facts will. Everything we know is a piece of the puzzle. It's up to us to methodically put the pieces together until the puzzle makes sense."

Puzzles. Cassie was in danger and this policeman wanted to play with freakin' puzzles? Quinn fought the urge to heave the empty chairs against the wall. What Cassie needed was to be in another town in a motel with him guarding her, holding her close and keeping her safe. Yet, here they sat eating tasteless tacos and talking puzzles.

The policeman guzzled a soda and then removed the top to a black dry erase marker. "Let's start with a timeline. Quinn, when did you join the State Department?" Arlo jotted the date Quinn gave him. "When were you invited into the meeting that temporarily assigned you to the DEA?"

"Look, I mean no disrespect, but this is a fuckin' waste of time. Our first order of business ought to be getting my ang...Cassie out of town. Let me borrow a car or rent one. I'll take her someplace fifty, sixty miles away. Meanwhile, you all can play this puzzle shit cause it ain't workin' for me."

Arlo planted his fingertips on the tabletop, leaned toward Quinn and stared him in the eye. "What happens if the two of you are followed? You've been watched for three years and were too damn dumb to realize it. You think now, all of a sudden, you can detect a tail? I don't think so."

Quinn jumped out of his seat, ready to crawl across the table to grab the arrogant bastard by the throat. Noah and Jace both grabbed an arm to hold Quinn in place.

Wolf motioned to the corner of the room. "Get the hell over there, Gallagher. Now!" Both men stormed to the corner indicated. Wolf stared at his feet for a minute as if he were choosing the right words. "If *my* Becca was in Cassie's place, I'd be every bit as pissed and scared and determined to keep her safe as you are." He took a deep breath and clasped Quinn's shoulder.

Quinn didn't like being handled and jerked away from Wolf's grasp. "But she's not your woman. She's *mine*."

Wolf shoved him back into the corner with a strong punch to his chest. "And she's my little sister, dammit. I have protected her for eight years. You think I'm not scared? That I'm not mad as hell? That I don't want to tear down this fire station, brick by fucking brick? You're not the only son of a bitch in this town who loves that girl to death."

Quinn ran a hand over his hair and was surprised at how much it shook when he lowered his arm. "I've never loved like..."

"Hell, neither have I." Wolf lowered his voice. "But I can double-damn guarantee you, Becca, my prickly redhead is my entire life."

Quinn jammed his fingertips into the front pockets of his jeans. "So if someone threatened Becca, you'd sit back and do this puzzle shit?"

"I'd get a grip and do whatever...*whatever* it took! You've got two minutes to get your shit together, and if you're half the man I think you are, you'll apologize to Arlo. Then you'll answer his stupid-assed questions, because this whole puzzle process is driving me every bit as batshit crazy as it is you." Wolf pivoted, his hands curled into fists, and strode to his chair.

Facing the wall, Quinn beat his forehead against it four or five times as he thought of those who had or might be torn from his life. First, his men. Then, his dad. Now, perhaps, his angel. He chuckled. For the first time in nearly four years, a certain dark-eyed woman did not tumble onto his list of losses. Maybe he was doing a bit of healing—or growing up. And the feisty green-eyed woman who'd prompted it all was in peril.

Quinn made the eight-foot trek, that seemed four times as long, back across the room to come face to face with the police detective. "I owe you an apology. I acted like an ass." He extended his hand, which Arlo shook. "Ask me whatever you need to know and I'll help you as best I can."

Arlo nodded. "Good. Let me repeat the question while you take your seat. When were you invited into the meeting that temporarily assigned you to the DEA?" He wrote the date Quinn provided. The policeman asked who was present at the time and added their names, then also wanted to know who each person's superior was before adding their names to the list.

Much to Quinn's chagrin, time dragged on, but question by question, Arlo constructed a picture of facts and names. He also shared how his team had learned the text Quinn received was from a burner phone, so that lead was dead. Even so, it remained on the timeline.

Arlo's cell rang. He answered the call, took notes, cussed a few times and issued a couple of orders. Once he ended the call, he turned to the group. "Looks like the driver of the bike was most definitely after your girlfriend, Quinn. No doubt about it now. A

Florida motorcycle license plate, starting with the numbers Ryder remembered, was found by one..." he glanced at his notes, "Milt Garland, shoved into the crack of your mailbox in the vestibule of your apartment building."

"Son of a bitch!" The table shuddered under the force of Quinn's fist. The man just kept getting closer and closer to Cassie. "One of us needs to be at the hospital with her all the time. We can't leave her alone."

"I've got an officer assigned outside her door. Wolf asked that she not know she's being placed under protective custody."

"I told Becca and Dr. Paxwell I'm hoping the rest of the girls will think the policeman is there for someone else, if they even notice him at all." Wolf reached for another taco and pulled back, almost as if he'd lost his appetite. "God, I hate this."

Jace leaned toward Wolf. "I think we need to tell the whole family. I don't think it's fair they don't know their baby sister is in danger. Besides, with Megan being a nurse at the hospital, that gives us an extra pair of eyes. Maybe she could switch duty with someone else and get temporarily assigned to Cassie's floor."

Wolf shook his head. "And just how the hell do we keep it all from Cassie? She's under enough stress right now."

"I gotta disagree with you on this, Wolf." Quinn snapped open another can of soda. "She's stronger than we think. I'm going to her room as soon as we're done here and telling her everything. We've already worked through some issues that troubled her. I have a feeling this will make her damn mad and speed up her healing. You know what a pistol she can be."

Wolf chuckled. "True that. The kid has worn me down more times than I can count. And, brother, if you truly plan on marrying her, you better grow an extra set of kahunas, cause you're going to need them dealing with her."

"Yeah, her mind is always working on how to get one ahead." Jace looked at Wold and grinned. "Wolf, remember how she glued your jockstrap shut before the big football game your senior year?"

Wolf laughed. "I'd almost forgotten. She was what? All of ten? Damn brat." He pointed at Quinn. "Yep, now that I think about it, you might deserve some of her shit. She can be sweet as all get-out and vengeful as a hurricane too."

"You think I haven't learned that already? Now, back to this asshole coming into my building. He knows where Cassie works, what kind of car she drives and where I live."

"To put his license plate in Quinn's mailbox. Sounds like the bastard is playing with our boy, here. Edging him on." Ryder crushed his empty soda can in one hand. "Still, trust old eagle-eye Milt to see it."

"Oh, he saw it all right." Arlo slammed the top onto the dry marker. "One of my men is bringing him here. Claims he won't tell anyone but Quinn and Ryder who he saw. Took a picture of the intruder with his cell phone, and his dog, Killer, bit the man on the leg. So now we got a man with no license plate on his bike and a limp when he walks."

"You think an effing Chihuahua can inflict that much damage?" Quinn wanted to laugh at the absurdity of it all. As excitable as Milt was, the picture was probably blurred or missing a head. Yet, here they sat, waiting for agent Milt Garland, double-oh-four and a half to show up with his photographic masterpiece.

As soon as this meeting was over, he was taking personal leave and going to the hospital with Cassie. Dr. Paxwell and her orders be damned. They could choose another month to stay apart, like November...of twenty-seventy-nine.

"By now, our man is probably using stolen license plates," Noah reached for another taco. "Do you have any reports of stolen plates or a ditched bike found anywhere?"

Barclay took a bite and chewed. "Could have the bike in a shop for a custom paint job. Stripes or design work. Or a complete color change."

For the tenth time, Quinn's gaze went over every detail Arlo had scrawled on the large whiteboard, his mind processing, eliminating and zeroing in on the facts laid out. He needed help. Cassie needed protection; the best he could provide.

The memory of the fury and shame in Buck Gallagher's eyes, the echo of contempt in his voice as his words attacked Quinn like verbal shrapnel after his failure in Chile, burned like acid in his gut. Hell, he'd spent his entire life trying to win the old man's approval. If being shot while serving his country didn't qualify, then nothing would. Where his male parent was concerned, Quinn didn't give a damn. Yet, damned if he wouldn't do anything to keep Cassie safe, including swallowing his pride. He stood and walked toward a bank of windows before dialing a number he'd known by heart since childhood.

"Dad, I need your help."

A long-suffering sigh sounded over the phone. "What kind of trouble are you in this time? And haven't I told you not to call me by that title?"

Telling him to fuck that shit was on the tip of his tongue, but Cassie's safety meant too much. "You're the only one I can trust. Will you give me five minutes to ask your opinion on something?"

While the words barely escaped the tight confines of Quinn's resentment-packed throat, hearing them seemed to knock some of the wind out of the old man's sails. His favorite chair squeaked, just as it had for years. "I'm listening."

"First off, how's Mom and Grandpa Hudson?" God, the pain of missing them was so acute he didn't know if he could get through the conversation without falling apart. The last time he'd seen his mother was at Walter Reed Hospital after his return from Chile. He was being treated for two bullet wounds and an infection. She'd cried and pressed kisses to his face. What he wouldn't give for one of her hugs right about now. A mother's hug that silently proclaimed everything would be all right.

"They're both fine, but that's not why you called, is it?"

"No." *Same old heartless bastard.* Maybe this wasn't such a good idea. His gaze swept over the whiteboard again. "A few days ago, I put out feelers for openings at the State Department and the DEA."

"Tell me something I don't know."

"Within hours, I got a text threatening the young woman I'm in love with, if I returned to government work."

"Go on."

"An ex-SEAL, trained in surveillance equipment, found bugs and hidden cameras in my apartment. Cassie was nearly run over and then followed by a motorcycle. A friend was able to get the first two digits of his license plate. Just now that license plate was found, bent in half and stuck in the crack of my mailbox, at my apartment building."

"Someone doesn't want you to come back."

"Yesterday, I emailed everyone I'd contacted a couple days ago, thanked them for their trouble, and told them that I'd decided to stay on here. I hoped that would end the danger for Cassie, but..."

"But it's not stopping what's already been put into motion. Let me call you back on a different phone." The line went dead.

A little more than a minute went by before Quinn's phone rang. Caller ID said Caller Unknown. He answered and Buck spoke. "Where is Cassie now?"

"Are you using a burner?" The person who'd sent the threatening text had used one. His dad hadn't reached his high level of government security without being a ruthless son of a bitch. Damned if he'd tell him where she was.

"I'm using a secure line. Tell me how I can help you?" Old resentments surfaced. Since when had his old man ever offered to help with anything? His trust level for his father was minus zero. What the hell was he thinking to call him? He was beyond desperate to help Cassie, that's what.

The door to the conference room flew open and Milt charged in, his face nearly beet red with excitement. Strands of grey hair stood on end as if he'd been attacked. The pupils of his hazel eyes were dilated. His hand trembled as he extended his phone to Ryder. "I got him. I got the son of a bitch's photo."

Barclay pulled out a chair for Milt to collapse into.

Jace handed him a Coke, but Milt shook too badly to open it. "Someone get the oxygen tank and the first aid kit." Jace snapped the can open and gave it back to Milt; he helped the old man hold onto it so he could get it to his mouth.

Quinn stepped behind Ryder and peered over his shoulder at the photo on Milt's cell phone. To his surprise, the picture was in sharp focus and, although it didn't show the front of the man's face, it did show his neck. All the air whooshed from Quinn's lungs. "Holy Mother of God. It can't be!"

"Son! Son!" His dad's voice yelling over the phone finally registered.

"It's T-Bone! Chris Mason. The only one of my team from Chile to survive. He told me he was in Montana. Asked me to come work for his band of mercenaries. Why is he in Florida? What the hell is going on?"

CHAPTER NINETEEN

A male nurse, wearing a mask and pushing a wheelchair, entered Cassie's room. "How's it going, sweetie? Your doctor ordered an MRI." His voice was barely heard. He coughed as he glanced at the clipboard. Just her luck. She'd end up with the nurse's bronchitis, laryngitis or whatever he had. Really, how much did those little white covers work at prevention?

"First, would you give me your full name and date of birth?"

Why did she need an MRI? She hadn't had one since…when? She couldn't recall. "My name is Cassie Jacqueline Wolford and I was born on January the fourteenth, ninety-three. Why do I need an MRI? Does Dr. Paxwell think my brain is diseased or something?"

The nurse coughed and looked at the clipboard again. "Hon, they don't tell us anything, except what to do next. It says here, we're supposed to have an MRI with dye."

"Oh? Are you getting one too?" Why in God's name did nurses talk like that? And should he really be working if he had some kind of a cold or bronchitis? Yet, she knew her sister, an RN, often dragged herself to work when she really wanted to crawl into bed and sleep off whatever ailed her. "Nurses aren't supposed to get sick," Megan would say.

"You're not allergic—" he coughed again. "Sorry. You're not

allergic to anything are you? Iodine? Shellfish? Latex." He pulled a hypodermic needle from the front pocket of his blue checked scrubs and removed the plastic cover from the needle.

"No. No, I'm not allergic to anything. Although I'm not overly fond of needles." *Especially when the nurse jabbing me with one is obviously germ-ridden.*

"Well, lucky for you, then. You got ol' Jimmy instead of Donna. Patients complain when she gives them shots." He rubbed an alcohol-soaked swab of cotton over the vein in Cassie's neck and injected the solution.

"We inject the dye here, so it's closer to the head. It's a double combination shot. Part dye for the imaging and part relaxant for the nerves. Just a little prick. Kinda like my last date." He laughed, injected the medicine and then stooped to tighten the belts which secured her into the wheelchair.

Cassie wasn't so sure she liked the male nurse. She hated being spoken to in a condescending way. And who ever heard of getting a shot in the neck? Just wait until she saw Megan; she'd ask her sister, the RN. Also, what was with wearing a turtleneck under his blue scrubs? Had he been getting chills too?

Within seconds, the burning spread through her system and her tongue swelled so she couldn't speak plainly. Her head became heavy, and she wanted to sleep. Panic hit her hard. Maybe she *was* allergic to whatever was in this injection, but she couldn't form the words coherently to make Jimmy understand.

He opened the door and pushed her through. "Here we go, darling. Just relax. Those nasty old MRIs don't hurt a bit. Ever had one?" He threw a wave at a policeman. "See you in a couple hours, officer."

What was a policeman doing outside her room? Was a criminal being housed somewhere on her floor? Why couldn't she talk enough to ask? Why did her throat hurt to swallow? She'd felt fine until this nurse gave her that damn shot.

They stopped at the elevator doors and, when they opened,

Jimmy shoved the wheelchair on. "Could someone press floor two for me, please?"

By the time they'd reached the second floor, Cassie could barely keep her eyes open. At this rate she'd sleep through the MRI.

****

After Milt had a few hits of oxygen, his coloring improved and his breathing slowed. His lips were no longer blue. Jace, one of the station's EMT's, pronounced his pulse an acceptable rate and his blood pressure in a more normal range.

Arlo slid a chair in front of the older man and sat. "Feel up to answering a few questions?" He flashed Milt his badge. "I'm detective Arlo Jacobs, assigned to this case." He pointed to the whiteboard. "We've been writing down everything anyone knows or has seen or heard. Can you tell me what happened earlier?"

Milt tugged on the blanket Jace had wrapped around him. "All...all hell broke loose." Then he farted.

Arlo slid his chair back a foot or two.

"I'm Quinn's downstairs neighbor. Probably his best friend."

"That he is." Quinn patted his narrow back. The man was so lonely with his wife deceased; he soaked up anyone's attention. Throw him a kernel of kindness, and he was your friend for life. He was a decent man, always ready to help. Quinn opened and handed Milt a bottle of water. "Drink this, buddy. You've been through a rough ordeal. You need rehydrating."

Milt beamed under Quinn's meager attentions and gulped the water. "Quinn asked me to keep an eye out for a black Kawasaki Ninja bike. We, in the security business, refer to them as crotch rockets." He drank more water. "I turned my recliner so I had a better vantage point from which to do my reconnaissance out the front window. Kept a pair of binoculars on the end stand. Was just finishing up my second bag of pork rinds when I heard that bike howling down our street like the devil hisself rolling into town to wreak havoc."

He shook his head once and gulped more liquid. "Zipped his Ninja in the spot right beside Quinn's Jeep. I used my binoculars to jot down the license plate number." His trembling fingers reached into his shirt pocket and handed Arlo a neatly printed number. "I watched him unscrew the license plate, too, and take it off." He turned to Quinn. "Sorry to tell you this, but he used that very same screwdriver on your tires. You got four flats, buddy. Got two pictures of him doing that damage with my cell too." He motioned toward the phone Ryder was holding. "Just index backward and you'll see them."

Poor Milt's jaw was swollen and starting to bruise. Quinn squatted in front of him. "Did that bastard hit you?"

The old man nodded. "I opened my door in the hope I could take the picture, nonchalant like so he wouldn't know what I was up to, but Killer charged out and attacked him. Smart dog, Killer. He knows when a person's no damn good." Milt nodded once.

"I got the picture just fine, but when I cussed out the man for kicking my dog, he cold-cocked me." The old man turned to Noah. "For those of you who ain't in the security business, that means he hit me before I knew what was about to happen."

To Noah's credit, he kept a straight face.

"Jace, could you get our hero here an ice pack. *Damn* that man for hitting you." Quinn clasped Milt's shoulder and gave it a gentle squeeze. Next to Cassie and the men on the force, this gassy old coot was his favorite person in all of Clearwater. He could have been beaten all to hell and back—or worse. All because he wanted to help a friend.

Wolf's phone rang and he answered. "What do you mean Cassie's disappeared?" His booming voice reverberated off the meeting room's walls.

Everyone stood.

Quinn's heart stopped beating and simply dropped to his feet like a leaden wrecking ball. No, T-Bone couldn't have gotten her. His angel was under police protection. His heart ticked back to life and then absorbed a hellacious strong dose of I-will-be-damned anger that pounded in his ears like tympani drums, while his chest constricted to the point he didn't think he could draw his next breath. *I will kill that bastard if he took her.*

"I'm going to rip that poor excuse of a cop a new one." Arlo punched some numbers on his phone, speaking to the officer stationed outside Cassie's room. "My man claims a male nurse took her down for an MRI about an hour ago. Nurse said they might be gone a couple hours for the procedure."

Wolf tossed his cell on the chair and glared at Arlo. "Jenna already checked with the head nurse on the floor to find out why Cassie wasn't in her room. None of the nurses had a clue. One of them asked your *very observant* man, who passed along the same information. The head nurse called down to imaging to check, since sometimes test requests are slow to reach the nurses' station. No test had been ordered for Cassie. No one in the MRI unit has seen her." By now Wolf was all but screaming, his face red and his fists clenching. "In fact, no one in that *whole* damn hospital knows where the hell she is!"

The other beat of Quinn's heart, the better half of his soul, the sunshine to his darkness, was gone. Neither his mind nor his heart could comprehend it. No, this nightmare could not be happening. A cold chill zipped through his system, leaving his skin clammy. Trembling started in his head and quickly moved to every part of his body until he visibly vibrated. Had Chris—he'd no longer think of him as T-Bone, nicknames were for friends and friends didn't harm the people he loved—had he hurt her? Was his angel frightened? Was she wondering why Quinn didn't come and save her? Where in the *hell* could Chris have taken her? His legs gave out and, in wobbly slow-motion, Quinn fell onto his chair.

As though Jace were speaking in a long, hollow tunnel, he proclaimed Quinn in shock as he took his blood pressure. He draped a blanket over him and forced him to drink a bottle of vitamin-fortified water. When Quinn's phone dinged with an incoming text, he shook so badly he could barely slide it from the pocket of his jeans.

Jace slipped it from Quinn's unsteady hands and read the text for everyone. "*Can U find her before I kill her?*"

Quinn roared with fury and futile frustration. On legs that were shaky a minute or so earlier, he stood and heaved an empty chair across the room. Rage replaced Quinn's shuddering shock. Why? Why would Chris want to kill Cassie? Why not simply walk up to Quinn and put two bullets through his heart and one through his head? Why destroy the most beautiful soul who ever breathed?

Quinn tossed aside the blanket and began to pace. "I will kill the son of a bitch. Ryder, I know you're always armed. Give me a damn gun. You got a knife strapped to your leg?"

Wolf got in his face. "Quinn, sit your ass back down. Arlo, you might want to leave. We'll be forming an extraction team and we *may* use methods you cannot approve of, according to the vows you took to become a police officer."

Their conversation grew louder as each one made a point in his favor.

"Arlo, I respect that you deal in a world of right and wrong, black and white. But for a day or two, we'll be dealing in whatever it takes to achieve the desired objective, which in this case is saving my sister. Some things we'll talk about, maybe even do, you won't want to know."

Quinn's phone rang. This time he was able to snatch it from where Jace placed it on the table. The caller ID once again read Unknown. "Listen you son of a bitch. If you've harmed one hair on her head I will scoop your eyeballs out with a jagged-edged spoon. Then I'll skin you alive with a razor-sharp two-inch knife. Slowly and with great delight. Do you understand?"

"Son? I didn't think you had it in you. Damn, you had chills going up my back." The old man's voice was laced with pride. If only he'd shown that kind of approval for Quinn earlier in his life.

"Dad?" *Yeah, sure, my threatening to torture someone would make you proud of me, wouldn't it?*

"Did Chris abduct Cassie?"

"I just got a text from him."

"You were right. He's got property in Montana, but he's also got a warehouse in Tampa. You want the address?"

Quinn smirked. "Do I want the sun to come up tomorrow? Hold on. Need paper and pen." Someone placed the items in front of him. "Okay. I'm ready." He scribbled the address his dad gave him. "Thanks. I…" he cleared his throat. "I wasn't expecting this."

"There hasn't been a day in over three years that your mother hasn't told me how wrong I was in how I treated you. I wouldn't put up with that kind of bitching from anyone but her. I love her like, well, you find a woman you love to the point of madness, by all that's holy and unholy, you do what you can to hang onto her."

"I found my love three years ago, but was too dumb to admit it."

His dad chuckled—or was he having an asthma attack? The sound was so foreign to Quinn, he wasn't sure. "Then, by damn, you rescue her."

"We're organizing a team now."

"You'll do best with Noah Steele as your leader. He's got the most experience. Dan Wolford's no slouch, but he's too emotionally involved, Cassie being his sister." *How the hell does he know all this? Does he have a dossier on every person in my life?* "Your mother and I are flying down, arriving in four hours. I figure the best place to hook up with you would be the fire station after the extraction. Will they grant us admittance?"

"I'll see to it."

"Any equipment you need, you call this number. You go get her, son. I'd kill any bastard who tried to take my wife away from me. And I'd kill without a moment's hesitation. I expect you to do the same for your woman. I'll use any kind of power I have to back up whatever you and your friends decide to do. Is that clear?"

"Yes, sir. I can't thank you enough."

"Grandchildren. Your mother wants grandchildren." The line went dead.

Well, hell, if that wasn't the strangest conversation he'd ever had with his old man. He'd actually given him fatherly advice, spoken to him with pride and genuine concern. Expressing a strong degree of possessiveness for his wife wasn't unusual. His dad had always doted on his mother, demanding to know where she was and who she was with every moment of the day.

On the other hand, his mother had always been attentive and very involved in Quinn's life. Had that been the problem between him and his father? Was his dad envious of the attention his wife heaped on him as a youngster and teenager? He couldn't analyze it at the moment. The only things he could think of were finding Cassie and killing one Chris Mason with his bare hands.

Wolf and Arlo were still exchanging words about who would and who wouldn't be involved in the rescue of Cassie.

Jace shifted his chair to talk quietly with Quinn. "I take it that was your dad?"

"Yeah. Strangest, damn thing. I called him first because I was so frantic to help Cassie, swallowing my pride seemed miniscule, you know?"

Jace nodded. "I'd do the same for Wendy Anne in a heartbeat."

Quinn still couldn't grasp it. "Next thing I know he's giving me advice, hunting down property Chris Mason owns. He and my mother are flying here. Why, I haven't a damn clue. And he said if we needed any government equipment to let him know. After all these years—all my damn life—of trying to make him proud of me, he sounded like he was."

"You're right. That is strange. Sounds like maybe he had some growing up to do too. Give him a chance." Jace winked. "Bet'cha Cassie has him eating out of her hand in the span of an hour."

"I hope you're right." Quinn could barely choke out the words. *I hope we get her back so she can give the old man hell.*

Arlo finally left, taking Milt's phone containing pictures of Chris along for evidence. Wolf wiped off the whiteboard. "All right, children. Now that we know who the bad guy is, we don't need all of this shit." He glanced at Quinn. "What about Milt? Is he staying?"

Quinn gave the old coot the once-over. To edge him out of the action now would be just cruel. Hell, thanks to him they'd been able to identify Chris. "He's in."

Ryder slapped Milt on the shoulder. "Hell, yes. He's got experience in the security business and everything. He needs to stop eatin' those pork rinds though. Can you fire a weapon, Milt?"

"Shot a B-B gun once."

"See?" Ryder winked. "The man's experienced in firearms too."

Wolf marched over to Milt, stooped in front of him and aimed a stern expression that made the old guy squirm for a beat. "But can you follow orders without arguing? Because we aren't going to have time for any drama. Noah's the best man to head this team. Whatever he says, goes. There will be no back talk. Just action to get my baby sister back—unharmed."

Milt nodded. "I'm your man. I love Cassie as if she were my granddaughter. Ain't no one on this earth any sweeter, nor anyone who can throw a tantrum any more comical than her. God, that girl can make me laugh." He leaned forward and looked Wolf in the eyes. "Now listen, I've got a Cutlass V-8 that runs like the wind when you open her up. Has a huge trunk to hold guns and whatever equipment you need."

"Runs like the wind?" Quinn exploded. "Hell, it couldn't go over thirty on the way to the hospital last night."

Milt narrowed his eyes at Quinn. "That's cause you needed a good, hard talkin' to, son. I drove like a snail for a reason. Did you good to agonize a bit over what you said to that lovable young woman. Made you face up to the fact your actions have consequences, flashbacks or no. You still have to consider other people's feelings." He turned his attentions back to Wolf. "Have no fear. My car will purr at a hundred and ten, don't you worry about that."

Wolf stood and grinned in a manner that could only be described as pure evil. "Damn, I like this old motherfucker. Noah, start doing your magic and get a plan organized." He patted Milt's back. "Looks like we got our driver right here."

Noah lowered the movie screen. "I've used our location software—"

The station's alarm went off, and everyone in the room groaned. The dispatcher's voice sounded loud and clear as she announced the location of the fire. Noah held up his hand. "Remain where you are. I called in six extra people, four from another shift and two from another station to help us out for a couple days. We're covered. Greg and Eduardo will be in charge while we go after Cassie."

"Chris won't expect me to know the address of his warehouse." Quinn glared at Ryder. "I asked you this before. Need a gun and a knife. I can be in and out in a few minutes. He'll be dead and Cassie will be with me." He stood and paced the room, nerves crawling up and down his skin like ants. "I can't sit through another long session of listing facts and figures and making damn charts." His hands opening and closing. "I need to get to Cassie!"

Wolf stood, puffed out like a cobra ready to attack. "Sit. The fuck. Down. You think I don't feel the same way? You think Jace and I don't want to go to this warehouse, half-cocked, charge in and maybe make a helluva mess of things? Maybe get our Cassie killed in the bargain? We've got a hostage situation here. Forget that it's Cassie. Think only of the hostage. The hostage is our mission. And our mission will succeed."

The two men stood and glared at each other for several tense minutes.

"You know I'm getting damned tired of you ordering me around. Fuck all, man, you are not my big brother."

Wolf showcased that evil smirk he had. "I will be once you marry my sister. Think about it. A good, sound plan. Well executed. Smoothly and successfully achieved."

Quinn evaluated what Wolf said, found it sound and sat. *Damn, I'm so tired of fighting everyone.*

Noah popped open another soda. "Like I was getting ready to say, I've already entered the address to Chris's warehouse." He punched a couple of buttons and the screen filled with the image of the brick building, deserted by all appearances, with boarded-up windows, and located in a rough-looking neighborhood.

As Noah tapped a directional key, they scanned the three-hundred-sixty degree view of the building. "Barclay, why don't you work on the best and quickest route to get us there since you're more familiar with that area? And the fastest damn route out, preferably open highway where Milt can show us what that Cutlass of his can do in case we're followed."

"There won't be anyone left to follow us," Wolf stated.

Ryder nodded in agreement. "In and out. Clean kills. Boom. Done."

Milt swallowed so loud everyone in the room had to have heard him.

Quinn, who'd finally bought into the wisdom of Noah's detailed planning, rested his elbows on his thighs and dipped his head to peer into Milt's eyes. "You going to be okay with this?"

"I..." The old man's face paled.

"You'll probably be in the car the whole time, keeping the engine running. Jace will be with you, too, unless we signal him for help. But I don't suspect we'll need him. Between the five of us in and around the building, we'll be one hell of a surprise."

Milt nodded. "Asshole kicked Killer. Made him cry."

Ryder glanced up from the list of weapons and ammo he was compiling. "I'll make sure he never kicks another dog, buddy."

One by one, ideas were shared, discarded, improved upon and written on the whiteboard. Soon Ryder had the list of equipment they'd need. Some was readily available. The rest, Quinn procured with a call to his dad, who asked for thirty minutes to arrange a pickup spot.

Barclay and Ryder took off to do some recon of the building and the neighborhood. They were to take note of any security cameras. Depending on the foot and car traffic, Ryder would install some listening devices and a couple of cameras of their own. Signals were arranged. Meeting places planned. Jobs assigned according to everyone's past military experience and training.

Quinn, Wolf, Jace, Noah, Barclay, Ryder and Milt had dubbed themselves the Unholy Seven—and damned if they wouldn't be.

CHAPTER TWENTY

Cassie's nose wrinkled at the putrid odor of something decaying as she slowly woke up. Where the heck was she? This didn't smell like a hospital. The room was totally dark. Was she in the MRI tube? Shouldn't there be some mechanical noise?

A few men talked excitedly in another room, almost as if they were playing video games. One raspy voice was that of the nurse. Nothing made sense. What the heck was going on? She tried to roll over, but couldn't. Raising her head from the pillow, she struggled only to find her arms and ankles were tied to the bed.

The door flew open and a bare bulb snapped on overhead. Two men walked in. They looked enough alike to be brothers.

"So, you finally woke up? The buzzer I put under your pillow works great. As soon as the weight of your head lifts, the control board in my game room lights up."

"You're my nurse. Jimmy. Where am I?"

He pulled a chrome handgun from the back of his jeans. "You're one bullet from hell, Cassie Wolford." His other hand cupped her breast and she nearly vomited at his touch. "At least after I'm through playing with you." His laugh was maniacal. "What do you say I tear off this nightgown and take a selfie of my hand on your bare boob? I'll send it to your boyfriend, and he'll go freaking insane."

Cassie tilted her head to get a better look at him. He'd changed out of his turtleneck and scrubs into a t-shirt and baggie jeans. There were thick scars around his neck. "Aren't you T-Bone, Quinn's friend?" He'd told her about finding his only remaining team member hanging by a chain in a deserted warehouse. Why would he turn against Quinn?

He pressed the barrel of his gun under her chin. "I was never his friend. *Never*. Being head of the team in Chile should have been my job. DB had promised it to me. My security clearance was higher. My experience more extensive. But, no, Buck Gallagher saw to it that the position went to his son. Thought the undercover involvement would make a man out of him."

T-Bone snorted. "I'll confess the little shit did a decent job. Learned a lot of good intel. Too much, in fact. I had to keep Renata busy humping the kid so I could go about my business. Poor schmuck insisted the mole was back in DC." He ran his tongue up her cheek, and she shuddered. "Hell, one of them was me all the time."

The other guy slipped his hand under her nightgown, up her leg. "Chris, why don't we just go ahead and do her? We can videotape each other. Aw, fuck, she ain't got no hair. She shaves her cunt. What a fuckin' turn-on." His finger stroked over her and if she could have gotten her hands on him, she'd have choked him until his eyes bulged out.

"Not now. Maybe tomorrow, Kyle, after the younger two leave."

Chris produced a hypodermic needle. "You're going to have a long night without something to help you sleep."

Kyle kept touching her and peering at her privates as if he was fascinated by it. He rubbed his obvious erection. "She's a no-good cunt. Let me have her now."

If Chris put her to sleep again, what was to keep horny Kyle from coming in here and doing things to her? She had to make a plea.

"No, you'll make me sick and then I won't be of any use to you." She didn't want his dirty hands giving her an injection. Here she lay, tied up on some filthy mattress, in a deserted building with a gun pressed to her neck and she was worried about someone needing to wash his hands. What about the hand that kept stroking her intimately? Her skin started to crawl, and she fought the urge to throw up. She hadn't wanted any man to touch her there except Quinn.

Chris slipped the gun into the waistband of his jeans before he tore open a packaged alcohol wipe with his teeth and rubbed the material over the inside bend of her elbow. Struggling was no use with both her arms and ankles tied to the bed with ropes.

"It's not that potent. Just a small amount of Lorazepam, enough to put you out for a few hours so I don't have to keep checking on you." There was a prick and a slight burning where he injected the drug.

"You'll be out for three or four hours while my brothers and I play the latest Skylanders SWAT Force game. We like the volume high, so we can get the game's full effect. That's one nice thing about this part of town. No one bothers us if we make a little racket."

He ran his tongue up her face again and she swallowed the bile that rose in her throat. "See how thoughtful I am to put you to sleep so you don't hear the noise?" He cupped her breast again and pinched her nipple to the point of pain.

She refused to show any response.

"By the time you wake up, I'll be ready for a little diversion. Think I'll take that selfie for Quinn. Kyle and I might both have to screw you a few times before I kill you." He laughed. "Yeah, set up a camera and record it for Quinn to watch.

I never got to do that when I screwed Renata. We had this little signal though. If Quinn spent the night, she'd sing to him in the mornings. Then I'd know not to come knocking at her door. Tell me, does he still mourn her?"

Cassie's eyelids grew heavy and her thinking fuzzy. She imagined he talked about Montana and taking her there so he could keep torturing Quinn with pictures of them together. If this whack-job thought he could hold her captive and live to tell about it, he'd never met a Wolford before. He couldn't keep her drugged all the time. The first chance she got she'd show him what the ugly in the word bitch meant. Okay, so she was never good at spelling, but she knew how to crush a man's balls.

****

Milt could barely close the lid to his trunk. "Good God A-mighty, I haven't seen this many weapons since that movie with Bruce Willis, that weird John Malkovich and Helen Mirren. Man, she's one hot dame."

Quinn helped him slam the lid. "You mean 'Red'? Cassie and I loved both those movies. She keeps telling me to shave my head like Bruce." Just the mention of her name and all the things they'd done together, everyday things like jogging, watching movies and texting like crazy, reminded him of happy times. How could he have loved her so much and never realized it?

Milt stepped closer and glanced at the rest of the guys before he spoke. "I'm a little worried about you."

"How so?"

"What if you have one of those flashbacks in the middle of all this?" The old man flung his hand in the direction of the men separating equipment into piles. "You got any techniques you use?" Quinn looked away and shook his head. "Melvin, that's my brother who got them, used to use a focal point when he felt one coming on. Sometimes they hit him so fast he didn't have time to do anything, but when he felt the shakes and the sweats start, he'd relive the high-school championship basketball game. The other team was one point ahead, and Melvin had the ball. He dribbled down the court, glanced at the clock and saw three seconds left in the game. Three seconds, man. He was never the best at long shots. He was better under the rim, but his team needed him.

So he made the long shot and the basket and won the game. He relived that moment time and time again through a helluva lot of flashbacks."

Does this old man know how freakin' much I hate basketball?

"If I was you," Milt tapped Quinn's stomach, "I'd think about the day Cassie unloaded your U-Haul and got ahold of your saxophone. If that wasn't a day and a half." He snorted. "Her making that awful racket and every dog in the apartment complex howling like it was a full moon. Think on that, son. Make it your focal point. Hang on to it for dear life until the flashback passes."

Quinn stared at the man. God, he loved the old fart. He could get on a person's nerves in a heartbeat, but he cared about people. "Thank you, sir, I'll try my best to do that."

"Good boy. Good boy. I gotta tell you, for a retiree whose high point of the day is spying on the neighbors, this night is one kick in the ass." Milt practically bounced on his sandaled feet.

"You'll have to check with Noah for instructions on how much of this you can share with anyone. He'll debrief you on this entire mission."

Milt's head bobbed. "Top secret, huh?"

Quinn glanced over his shoulder at the rough-looking man who'd delivered the arms and ammo. There was something half creepy about the dude. "Yeah, Milt, top secret. This whole operation might be labeled that way."

Like how did Quinn's dad know about Barclay's beach cottages? Only his closest friends at the station were aware Barclay had recently inherited the property from his uncle. His family legacy was five small, beachside bungalows too dilapidated to rent to tourists. Yet Quinn's dad was familiar with these cabins in Indian Rocks Beach, not far from the Intracoastal Waterway bridge that became the well-traveled highway into Tampa. Still, Quinn had to admit, Barclay's private property, hidden among palms of various sizes, was the ideal place to make the switch of equipment.

An hour earlier, when the muscled, silent man had opened

the back doors of a black van marked "Sam's Catering", every ex-military man on the team acted like they'd gotten an instant woody. Words of "come to poppa," or "I'm in love," and "fuck me running" floated in the dark night. There were cases of guns, infra-red goggles, mobile communication devices, hand grenades as well as 30mm grenades, M320 grenade launchers mounted on M4 carbines, Mk48 machine guns, ammo, body armor, and both magazine and grenade pouches.

Now that the cases were either loaded into Milt's trunk or stacked on the ground to divide between the men, the driver of the black van reached across the front seat and retrieved a clipboard. "Which one of you gentlemen is Quinn Gallagher?"

"That would be me." He moved to stand in front of the stranger.

"According to my instructions, I need both you and retired Major Noah Steele to sign these forms." Quinn scrawled his name before handing the clipboard to Noah, and who the hell knew he'd been a Major? Noah had certainly kept that bit of information to himself. Once Noah signed, he handed the pages back to the man with a military bearing.

"Here's an envelope for each of you." He saluted them both. "Gentlemen, it's been a pleasure." Whoever he was hopped in his van and drove off.

Noah tore open his manila envelope and removed the thick set of papers. Using a flashlight, he scanned the pages. "Well, hell, guys, looks like we are now a temporary team of mercenaries, operating under the name Steele and Associates, assigned by the US Government to arrest one Christopher Mason and any of his accomplices for espionage, treason and kidnapping. We are authorized to use lethal force, if necessary." A round of "hoo-rahs" and "fuckin' A's" were uttered.

"Hell, we even get paid, and damn fine, too, thanks to these enclosed checks from a DB Enterprises Incorporated account at Bank of America." Noah turned to Quinn. "How did your dad know the name of every man going on this mission? Even Milt?"

"Hell, beats me." *I'm beginning to feel like he's looking over my shoulder every freaking minute of the day.*

Noah stared at him for a few seconds. "According to these orders, anything we do from this point out is legal as shit on a shingle." He held a card. "For all fatalities, we are to call this number for pickup. We're to use the same number if there are any survivors, although it is not advised there be any. They are our clean-up crew."

"They've ordered a kill mission." Wolf exchanged looks with Noah.

Ryder elbowed Quinn. "Damn, your old man must carry some heavy influence. Open your envelope and tell us what yours says."

Quinn broke the seal and removed two sheets of paper. The first was handwritten. Short and concise. "Forgive me. According to your mother, I've been a pompous fool. And we both know the woman is never wrong. Stay safe so I have a chance to make things right." On the second sheet, in a broad stroke of a Sharpie was one word: "Grandchildren!"

"Yeah, well I've got another word for you, buddy." Wolf elbowed him. "Wedding. You knock up my sister before you put a wedding band on her finger and I'll slice off your effin' balls."

The whole team was shining penlights over Quinn's shoulder, laughing at the one-word command and Wolf's reaction to it.

"Pompous ass never did have an ounce of patience." Still, the thought of Cassie carrying his child wasn't such a bad idea. Maybe in a year or two. For now, he'd count himself the luckiest guy alive to cover her heart-shaped face with kisses and tell her how precious she was to him. This mission had to succeed or both of their lives would end in one manner or another.

Ryder and Jace took the dark-blue van Ryder kept equipped with surveillance monitors for use on his second job. Once in place up the street from the warehouse, plans were for Milt to exit the Cutlass and join Jace to monitor all audio and visual communication.

Following the van, Milt drove the Cutlass into Tampa with

Wolf riding shotgun. Noah, Quinn and Barclay took the backseat.

Once they eased their vehicles into place, they put on their night-vision goggles and mobile communication devices. Milt shook each man's hand before he hopped into the van with Jace.

With quiet efficiency, the rest of the team slipped into their body armor and slung ammo and grenade pouches around their necks. Each took an M4 carbine with grenade launchers attached and an Mk48 machine gun. Noah did a final check of his own sniper rifle mounted with an infra-red scope.

While checking the volumes on everyone's mobile communication earpieces, Jace told them that microphones Ryder had set up earlier indicated four occupants of the building were busy playing a video game. "Sounds like Chris is whipping everyone's ass."

"Wait until he finds out what it's like to really get his ass whipped." Wolf reached for his machine gun, looping belts of ammo over his shoulders.

Noah took off on a silent run, his objective to take a sniper position on the roof of the building across the street. Barclay, the Ice Man, who had the reputation of moving like a ghost, would enter the building before anyone else. Ryder was going in as point man, followed by Wolf. Once Barclay, Ryder and Wolf gave Quinn the "all clear" signal—three taps to their mouthpiece—he was scaling the side of the building after his woman. By prior agreement, no vocal communication would take place to alert Chris or his cohorts. The three inside guys would take care of any occupants in the building. Noah would take out any who tried to exit the building and run. And, come hell or high water, Quinn would rescue Cassie.

The body-heat sensors Ryder had put in place, when he and Barclay did their earlier recon run, showed four humans in a room on the second floor and another in a prone position in a room down the hall. Jace transmitted the information to the men. Milt evidently counted the windows to the room that held the prone body they suspected to be Cassie and relayed that count to Quinn's earpiece. Quinn raised his hand in acknowledgment.

The plans they'd gone over and over, back at the fire station and again under the palm trees at Barclay's deserted cabins, until every step was embedded into their brains like how to change a flat tire on a car, were for Quinn to get Cassie free and clear of the building before the inside threesome opened fire. Plan B was for him to protect her with his life—as if he wouldn't anyhow—if the rest of the team were discovered before he got her out. And if a flashback started, he'd think about Cassie playing the hell out of Uncle Mat's saxophone—if he had the time before it overtook his mind.

Quinn tossed a grappling hook to the sill of the window Milt had indicated and climbed the side of the building, looping the rope around the arch of his foot for support. He pulled the crowbar Velcroed to the side of his leg and began the process of prying the rusted nails from the boards covering the window. Breezes blew palm fronds against his face, jogging his memories of the rain tropics of South America. *Focus on the mission. Only the mission. Only Cassie.*

He swayed back and forth until he braced himself against the building with his other foot. In the end, doing so was a good thing. It gave him extra leverage to pull out what few nails there were. And, thanks be to God, the glass that should have been behind the boards was gone. Two large palm trees and their fronds that brushed the side of the building, reminded him of the coves and inlets on the coastline of Chile.

He placed the two boards and crowbar on the floor of the darkened room as quietly as he could and crawled inside. By the sound of Cassie's gentle snoring, she was asleep. To keep her from waking up and making any fuss once she realized he was there, Quinn tapped his mouthpiece two quick times and then once to signal to the rest of the team he was inside.

He waited for their copy signal.

And waited.

Sweat poured from his body. His hands shook. What if none of his team was alive to respond? What if this mission failed too? He breathed deep, the memory of Cassie honking on the sax reverberating through his mind until he heard two quick taps followed by one from each of his squad members.

It was then he recognized he'd slumped onto the floor, leaned against the wall, his knees drawn to his chest and his gaze fixated on the woman he loved, lying on the bed. As awareness took hold, he realized he'd been chanting her name in a gravelly murmur.

CHAPTER TWENTY-ONE

The hand that clasped over Cassie's mouth jarred her awake, sending her into panic. Her heart pounded in her ears. It was a hand, right? Or was she dreaming? At least the hand wasn't touching her privates or her boobs.

Lips moved against her ear. "Angel?"

She *was* dreaming. The whispered word was soft and strangely urgent. Only one person called her by that nickname. Oh yeah, she had to be dreaming. Safety warmed and flooded her soul at the sound of his voice. How could Quinn know where she was or how could he have gotten inside the building unnoticed? Whatever. This was one great dream.

"Angel. Nod once if you can hear me, baby."

She complied. *If this is a dream, please let it continue through the night. Let me find shelter in the sound of Quinn's voice.*

"We've got a team here to get you out. Wolf, Jace, Ryder, Barclay, Noah. Hell, even Milt is here. But you must be quiet. No noise. Understood?"

Her drug-hazed mind slowly comprehended what he was saying. Was this...could this really be happening? She shook her head.

He repeated his words, and they permeated her sleepy, drug-induced mental state. A team? They'd come to rescue her? Those men wouldn't touch her again? She started sobbing, and Quinn pressed kisses to her face, whispering words of reassurance. "I love you. Did you think I wouldn't come for you? I'm going to remove my hand now. Remember. No noise." As soon as his hand left her mouth, his lips covered it, pouring out all the worry and relief she could sense pulsating from his body.

When the kiss finally ended, she whispered, "Put your ear to my mouth." He did and she told him about the buzzer under her pillow. Once the weight of her head left the pillow, the buzzer would alert Chris.

He shifted his head to whisper in her ear. "I'm going to cut your ropes. Then alert the guys. Be prepared for some gunfire. No screaming. Just do whatever I tell you. Okay, angel?"

She nodded. Gunfire? The guys must have brought along some pistols.

Quinn slipped a knife from his boot and cut the ropes at her ankles, briskly massaging them to get the circulation going. "I brought along slippers for your feet. Stretchy like we use for fire victims." His voice remained at whisper level. He covered her feet with the slippers and then ran the knife under the ropes at her arms and wrists. His strong hands rubbed her arms and he kissed the pulse points of her wrists while he rubbed the areas around them. Once more he put his lips to her ear. This time the ornery cuss ran his tongue around the edge of it. "Hold on while I notify the team."

He ran one hand through her hair as if he couldn't bear to stop touching her and depressed a button on whatever he spoke into. "Have a situation. Bastard put a weight-controlled button under her pillow. As soon as she lifts her head, a buzzer will go off to alert them."

"Copy. In ten seconds, move her and get the hell out." Was that Noah's commanding voice? "Synchronize now. Point. Zero."

Quinn depressed the Indiglo light on his watch, counting under his breath.

A blast shook the building, followed by three more. Plaster

shifted down from the ceiling like baby powder. *Good God, what kind of pistols are they shooting?*

In one smooth movement, Quinn lifted her from the bed, slung her over his shoulder and carried her to the window. She peered around his body to see how far up they were. Thank goodness they were only one floor off the ground. If they fell, they'd only suffer a broken leg, or something. She raised her head to look around. Milt jumped from the back of a dark van and scurried for his Cutlass. Quinn wrapped his hands around a rope and slid down, using his boots as anchors on the section of the rope below them.

Once they hit the ground and were on the run, he pressed his mouthpiece again. "Clear of the building and hauling ass for the Cutlass."

In a matter of seconds, the whole side of the building blew out, bricks flew everywhere. Dust and debris floated through the air like falling leaves. Wait, these guys had more firepower than little old pistols.

"Give me the total collateral damage." Noah's voice sounded again. Was he in charge?

"Two, sir. Our main objective and his brother, or so he claimed. Two wounded and in a world of hurt." Wolf laughed, of all things. "One might have to sit down to piss from now on, thanks to Ryder and the other smart-ass is going to need a knee replacement."

Out of the smoke of building destruction and fire, three soot-covered, smiling warriors approached, dragging two men.

"Put me down. I want Wolf." Quinn set Cassie on the ground and she took off running. Wolf dropped his hold on the hurt fellow and opened both arms for her to leap into. "Baby girl," the big tough guy choked out.

"Thank you for saving me. I've got the best oldest brother in the whole wide world." Her tears started again.

He swung her back and forth in a grasp so tight she could barely breathe. "Damn straight."

She hugged and thanked Ryder and Barclay. Then her gaze swept to the two men on the ground, bleeding and crying. "You!" She pointed to the one holding his knee. "You put your hand under my nightgown and remarked about my bald hootchie." She kicked him twice in the stomach. Took a step away before deciding that wasn't enough. She marched back, grabbed him by the hair and punched him in the eye. "No one has the right to touch me there."

Obviously sensing trouble, Quinn jogged over and placed the barrel of his rifle to the man's temple. "Trouble, angel?"

"His...his name's Kyle and he touched me someplace private and...and then...he called me a cunt."

"Oh, he's gonna have to die. No one calls my baby sister a cunt," sneered Wolf.

"We've been authorized to use any force necessary. Do what you think is right." Noah's footfalls sounded closer. Several of the streetlights were out; this area was really downtrodden. Through the haze, his shape finally took form as he approached from across the potholed street, his rifle slung over his shoulder.

Ryder stepped on Kyle's wounded knee and he cried out in pain. "A man who would treat a lady like that would probably rape her and not give it a second thought."

"He threatened to. He and Chris were going to set up a camera and tape them doing things to me." Now that the danger was over, she started to tremble. Her teeth chattered. The violation of having her genitals touched by a strange man would replay through her mind for a long time. Quinn enveloped her in his arms and kissed her face several times before turning her over to her brother.

"Wolf, you want to take her to the van so Jace can treat her for shock? Tell Jace I put some of her favorite chocolate bars in his first aid kit. I want to talk to this asshole for a minute."

Quinn pivoted toward the brother Chris called Kyle. "You touched my woman? You dirty, filthy bastard touched my woman?" By this time, Noah had joined them.

Cassie grabbed Quinn's arm. "Don't you dare do anything you'll regret for the rest of your life."

His expression, when he turned it on her, was feral. "Don't you get it? You *are* my life. And I'll hurt any bastard who tries to take you from me."

Wolf scooped her up, cradling her in his arms, and ran for the van.

"What will Quinn do to that man? I won't have him going to jail for murder. I have a wedding gown on layaway."

"And a veil." Wolf winked. "Let's not forget the veil edged in alternating rows of seed pearls and Austrian crystals."

"You've been listening."

He opened the back door and handed her in to Jace. "It's not like I've had any choice in the matter. Keep her in here. Quinn has a man he needs to teach some manners to." Jace wrapped a blanket around her and hugged her close. "Quinn told me to tell you he put chocolate bars in your kit for Cassie. The way she's shaking, she could probably use some sugar."

****

"What do you think?" Quinn poked Kyle's neck with the barrel of his rifle. "We've got authorization to kill him." The bastard had touched his angel and scared her.

Ryder slipped a long knife out of his cargo pants and sliced the zipper out of Kyle's jeans. "I say we cut his pecker off so he can't ever hurt another woman like he planned to do to our baby doll."

Not a bad effing idea in Quinn's opinion.

"Good idea." Noah leaned on his rifle. "For the charges he's got against him, he'll be in jail the rest of his life. His cell husband won't care if he's got a pecker or not. All he'll be worried about is his ass."

By this time, Kyle was a blithering crying fool. "I didn't mean nothin' by what I said to her."

Quinn knelt next to him and grabbed him by the shirt. "Did

you or did you not call my future wife a cunt?"

The stupid fool had the nerve to laugh. "Hell, what's wrong with that?"

Noah pulled a quarter from his pocket. "Heads, he dies. Tails, his pecker goes."

****

By the time Noah called the pickup number on the card included in his government manila envelope, Wolf, Jace, Cassie and Quinn were in the Cutlass with Milt. Ryder, Barclay and Noah would take the van back to the fire station.

First stop for the family in the Cutlass would be the emergency room to have Cassie's blood checked for traces of whatever drugs she'd been injected with and to apply clean bandages to her cutting wounds. While she was being examined, Milt and Jace would go to her apartment and pack her several changes of clean clothes and her toiletries. Because once Quinn got her home to his place, he wasn't planning on letting her out of his sight until he began to calm down, which he feared might be in twenty-two or twenty-three years. He held her on his lap as close as a person could be embraced and still breathe. He'd almost lost her. The most important person in his life and he'd almost lost her to crazy Chris.

Cassie ran her hand over his hair. "You can loosen your hold. I won't disappear."

"Don't talk to me. I'm so damn mad and so grateful at once; I know I won't make a bit of sense. I want to kiss you all over and paddle your ass at the same time." He buried his face in her neck. "I have never loved anyone the way I love you. I've never needed anyone the way I need you."

She held him to her for a few moments, stroking his head and shoulders, no doubt trying to ease some of his tension. "What did you do to Kyle?" She cupped his face in her hands and peered into his eyes. "I want the truth. What did you do to him?"

"One of us fixed him so he can never harm another woman. He's alive. He's just not the man he once was. Anything beyond that is a government secret. Besides, you're the one who gave him a black eye."

His angel leaned in and placed her lips to his ears. "He touched me where only you're allowed to touch me. And he called me a dirty name. I can't wait to take a long, hot bath to wash away his touch."

"Whatever you want, baby. There's just one thing. My parents flew down tonight and they want to meet you."

"After all I've been through these last twenty-four hours, now I'm going to have to meet your mother and Buck?" She held out her bandaged arms as if to signal her embarrassment. "I didn't think you and your dad spoke."

"I was so scared when I found out you were in danger, I called the only person who I knew could help—and he did. Somehow, thanks to all that's happened today, dad and I have reached a tentative truce. Believe me, no one's more surprised than I am." Quinn slipped the cell from his pocket and dialed his mother.

"Son? Son, do you have her? Is she safe? Are you okay?"

"Yes, we're both fine, but exhausted. We're taking Cassie to the hospital for lab work and a thorough physical. Where are you now?"

"The plane just landed and we're on our way to the car rental place."

"How long will you and dad be here? We don't know how extensive Cassie's examination will be at the hospital. We'll likely be too tired for conversation tonight. Could we meet for breakfast in the morning?"

"Why, yes of course." There was a note of disappointment in her voice. It had been over three years since they'd seen each other. "That might be best. We're rather tired ourselves from hurrying to meet the flight. Where shall we meet?"

"How about Sandy Seashells at eight? She makes the best eggs

Benedict, and I know how you like those." He gave her the address and she wrote it down.

"But you're both all right?"

"We'll know for sure after the blood work. They gave her some injections and we have no clue what they were."

"Oh dear. What terrible, terrible men."

"Is Dad nearby. May I speak to him please?"

Her voice warmed. "Yes, he's right here."

"Son?"

"I can't thank you enough. The equipment and the support was all top-notch. Without your help, I wouldn't have her."

"Well…" He coughed and cleared his throat. "Did I understand your mother's end of the conversation correctly? We're waiting until tomorrow morning to meet?"

"Yes, we don't know how many hours we'll be at the hospital having her checked out."

"I ah…" he laughed or wheezed again. "I understand she gave one of the men a black eye for calling her an obscene name."

Damn, how does he find this stuff out so fast? "Yes, sir, she did. The girl's got a mean right hook. She's a cross between a kitten and a tiger."

Cassie straightened on his lap. "Hand me the phone." She made a beckoning motion with her fingers. "I mean it, hand me the phone." He gave her the cell. "Mr. Gallagher? My name is Cassie Wolford and I want to thank you for all the help you provided in my being rescued. They were nasty men with mouths as foul as the sewer. Not that I'm averse to cussing someone out, you understand, I just think you ought to know them first, and, sir, I didn't know those ass-wipes."

His father's laughter boomed over the phone.

CHAPTER TWENTY-TWO

"Jace, does Wendy Anne know about all this excitement? You know how she worries. Did you call her?" The whole family tended to overprotect Jace's wife. She was entering her sixth month of pregnancy, after losing their first child.

Jace seemed lost in his own world, staring out the side window of the car. "No, she has no clue. She thinks I'm at work. But then we didn't tell her about the text either."

"What text?"

"What text? Oh, the one Quinn got the other day from that guy, threatening to kill you if Quinn went back to work in DC. You know, that's one thing I still can't figure out. What difference would it have made to Chris if our man went back into government work? Chris was doing his own mercenary thing. Right? I can't get it all to settle right in my head. Something's off."

"When did you get the text?" She tried making eye contact with Quinn, but he stared at his thumb, rubbing gentle circles over her knuckles.

"Maybe the dude was afraid of being discovered and arrested. He probably knew Quinn would keep digging through files until he figured out who wiped out his team." Wolf emptied the bottle of water he drank. "Man, I'll be glad to get a shower later. Once we know Cassie's all right, I'm going home to Becca to snuggle in for the night."

She slid off Quinn's lap to sit between him and Jace. "*When* did you get the text?"

Quinn rubbed his forehead and tensed. "The day you unloaded my U-Haul in one of your hissy fits."

"So, the first time we made love, you knew my life was in danger and you never thought to mention it?"

"Whoa!" Wolf held up both hands. "TMI in this car right now. I do not want to know my baby sister is having sex."

"Butt out, Wolf." She shifted in the seat to stare at Quinn. "You sent me off afterward as if I was nothing more to you than a one-night stand, knowing some wacko out there had me in his sights?"

He exhaled a shaky breath. "I didn't want you to be scared."

"So, when did you tell Wolf and Jace?" And *not* me.

"Last night, after we made up in the hospital."

"After you told Dr. Paxwell how much you respected me and my intelligence and my strength." The joy slowly seeped from her body like air from an inflated balloon. "Did you tell my sisters?"

"No, we were still arguing that out." Wolf glanced over his shoulder at her. "Jace wanted to, so they could keep a closer eye on things, but I was afraid you'd find out. Quinn wanted them to know, too, but I felt you were under enough stress, having started with the cutting again."

"Maybe, had I known, I'd have paid more attention to my instincts about the nurse Chris was imitating. I got this really bad sense about him. He didn't act like a real nurse. Nor did it seem kosher that he gave me a shot in the neck. Maybe, had I known, I could have protected myself. Wait. That policeman in the hallway. He was for me, wasn't he?"

Quinn clamped his broad hand over her thigh. "Calm down, angel. We were only doing what we felt was in your best interests."

"So I was in enough danger to have a policeman stand guard over me, but I wasn't important enough to tell?"

"Being in the hospital the way you were, what could you have done? That guy who followed you on the Kawasaki the other day?" Milt glanced in the rearview mirror when he stopped for a red light. "That was Chris. You were in more danger than you can imagine, sugarplum, and these guys were just trying to protect you the best way they knew how."

"How old am I going to have to be? Thirty? Forty? Fifty? How old before you all deem me strong enough to take care of myself?" She was tired and sore and in need of a bath. Yes, she was being cranky but, dammit to hell, she'd had a long, hellacious day. Her nerves were shot.

Quinn snatched his hand from her leg and glared at her. "Maybe when you start behaving in a more consistent manner, then we'll know how to treat you. One day, you're the sweetest person on this earth. The next, you're ready to fight whoever gets in your way. On another, you're on the phone to one of your big brothers because your car's not running the way it should or you can't get the stove to work right. Then, when things get really tough, you resort to the teenage behavior of cutting. So which Cassie are we dealing with here, because I'm damned tired and I'd like to know."

Quinn tapped Milt's shoulder. "Pull over up here. I'll call for a taxi. I've had enough of Cassie's tirades. I need to be alone for a while."

"You're an asshole for talking to me like that."

He smiled in an almost cold-hearted way. "Hell, I've always been an asshole. You just now figuring that out?"

Milt eased the Cutlass to a stop, and Quinn waited for him to get out to open the door from the outside. "Have you given any thought to the fact that all of us put our lives on the line for you tonight? We risked everything for you and you want to throw a teenage bitch fit because you were left out of the loop.

Well, try thinking what the last forty-eight hours have been like for your brothers and for me. You know, trying to carve out a spot in your life is damn hard for any man when your big brothers are always going to come first."

He leaned toward her until they were nearly nose to nose. "And a woman's pussy is called a cunt. Grow the fuck up and learn to say it." The door opened and Quinn jumped out. He strolled across the street with his hands jammed in his jeans pockets. His head down and shoulders slumped, he walked out of her life, but most definitely not out of her heart.

Milt settled himself behind the steering wheel and started the car's motor again. "He's coming down from that flashback he had. My brother sometimes acted the same way."

Wolf's phone rang and he answered. "Okay. Will do."

"Was that Quinn?" Jace turned from the window.

"Yeah, he wants to know how she is once the physical is over."

"Like he cares." She folded her arms and shifted in her seat. The things he said to her were so not true.

"What Quinn said held a lot of truth. You keep bragging how you're twenty-one, yet you still expect baby sister rights." Jace glanced at her, his eyes narrowed in an expression almost accusing her of something. "Wendy Anne said nearly the same thing to me once. That she felt at the bottom of my female priority list. I almost lost her to you sisters soon after we married. Not that she doesn't love you all. She does. Sometimes, she just feels lost in the crowd. We're a close-knit family. Not everyone can handle the strong bond we share."

Jace ran a hand behind his neck and kneaded the muscles there. "Quinn had a flashback tonight, trying to rescue you. I never understood the torment of that experience until I heard it coming from his soul. With Milt and me hearing every bit of communication going on, it was rough hearing Quinn fighting his demons. Made chills go up and down my spine. He finally worked through it by chanting your name over and over."

"Damn near brought tears to my eyes." Milt shook his head as he pulled up to the emergency room entrance. "You brothers take her on in. I'll find a parking spot and wait in the waiting room once I get some coffee." He got out to open everyone's doors and glanced back in the direction from which they'd come. "I hate the thought of him out there all alone. Claimed he'd call a taxi, but I bet he's not in the presence of mind to do it. He'll just keep plodding along until he sees home or the station or some other spot he recognizes."

****

A gentle rain had started sometime during Quinn's trek home; he couldn't recall when. Before long, the squishing droplets had turned into a stinging precipitation, plopping off wide palm fronds. He'd found Cassie and lost her again, all in the span of an hour or more. A wiser man would have kept his damn mouth shut, but sometimes she drove him fucking nuts. He loved her, but, hell, she needed to understand a man had a right, a duty, an innate need to protect his woman.

An all-night restaurant sat at a corner, its lights blinking a cheap-ass red and yellow welcome. He stepped inside and slid into a booth. The odors of burgers frying and coffee brewing made him realize his stomach was so hungry it was chewing on his backbone. He ordered a cheeseburger special with extra fries, apple pie and coffee. It didn't take him long to wish Cassie was there to share the meal with. God, what had he done yelling at her like that?

He beat the bottom of the ketchup bottle with his palm. Okay, so maybe not telling her about the text was wrong. Maybe. But if he had it all to do over again, chances are he'd do things the same way.

Still, the issue with the text wasn't the only thing stuck in his craw. Having her break free from his arms to run into her big brother's chafed his ass like hell too. He'd played second fiddle to his dad's career and his mother's devotion to her husband. Damned if he'd come in second or third place to her brothers. Until tonight he'd never noticed or comprehended the strength of her connection to them. And, fuck all, it shamed Quinn that he was jealous of her family, especially when they'd treated him so well.

He paid his bill, left a generous tip for the waitress who looked as exhausted as he felt and then turned the corner toward his neighborhood. His apartment complex finally came into view and he trudged one rain-sodden boot in front of the other. A hot shower and he and Furball would sleep for hours. Right now, he didn't care if he made it to work on time or not. He didn't much care about anything.

His jeans were so wet he could barely get his fingers in his pocket to retrieve his keys. He opened the door and was surprised that Furball lay on the top of his computer. The only time the cat laid on it was when the laptop was warm from recent use. "Did you and your bottomless pit of a stomach miss me?" Quinn bent to untie his boots and take them off before dragging mud through his apartment. The first thing he saw behind his feet was a pair of shiny black leather shoes. The second was total darkness.

****

The incessant ringing of his cell phone slowly pulled him from his unconscious state. Furball's sniffing his face and hair further woke him. He finally shoved the cell from the pocket of his damp jeans. "Yeah." Christ, his head hurt.

"I was beginning to worry." Wolf's voice boomed over the phone and Quinn winced at the loud noise. "This is the third time I've called you."

He gingerly touched the pulsing spot on the back of his head and looked at his bloodied fingers. The room spun when he tried to sit up. "Someone was in my apartment when I got home. He hit me across the back of the head and knocked me out. As soon as the place stops spinning, I'll get up off the floor." He relaxed against the linoleum of his foyer. "Until then, I'll just lie here…

Wait! Cassie. Is she okay?"

"She'll be fine after some rest. We're on our way over. Don't move." The line went dead.

Don't move? Hell, as if I could with my apartment turned into a fuckin' merry-go-round.

The next thing he knew four pairs of eyes were peering down at him while four pairs of knees pushed into his sides. How did they get in his apartment? Oh yeah, Milt kept a set of keys.

"He's white as a sheet." Cassie pressed feather-light kisses to his face.

Quinn reached to cup her cheek. "Angel, will you be okay? What did the doctor say?"

"He said I'm to crawl in bed with the best-looking man I can find and stay there for hours and hours."

"Lucky bastard." Too bad it wouldn't be him. Not after the way he'd talked to her.

Jace rolled Quinn onto his side and examined his head. "Look at the size of that goose egg. Someone get me a clean, wet, soapy washcloth. I need to see how bad it is after I remove the dried blood."

Cassie hurried off.

Wolf tugged off Quinn's wet t-shirt. "What happened? Can you remember? Cassie, get him some dry clothes too. He's drenched."

Damn, does he need to yell? I already have bombs going off in my head.

"I walked home in the rain. As soon as I stepped inside I wanted to take off my wet boots. The cat was lying on the lid to my laptop, which was odd, because the only time he lays there is when it's warm."

"Like after someone's been using it?" Wolf glanced at the computer on Quinn's desk.

"Yeah. Then I bent over to untie my boots and I saw these shoes behind me and some bastard hit me in the head."

Cassie returned with a wet washcloth and an armful of clothes.

Jace started cleaning off the wound. "He ought to have stitches. I'd say about five or six."

Quinn wasn't going back to the hospital. "Hell no. Put some butterflies on it. My hair will eventually cover the scar.

"I can drive him." Milt looked and sounded exhausted.

"No. You need to take care of Killer. He's been alone all day and night. You get some rest. Honest, man, I'm not going to the hospital. Go on home, now, and thanks for everything. We'll talk tomorrow evening. I'll take you out for some Italian, that place you like with the cute waitresses."

Milt beamed. "You got it, buddy. If you two young guys can handle him, I'm going downstairs and hitting the hay." His knees creaked when he stood. "Man, I wouldn't have missed today for anything. I felt useful again. Getting old sucks. A man feels damn invisible." He opened the door and ambled out.

Wolf was on the phone. "Ryder. Got another situation. When Quinn got home, someone was in his apartment and knocked him out. He's going to need some stitches. Looks like whoever it was snooped on Quinn's laptop. I'm thinking his apartment might need to be swept again. Thanks, pal." Wolf ended the call.

"He's coming over to check the place out." He thumbed in a number. "Becca, baby, can you come over to Quinn's place and drive us to the ER? Someone hit him in the back of the head and he's going to need some stitches."

"I don't need any fucking stitches." Was everyone freaking deaf in this family?

"Thanks, gorgeous."

****

Six stitches later and Cassie had her damn wish. With her encouragement, emergency room staff had shaved his entire head. And damn if she hadn't taken to calling him Quinnie Bruce. But at least she was talking to him, and maybe they stood a chance at working things out.

Ryder called him just as they were ready to leave the hospital. He'd found six cameras and eight listening devices. He only removed seven of the bugs, hooking up the eighth, found in the kitchen, to a voice-activated recording of Furball meowing and purring looped in with some Lady Gaga tunes. Ryder's thinking was if none of the bugs recorded any sounds, whoever was putting them in would only return and install more.

At that moment, all he wanted was a hot bath and a soft bed. The fact that his angel insisted on joining him was almost lost on his exhausted mind. After their baths, they snuggled between the sheets and, under the influence of both of their pain medicines, they quickly fell asleep in each other's arms.

Until the alarm went off at seven o'clock for them to meet his parents for breakfast.

His raging hard-on ached so badly for release against the warm, rounded bottom she had shoved against his groin, he kissed her neck and shoulders while his hands fondled her breasts. She rolled over in his arms and pushed him onto his back.

"I was wrong to leave your arms yesterday to run into my brother's." She slithered down his chest and abdomen and then twirled her tongue around the head of his cock. "I won't ever put anyone before you again." Her lips curved in that lovable ornery way she had. "Quinnie Bruce." Then she licked the drop of pre-come from the slit in his head and worked magic with her tongue and mouth.

He fisted her hair. "Angel. God that feels so fucking good." She took all of him into her mouth until the tip banged the back of her throat. Then she reached for his nipple ring, gave it a few tugs while she sucked and licked, sending him right over the edge of sexual madness.

CHAPTER TWENTY-THREE

Cassie removed her bandages before dressing to meet Quinn's parents. Her cuts were healing nicely. She wore a pale purple long-sleeved cowl-neck sweater, dark purple jeans and black low-heeled boots. Although she kept telling herself she didn't need to make an impression, she still battled the flutter of gigantic butterflies.

"Should I wear my hair up or down?" She twisted and turned in front of the mirror, holding her hair off her neck, thinking of how she could pile it on top of her crown.

"Now, that's just plain mean." Quinn leaned against the doorway to the bathroom, his arms folded across his light blue button-up shirt. The back of his head was too swollen to slip on one of his typical t-shirts. "You made them shave my head and now you want *my* advice on how you should wear *your* hair?"

She snuggled against him, enjoying the smell of his woodsy soap and cologne. "I don't see why you're complaining. You didn't mind fisting your hands in my hair earlier."

He laughed and smacked her ass. "Wear it down and tousled so they know what an inconvenience meeting them for breakfast is." He backed her against the wall, his hands on her hips. " Cause I could be riding you long and hard right now. There's something on the bed for you."

She pulled back and glared at him. "Oh, I'll just bet there is."

"Look at it while I feed Furball and give him some fresh water."

On his freshly made bed lay a calendar opened to the month of June and a red magic marker. A post-it note was stuck to the calendar. "Pick any date not X'd out and drawl a circle around it." She sat down, calendar in hand and stared at the month. The only days not crossed out were Fridays, Saturdays and Sundays. What was she doing? Planning for a day of scuba-diving? A weekend at Disney World? What?

She carried the calendar and marker out to the kitchen and smiled at Quinn hand-feeding the cat treats. Sliding onto one of the bar stools between the kitchen and living area, she slapped the plastic calendar onto the counter.

"What date did you pick, angel?"

"What am I choosing a date for? Knowing what we'll be doing that day might help me chose."

He crossed the room and folded his arms on the snack bar directly across from her. His blue-grey eyes bore into hers and softened. "I'm hoping we'll be getting married."

Focused on the "M" word, her mind froze. Evidently her jaw gaped because Furball came over and stuck his nose in her open mouth and sniffed. "M...Married?"

"Yeah, I know it's customary for the man to present the future bride with an engagement ring first, but with my parents in town, I thought it would be nice to announce a date to them. That is if you still want to marry me."

"But it has to be June? Don't couples usually pick a date together?"

"I'm an alpha male and I make no apologies for it. Where you're concerned, I'll be possessive as hell, indulgent at times and adoring of most everything you do...as long as you put me first most of the time. I chose June because April's getting married in April. Wolf and Becca's big day is in May. If June's too soon, which month would you prefer? It gets so damn hot here in August, I'd rather not put on a tuxedo then. What are your thoughts?

October? November?"

"I want a house and I want babies."

One of his slow, sexy-as-hell smiles spread. "I think we can handle two children and a modest rancher."

She snatched the marker off the counter and pulled the cap off with her teeth. "Then, Quinnie Bruce," she circled the second Saturday in June. "We've just set a date to start making babies. Do I have time to send a mass 'save the date e-mail' to everybody?" She clapped her hands in excitement.

"You send your email while I call for a taxi. My Harley's at the station and the Jeep's got four flat tires thanks to Chris. Your car's not here. We'll start getting our lives back to normal this afternoon."

Cassie flipped open his laptop and opened a couple of programs. "Face it. You're marrying me. Your life will never be normal again. I'll just announce the date in the e-mail. We'll decide on the time of day and location later."

****

Quinn had his arm firmly around her waist when they entered Sandy Seashells, one of the best places to eat breakfast in Clearwater. A middle-aged man and woman stood when they walked in. He hugged the older woman, her blond hair shoulder length and eyes a clear blue. "Sorry we were late, Mom. We were setting a wedding date. This is Cassie Wolford, my future bride."

His mother pressed a hand to her expensive silk blouse. "A wedding date? Well, this is certainly news!" She wrapped Cassie's hands in hers. "I hope you'll call me Selena or Mom." Her warmth shone through. No wonder Quinn talked so fondly of her.

"Selena, I hope you'll save the second Saturday in June for our wedding. The whole weekend, actually. I could probably use your opinion on a lot of last-minute things."

A blush of excitement kissed her cheeks. "Oh, nothing would

please me more. Buck, our boy is finally getting married and settling down. Isn't Cassie gorgeous? No wonder he fell for her." She reached out to touch Cassie's angel necklace. "What a beautiful piece of jewelry."

"Thank you. This means a lot to me. It was a present from Quinn. He calls me 'angel' as a nickname."

Selena blotted her eyes. "Isn't that the dearest thing, Buck?" She glanced at her son. "He must love you very much."

If Selena was friendly warmth, Buck was some weird-assed ice.

"Why in God's name did you shave your head?" The self-important man sat and flicked his linen napkin over his lap. "You look like a dick with ears."

"Buck!" Selena elbowed him, sadness edging the deep blue of her eyes.

While the waitress poured them cups of coffee, Cassie glanced at her future husband, the muscles in his jaw twitched. Is this what he'd put up with from his father? Well, Quinn might be the alpha in their relationship, but she was the momma bear. And maybe it was time she made that fact clear.

She smiled and leaned toward Buck-the-jerk. "It was my idea he shaved. You see, his bald head matches my bald cunt."

Quinn spewed coffee all over his dad's pristine white shirt. Once he quit coughing, he wrapped his fingers around Cassie's chin. "God, woman, you do brighten my life."

From that point on, breakfast was strained. She was sorry if she'd added to the tension, but Quinn made it clear with little touches here and there that he wasn't upset with her. They ate off each other's plates, something they'd always done. She kept a close eye on the time and, on the hour, opened a bottle of medicine and tipped two pills into Quinn's outstretched hand.

"Why is he taking drugs?" Honest to Pete, if Buck's forehead wrinkled anymore, one could play it for a harp.

"He had six stitches in the back of his head last night." Quinn's hand squeezed her thigh in silent warning. "He had a work-related accident."

Selena's expression filled with concern. "So that's why his head is shaved?"

"Yes. If Buck would have been less rude, I wouldn't have needed to be crude in return, but no one insults my man and walks away unscathed."

"You're a very protective woman." Selena's cup stilled partway to her mouth. "I like that."

"I was raised in a protective family. A lot of it rubbed off. Even an alpha needs someone to take care of him, spoil him a little bit."

Quinn's pinky finger rubbed back and forth over her pussy— thank God for the tablecloth that hid what his fingers were doing to her. The blueberry pancakes trembled off her fork before it reached her mouth. "Need some help, angel?" He winked before jabbing a forkful of pancakes and feeding her a bite.

****

Two days later, Cassie rang the doorbell at Becca's townhouse. As soon as the door opened, her future sister-in-law enveloped her in a hug. "Can you believe it? Three brides in three months? This family knows how to do romance right." She was laughing when she stepped back. Her expression quickly changed.

"Cassie, what's wrong?" She led her into the living room where Einstein sat obediently on his chair. He wiggled and whined for Cassie's attention. She sat on the floor and patted for the German shepherd to join her.

"If you have the time, I need to talk to you as a reporter."

"Of course."

"I'm getting all these weird vibes and I don't know if I'm truly sensing something wrong or just overreacting to nothing."

Becca opened a desk drawer and pulled out a tablet and a couple of pens. She curled up on her sofa. "So you want to see if

I get a strange gut feeling too?"

"Yeah." She scratched behind Einstein's ears. "Or tell me to let it go, and I will, because I trust your reporter instincts."

"Tell me everything you know. Preferably in order, but it doesn't have to be. Our minds don't always recall things in a precise pattern." Becca pulled out her rubber band and fingered her long red hair into a tighter ponytail before winding the band around her tresses again. "Where do you want to start?" She held out a hand. "Do you want a can of soda and some cookies? I just made some snickerdoodles."

"Sure. Is that why it smells so good in here. It's the baked cinnamon and sugar."

Einstein whined.

Becca pointed at the exuberant dog. "You get one doggie chew. No cookies."

Cassie was sure the dog whined, "Awl, Mom."

Cassie moved to the other end of the sofa once Becca set a plate of cookies and two cans of soda on the coffee table. Einstein stretched out on the floor and chewed his rawhide treat, although one eye stayed on the plate of home-baked treats.

"Telling you this has to be private. I'll be sharing some of Quinn's relationship with his dad and I'm not sure how he'll feel about that."

"He's already told Wolf, hon. I don't think you're betraying a trust."

Cassie started talking and Becca took notes. Cassie reached for another cookie and stared at Becca. "When Chris had me captive, he told me something."

"Go on."

"He said after the shitstorm happened in Chile, Quinn insisted there was a mole in DC, in either the State Department or the DEA, but that he—Chris—had been *one of them* all the time."

"One of them. He used the expression 'one of them'?"

"Yes." Cassie shuddered at the memory. "When he pressed the

barrel of his gun under my chin, he insisted Quinn had never been his friend and that being head of the team in Chile should have been Chris's job. He claimed DB had promised it to him. That his security clearance was higher and his work experience more extensive than Quinn's. But Buck Gallagher gave the position to Quinn. Thought the undercover involvement would make a man out of him. Now, why would he help Quinn's career when he wouldn't even go watch him play football in college? Does that make sense to you? Because it doesn't to me."

"Evidently the man's career meant more to him than his son." Becca glanced at her. "You're sure Chris used the specific initials DB?"

"Believe me. I remember every word he and his brother said to me. Every disgusting word." She gave an involuntary shudder.

Becca stopped writing and stared off. "Let me check something for a second." She stood and opened the small middle drawer of the desk, removing a bank envelope. She dumped out a deposit slip and a check which she studied for a minute. "Did you know every man involved in your rescue was paid and paid quite well?"

"No. Quinn never mentioned it."

"Look at the check."

Becca handed it to Cassie who gasped at the amount. "Ten thousand dollars?"

"Now look at the account the check was drawn on." Becca pursed her lips.

"DB Enterprises Incorporated? Holy hell!" Cassie handed the check back as if she couldn't bear to touch it. The paper seemed dirty, somehow. "What are you thinking?"

Becca placed the check back in the envelope, returned it to the drawer and reached for another cookie before she sat. "Gut instinct? Whoever runs DB Enterprises is the real mole, or the chief mole, in the department. I'm betting he had a group of eager young men working for him, like Chris, and offered them promotions if they did whatever he ordered. Enter Mr. Gallagher, who wanted to help his son get ahead. Evidently he had more influence and used it."

"He made sure Quinn got that assignment in Chile."

Becca nodded. "Which could explain his anger when the mission went badly. He'd stuck his neck out to promote his son and then things went belly-up, making Mr. Gallagher look like a fool."

"A man and his pride."

"Oh yeah," Becca breathed. "You don't ever want to mess with a man's pride. So, Quinn resigns and things are fine and dandy for a few years. Until…"

"Until Quinn sends out feelers for job openings in the State Department and the DEA. Within hours, the text arrives threatening my life."

"Makes sense, doesn't it?" Becca guzzled her soda.

"Yes. Yes, it does."

Becca studied her notes. "We need to find out who this DB is. That could be a very big key." After reaching for her can of soda, she held it partway to her mouth. "Jace has his doubts, too. He said it was like Buck knew everything about Quinn's life, like he was keeping close track."

"Why do that when he refused to talk to him?"

"I know. Right? It's all weird. Jace said the old man came by the military equipment and the funds to pay them awfully fast when you consider how slowly the government moves in every other area."

"There's something else. When I met Quinn's parents, I could see no family resemblance between the three of them. While Selena has deep blue eyes, they're not like Quinn's. Buck is tall, thin to the point of being gaunt, blond thinning hair, green eyes and a weak chin. Neither parent has a strong, square chin like Quinn or dimples. I saw zero family resemblance."

"You think he was adopted?"

Cassie shrugged. "I don't know. There's like this emotional disconnect with his dad. He showed zero concern—zero, mind you—when he found out Quinn had stitches in the back of his head. Selena expressed the typical worry of a mother, but the old man could have cared less. He was rude to Quinn and I gave him a dose of attitude right back."

Becca laughed. "I'll just bet you did."

"The man's face turned beet red and his eyes all but shot shards of ice. He's not used to being challenged. I don't like him, nor do I care for the way he treats Quinn." Cassie leaned forward, her arms draped over her knees. "What if Buck was the intruder in Quinn's apartment the other night?" She glanced at Becca to gauge her reaction. "I heard Quinn talking to his dad on the phone, telling him he was taking me to the emergency room and didn't know how long it would take the doctors to run tests and check me out. We were going to meet them that night but were both too tired after the rescue, so Quinn set up a time to meet them for breakfast. Then we argued, and Quinn went straight home. Maybe he surprised his father's snooping."

"You think his father could have knocked him out?" Becca's eyes were wide with astonishment.

"When you think of a man telling his only son he is no longer his parent and he is not allowed to call him father or dad, then I think a person like that is capable of most anything." She pointed to Becca's notes. "Are you going to show these to Wolf?"

"Yes, honey, I am. We don't keep secrets. Trust is a big deal with us. When we first got together, I didn't trust men and he didn't trust reporters. It's taken us a lot of work to get beyond those trust issues, but we have, by being totally honest with each other. I'll have to talk to him about all this." She tapped her pen on the tablet.

"Quinn and I have a few issues, too, although we're slowly talking them out."

"Both Quinn and Wolf are alphas. They need to know they run the pack." Becca laughed. "Even if they don't always, we just get smart at letting them think they do. But there's nothing like being loved by an alpha. The passion will never die. And you will always have someone in your corner, on your side. Life can be tough. Having someone standing by you all the time makes it easier and more enjoyable.

"Will you investigate these things farther?" Cassie jerked her chin toward the tablet.

"Once Wolf and I talk it over, yes. Something's not right here. I think once I present the facts to my editor, he's going to insist I do a full investigation. Do you think Quinn's mother would talk to me if I called? I could begin the conversation under the guise of wedding preparations. Ask her if she'd like to come down to help chose a venue for the service."

"Yes, that might work. I'm betting Selena would be more open once she gets away from her iceberg husband. Becca, he even looks at Quinn as if he can't stand him. He gives me the creeps."

"Can you get me her number?"

"She gave it to me. I have it on my cell." She spun through her contacts. "Here it is." And read it off for Becca to jot down.

"This has a potential of being a case for treason. I have a friend who's a reporter at the Washington Post who would be all over this in a heartbeat and help protect my name. That will be Wolf's biggest concern—that I stay safe. Meanwhile, you'll need to talk to Quinn. We can't keep him in the cold or have him blindsided by this."

"I agree."

CHAPTER TWENTY-FOUR

Thanks to Quinn's encouragement, Cassie reduced her hours at the beauty shop to only accommodate her regular customers who'd followed her from her shop after it was destroyed by the fire. His thinking was she'd have more time to move out of the apartment she'd shared with Sara and Misty and in with him. Plus, as he loved reminding her, she had a wedding to plan.

Even as they enjoyed their time together, tensions simmered in the background. Quinn was pissed his father had changed back to the old iron-assed Buck he'd been before Quinn'd called about the threatening text, and Cassie couldn't seem to find the right time to bring up her suspicions about Quinn's father.

On the other hand, his mother was thrilled to be included in the early stages of the wedding planning. Selena and Becca spoke often by phone. Cassie called her every day too. It didn't take Selena long to confide how unhappy she was. The time had come to tell Quinn.

Determined to make tonight the night for the talk, Cassie fixed him his favorite lasagna and put it in the oven before charging back to the bathroom for a quick shower. She'd had a complete Brazilian wax earlier at the shop so he could enjoy her bald hoo… er…cunt. One way or another she'd get used to calling that part of her body by a word she'd always found offensive.

She sat on the edge of the bed, rubbing peaches and cream lotion into her skin when keys jangled in the lock.

"Angel?"

"In the bedroom."

"Is that lasagna I smell?" Quinn stopped and leaned a shoulder against the doorway, his eyes turned a stormy blue as they took their fill. "Lasagna and a naked woman on my bed." He slipped a pair of pink handcuffs from his pants pocket. "Only one thing could possibly make my life any better."

"Oh no, Quinn Gallagher. You are *not* handcuffing me to the headboard." Just to torment him, she shifted on the bed and raised one knee to give him a full view of her newly waxed cunt.

That slow, sexy-as-hell smile she loved so much spread, creasing his cheeks with those dimples that did it for her. He swung the handcuffs on his index finger. "Lay back angel. I've got a few surprises for you. Don't you like surprises?"

"Not if they come with handcuffs." She stuck out her lower lip, hoping he'd suck on it out of revenge for her arguing with him. *Actually, why am I arguing with him?*

She lay back with her hands over her head. "What kind of surprise do I get?"

"First the handcuffs or you don't get to see." He snapped the pink, fur-lined cuffs on her wrists and then propped a foot on the bed.

For Pete's sake!

"New sneakers? You had to handcuff me to show off your new sneakers?"

He pranced around the bedroom, his hands in his pockets. "Hey, this is a special occasion. It's not every day a man gets new sneaks. They reminded me of you." He raised a leg to show one off again.

She narrowed her eyes. "Grey sneakers reminded you of me?"

"It's the green, angel. The green trim matches your eyes. Now, spread your legs."

Her knees pushed together. "No."

Quinn made a tsking noise. The man was certainly in a playful mood. "Gee, too bad. I had another surprise or two to show you, but your legs have to be spread first."

She rolled her eyes. *Damn fool man.*

He reached a hand behind his shoulders and tugged off his shirt. Then he sat on the edge of the bed and untied his new sneakers. He glanced toward her, one eyebrow cocked. "I'm still not seeing that pretty bald cunt. Guess I'll put the handcuff key and the other surprise in the desk drawer." He sauntered toward the bedroom door. "In case you've forgotten, the desk is in the living room.

"I know where the damn desk is. I just dusted it the other day." Still, she spread her legs, thinking of how she would get revenge. "Okay, hot lips, I'm showing off what you want to see."

He stopped but did not look at her.

"And what is that object called?" The tone of his voice brooked no room for error. He wanted to hear her use *that* word.

"It's called a hootchie-cunt."

His shoulders shook with laughter. Did she know how to get to her man, or what?

Quinn slowly turned. "Being alpha in this marriage is going to be a constant battle with you, isn't it?"

She spread her legs wider. "Well, if you don't think you can handle it. I guess I've learned how to give awesome head for nothing."

He shucked his pants and briefs, removing two items before tossing the clothes on the floor. Then he crawled onto the bed between her legs, lowered his head and ran his tongue along her slit.

She moaned his name. Maybe the man did know some cool games to play. He ran his tongue around her clit a couple of times. Make that hot games, because she was definitely getting more heated with every stroke of his very talented tongue. When he drew her pleasure button into his mouth and sucked on it, she screamed his name in climax, while he wrapped his arms around her waist and held her to him until her spasms ceased.

"Are you ready to finish playing the game now?" His gaze slowly rose to lock on hers. "I've got something in each hand." He opened one. "In this one is the key for the handcuffs, and I promise to massage your arms to get the circulation going again. So, choosing the key has its benefits." He held up his other closed hand. "In this one is something that stops the circulation forever. It's called an engagement ring." He rose onto his knees and placed both hands behind his back, switching the contents from one hand to the other. Then he presented both at his naked waist, a pleased-as-hell smile brightening his features. "Chose one, angel."

Oh, no, he's not getting ahead of me.

"But I can't pick a hand with both of mine restrained. You'll have to open the handcuffs so I can touch the hand I think has the diamond hidden in it."

He threw his head back and laughed. "Jace warned me about you. Just tell me left or right."

She had him now. "Left."

He uncurled his fingers and a key rested against his palm.

"But that's *your* left. I meant my left. Besides, do you want to tell everyone you slipped a diamond on my finger while you had me handcuffed to the headboard?"

His sexy grin spread again and he tilted his head. "Yeah. Yeah, I think I do. Our kids will love the story." He kissed the square diamond set in a band of smaller diamonds before slipping it onto her finger. "See how nice it looks on your hand?"

"It's gorgeous. The most beautiful ring I've ever seen."

He used the key to unlock the handcuffs, massaging and kissing every finger, as well as her wrist until her circulation returned.

"You sure know how to propose to a girl." She winked. "Tie her to the bed and then slide on the ring."

Still, she'd taken it under false pretenses. How could she explain she was having his father investigated? What a mess she'd made of things and, in the end, she'd probably hurt the only man she'd ever loved.

He held her close, his lips near her ear. "I've never made love to a woman wearing an engagement ring. I'm betting it would be phenomenal." He kissed her long and slow, his tongue sweeping the inside of her mouth. His finger dipped between the bald folds of her pussy. "What do we call this?"

"A hootchie-cunt?"

He pinched her labia, the corners of his delectable mouth twitching. "I can see someone needs her ass paddled."

He wouldn't dare!

Before he decided to put that crazy idea into action, she made up her mind to be honest. "We have to talk about something I've done. I've been trying to work up the courage to tell you for two days. To my credit, I've been busy packing, moving and unpacking. The timing never seemed right."

He rolled onto his side and tucked her to him, her head on his shoulder and his hand cupping her ass. "Tell me, angel."

"I remembered some things Chris said to me at that warehouse."

He tensed, which was never a good sign. "And you're just now going to tell me?"

Oh God, here comes the explosion. When she told him, he would go batshit crazy on her. "I went to Becca and discussed them with her because I wasn't sure if what he said was anything important or if I was just overreacting."

He released her, sat and glared. "So, what you're telling me is, her opinion is more valuable than mine."

"No. No, not at all. I mean, I know it seems that way, but she's a reporter—"

"Fuckin' A it seems that way." He stood and jerked on his boxers. "You come to me with every problem you have." He jammed one leg at a time into his jeans. "Every *motherfucking problem*, otherwise, what good am I to you?"

He yanked his shirt back on. His new sneakers he kicked aside, and he stepped into his motorcycle boots.

"Where are you going?" The thought of his riding the Harley

when he was so pissed scared her.

"To Becca's. To find out what my future wife couldn't share with me." He charged out of the door, slamming it behind him.

Cassie slipped into her robe and called Becca to warn her one pissed-off man was on his way to her house. She'd have more company tonight than she expected.

****

Quinn rode like the wind up and down Gulf Boulevard. At one point he turned onto Sunset Bay Drive, got off his bike and walked to Prickly Pear Point. The sunset was especially beautiful, with more oranges than reds or purples. Watching it alone didn't help his mood any, but observing some children, chasing each other, squealing and teasing, helped him calm down.

He wanted children. He wanted to give them what he'd never had—love and total acceptance. While he'd gotten it from his mother, for some reason earning his dad's love was elusive.

A few days ago, when the emergency over Cassie's safety was tearing Quinn apart, his dad showed him support and pride, something he'd never had before. Now that she'd been rescued, his dad was back to being his normal heartless self. Gulls circled overhead, and Quinn witnessed their flight until he was ready to talk to Becca without acting like a complete ass.

By the time he got to Becca's place, Cassie's compact was parked in front of Wolf's townhouse. Figures. Any time she had a problem, she ran to her family, but never to him. Was this how it would always be? Damn, he was tired of being at the bottom of everyone's priority list. Was it too much to ask to be at the top of hers?

He locked the helmet to his bike and strode toward Becca's front door. As soon as he rang the doorbell, the door was yanked open. A pair of arms swept around his neck and legs wrapped around his hips before a pair of familiar lips captured his. Cassie tugged on his bottom lip, bit the hell out of it and sucked it into her mouth. Quinn pivoted and pushed her against the wall to take control and deepen the kiss.

When her warm tears ran down his cheeks, he pulled back.

"I'm sorry. I was so, so wrong. I've never had a fiancé before and I didn't realize I was doing things that would hurt you." She planted kisses over his face. "You'll have to teach me, because I'm sure I'll mess things up from time to time. But there's one thing you have to understand."

God, he could barely talk. Her soul-deep honest emotion really affected him. "What?"

"No one is more important to me than you." She kissed him again, more gentle this time, thank God, cause his legs were a little weak from the raging hard-on she'd given him.

"How long does it take you two to make up? I'm getting hungry out here."

"Stuff a sock in it, Wolf. I've got some major ass-kissing to do." She bit Quinn's neck. "When we get home tonight, I'm going to give you the best blow job you've ever had."

"That's a good start." His bad mood was already forgotten.

"Wolf and Becca and Jace and Wendy Anne are here to talk about everything. So is your mother. She flew down to talk to Becca after she interviewed her on the phone. We're about to have a family conference."

He glanced back the hallway. "Mom's here? Why?"

"I brought your lasagna over and there's other food too." She kissed his cheeks and then placed her forehead against his. "Is that okay with you?"

"Why did Mom fly down from DC? What the hell's going on?"

"We're about to have a family conference. Both you and your mom are part of our family now. I hope you're up to it."

Hell, with Cassie's lasagna waiting and a promised blow job in his future, he was up for most anything. Most importantly, though, Cassie had told him the magic words. Words that healed the heart of a little boy and the soul of a grown man. Words no one in his life had ever told him: "No one is more important to me than you."

CHAPTER TWENTY-FIVE

Cassie clasped Quinn's hand and led him through Becca's living room to the group gathered around her dining room table. The tension was palpable. His mother stood, her arms and bruised wrists outstretched. "Son."

Quinn cupped her hands, his square jaw set in both gentleness and concern. "What's happened to you?"

Her hand, devoid of rings, rose to trail his jaw. "You look so much like him right now."

He kissed both of her cheeks. "Like who?"

"Like Quinn Matisse, your father." She collapsed into his arms. "Forgive me, I can't live with this lie anymore. Buck Gallagher is not your biological father."

His large hands swept up and down her back. "Is that why he's always resented me?"

She nodded. "If it was possible to love two men at one time, I did. My engagement to Buck was a long one. He was more focused on his career than on starting our lives together. My cousins and I went on a trip to New Orleans where I met Mat, playing the most sensual music on a saxophone I'd ever heard. He romanced me and I fell in love with him. When I returned to DC, I was pregnant with you."

"Yet Buck allowed Uncle Mat to visit, to spend time with us."

She nodded. "Buck thought you were his, until he began to see the physical resemblance between the two of you." Her fingers brushed Quinn's face. "The dimples, the square chin and the unusual eyes. The older you became, the more you looked like your biological father."

Quinn walked into the living room and crossed his arms, his back toward them all. "Did Uncle Mat know I was his?"

"He told me he felt the connection of your souls. That he could hear his blood flow through your veins. He was part Creole with a fanciful nature."

"All these years, I thought dad hated me because I wasn't good enough."

"He hated you because he found out he was sterile. He could never father a child of his own. I've left him, Quinn. I can't take anymore."

"Good. We'll have to keep you safe for a while."

"She's staying here with me." Becca pursed her lips.

Cassie could only imagine the turmoil in Quinn's mind. She wrapped her arms around his waist. "Come on, my love. Let's eat and talk—as a family. Your mother is one of us now. We have plans to make."

Over hot food and cold beer, Cassie shared most of what Chris had told her while she was held captive. At one point, she had to stop looking Quinn in the eye and busied herself with passing around the food, making sure everyone had enough to eat.

Meanwhile, she argued with herself over revealing what Quinn's beloved Renata had also been up to. Some women would relish belittling their man's former lover, but why hurt Quinn that way? Hadn't he had enough thrown at him tonight? It seemed as though everyone important in his life had betrayed or used him in one form or another. She loved him too much. What good would it do to tell him?

He wrapped his fingers around her wrist and brought her hand to his lips, kissing her palm. "What are you *not* telling me, angel?"

He knows me too well.

She shook her head. "I refuse to say anything that might hurt you. We're concentrating on the mole issue and the DB business right now. That's what's really important."

When she tried to pull her hand from his grasp, he tightened his hold. "So, I could withhold information from you that might hurt you? Like, say, one of your brothers being hurt on the job, and it would be okay?"

Her eyes snapped to make contact with his. "This is different. Nothing good comes from inflicting pain on someone you love, with your whole heart, the way I love you." To her surprise a sob crawled up her chest and escaped. She looked away.

"Angel, come here." He tugged her onto his lap, and his mesmerizing blue-grey eyes bore into hers. "Suppose you let me decide."

Tears filled her eyes. "Don't make me say something to hurt you. I know how much you loved Renata."

"Renata was a lying bitch who helped get my men killed. Now, what else do you know about her?"

Cassie exhaled an audible sigh. "According to Chris, she was also having an affair with him. They had a signal. If you spent the night, she would sing in the morning to alert Chris you were still there."

Quinn blinked a few times and then cupped her cheek with a hand. "If it was you who cheated on me like that, it would destroy me. But Renata? No big fuckin' deal. I'm over her." He smiled. "Dr. Paxwell would be so proud to hear me say that."

I'm pretty pleased myself.

"I didn't know if you were still seeing the good shrink, or not." Wolf forked some fried chicken off the platter. "How's it going?"

"I've had three sessions. She's pissed because Cassie and I aren't staying apart like she instructed, but surely she knew when she issued that mandate that it wasn't going to fly. Even so, she's good. Tough as nails. Zero sense of humor."

Quinn smiled at Cassie. "Speaking of which, do you know I

had to handcuff Cassie to the bedpost to put this diamond on her finger?" He held her hand out for one and all to see.

"How come you didn't show that to us earlier?" Jace leaned across the table to get a good look.

"Because I was more worried about making up with my future husband than I was about showing off my ring. Jace, why don't you tell Quinn what you were talking about earlier."

"Remember in Milt's car I kept saying there was something I couldn't figure out? What difference would it have made to Chris if you went back into government work? After all, he was doing his own mercenary thing. I just couldn't get it all to settle right in my head. Something was off."

Quinn sipped his beer. "Yes, I recall."

"What we didn't know at the time, and Cassie was too upset to remember, was Chris wasn't the only one. There were other moles beside him, led by someone referred to as DB." Wolf shook his fork at Quinn. "The checks your dad included in that thick packet for Noah were checks made out to each of us. Checks issued by DB Industries Incorporated."

"DB? Oh dear, that over-bearing, cold-hearted bastard," Quinn's mother mumbled. "I just knew he was up to something all these years. His office at home was always locked. There seemed to be secrets around every corner. The last twenty, or so, years, he would get so testy if I inquired." She glanced at her bruised wrists.

Quinn's face went blank. There was no expression. He didn't even so much as blink. Everyone quieted and waited.

"Didn't you wonder how they knew who to make the checks out to?" Jace spooned some pudding into a bowl and handed it to Wendy Anne. "Hell, they even had Milt's name right and he's not associated with the fire station."

"I talked to each member of our squad privately," Wolf said. "I asked if they'd seen anyone strange inside the fire station. Ivy Jo said an Internet repair guy was there a couple days earlier. The day you got the threatening text. The repair guy claimed our system was scheduled for an update. She's new. She didn't know, but she was smart enough to make note of the make, model and license plate number of his van. Arlo checked it out and it's owned by DB Enterprises."

"Ryder swept the fire station today for bugs and found two in the meeting room and one in Noah's office."

Quinn picked up his beer bottle. His hand shook. "I re…" he cleared his throat. "I remember being in the men's room one day at the CIA when two young guys came in. They were talking about someone they referred to as DB. One was especially excited and forgot himself. He used the name Daddy Buck." Quinn put his hands on Cassie's waist. "Stand up, angel. I need to walk outside for some fresh air."

The man she loved walked outside in pain and alone.

Wolf leaned back and stared at her. "This is how you build trust between a man and a woman. Quinn has faced every painful time in his life alone. You don't have to say anything, but you do need to let him know he's not alone anymore."

Cassie opened the door, stepped outside and sat on the step of Becca's deck and waited. Quinn made two slow revolutions around the edge of the yard, his head bowed. What should she do? Speak? If so, what were the words he needed to hear? How could she ease his pain? When he began his third trip around the yard, she followed four or five steps behind him.

"Go back inside, Cassie."

"If I was hurting, would you leave me alone? Or would you protect me?"

"Baby, I'm not in the mood for this."

"Okay, you just keep walking. I'll just keep following. But I will not leave you alone. If we are a couple, then when one hurts, the other hurts."

He walked on some more and she kept behind him. His hands slipped into the pockets of his jeans, and he stopped. "I think Buck had my real father killed."

Cassie nearly stumbled into Quinn's back in shock over his remark. "You can't be serious! What makes you think that?"

"When you were being held captive, he told me he'd kill any son of a bitch who tried to take my mother from him. I think he was talking about my biological father."

"He's going to jail, whether it's for treason or misuse of government funds or murder. He'll have to pay for what he did."

"I'm changing my last name. I don't want it. I don't want anything associated with that cold, heartless bastard. Did you see the bruises he put on my mother's wrists?"

"Yes."

"I'd love to get my hands on him for hurting her." His head dropped back and he stared at the stars, "How would you feel about being Cassie Matisse?"

She circled him and pressed her hands to his cheeks. "You are the most important person in the world to me. I will take your last name, whatever it is. I need to be with you. I want to have your babies. And you, hot lips, need to be loved every day for the rest of your life, because you're mine."

www.ingramcontent.com/pod-product-compliance
Ingram Content Group UK Ltd.
Pitfield, Milton Keynes, MK11 3LW, UK
UKHW041209180426
11947UKWH00025B/1950
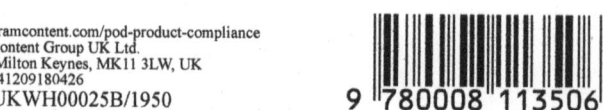